COMES IN WAVES

Praise for *Catching Feelings*

"I have yet to read Ana Reichardt's debut, book one in this series, *Changing Majors*. That is something I will soon rectify after reading *Catching Feelings*. There is an ease to her writing, and I was quickly drawn to Andrea, the adorkable lesbian who finds herself having to try to find her voice as the new leader of her team...I don't read a lot of YA novels, maybe because college was so long ago, I can hardly remember it. Reading this book made me feel wistful and long for those days of crushes and endless possibilities. Any book that evokes such emotions is one I will return to again and again. *Catching Feelings* is a wonderful sophomore effort by Ana Hartnett Reichardt. The characters are so relatable and their growth both individually and as a couple, was beautifully written. I can't wait to see what comes next from this author. Her star has only begun to rise."—*Sapphic Book Review*

"From start to finish *Catching Feelings* is such a great read... It is full of sweet moments to delight, heart-stopping moments to thrill and steamy moments to make your temperature soar. Andrea and Maya have to navigate college, competitive sports, and people who want to get in the way of their friendship and eventual romance. This makes for a compelling read that keeps you turning the page and ends up wrapping you in a warm hug."—*Lesbian Review*

By the Author

Alder Series

Changing Majors

Catching Feelings

Chasing Cypress

Coasting and Crashing

Romances

Crush

Comes in Waves

Visit us at www.boldstrokesbooks.com

COMES IN WAVES

by

Ana Hartnett

2024

THIS TRADE PAPERBACK ORIGINAL IS PUBLISHED BY
BOLD STROKES BOOKS, INC.
P.O. BOX 249
VALLEY FALLS, NY 12185

FIRST EDITION: AUGUST 2024

CREDITS
EDITOR: BARBARA ANN WRIGHT
PRODUCTION DESIGN: STACIA SEAMAN
COVER DESIGN BY INKSPIRAL DESIGN

Acknowledgments

It's hard to write a love story in a hurricane.

Comes in Waves was written during a tumultuous time of my life, but as I was finishing the first draft, my skies were clearing. A lot of emotion was poured into this book. And thanks to the support of my friends, my family, and my publisher, I was able to finish it.

Thank you to my editor, Barbara Ann Wright, and everyone at Bold Strokes Books for supporting me through thick and thin and making this book possible. Especially Sandy and Rad.

An enormous thank you to Nick and Kailyn for giving me shelter and a safe space to be creative. To my mom for being my superpower. To all my Atlanta friends for emergency beers and shoulders to lean on.

As always, thank you to my writing besties, Morgs, Kris, and Rivs, for the commiseration, laughs, and love.

And of course, thank you to Lauren for everything.

For those in rough waters

PROLOGUE

J,

I'm not sure how to be clearer, so I'm reverting to our childhood form of communication. I do not want to see you. Handle your business here, hell, sit at the bar at Crabby's and try to catch my attention. I don't care. You do not exist in my life anymore.

How could you? I clearly never existed in yours. I'm just a townie, remember?

Best,

B

CHAPTER ONE

Crabby's was packed the day I met her, tourists spilling from its beach-side patio to the sand where drinks were not allowed. But that didn't stop the finally free adults from sloshing their margaritas as they stumbled down the wooden steps, their floral-print shirts just a little too loud, the fabric a little too starched, and their drunken smiles a little too entitled.

It got like this every Memorial Day weekend when school let out and everyone fled to the panhandle. But Coral Bay was no Panama City. It was a small shrimping town whose streets seemed swollen in the summer, awash with tourists like clogged arteries. Seemed the high-rises inched closer up the coast every year. Closer to our home full of tackle shops, roadside seafood by the pound, and sandy backroads. The biggest thing in town was the Coral Bay Inn, the palm green and coral pink resort on the water that was in desperate need of a renovation.

Crabby's was the resort bar and restaurant where I worked—illegally—in the summers. During the school year, I helped wash linens and did odd jobs around the inn for cash. The owner, Marge, was tight with my Aunt Pat and let me help around the resort and bus tables, even though I wasn't quite fourteen. But I needed the money to fix the crappy little aluminum boat my mom had left me when she, well, left me. She always came back, though. That was the tricky bit.

"Breezy, can you preset table nine for me?" Mark asked. He scribbled something in his order book and jammed it in his apron, turning his attention to the windowful of hot food ready to be run. He balanced two plates of grouper and one of mahi down his muscular arm.

I tucked my stray bikini strap under my collar and tightened my ponytail. Mark was cute, and I didn't want him seeing me as some kid who was eager to go play on the beach with my friends after my shift. "Sure. What do you need?" I asked.

His eyes briefly passed over my body as he turned from the window. It was the first summer boys had noticed me. I stood straighter, hoping he enjoyed how my breasts had begun to fill my Coral Bay Inn button-down and how I'd finally figured out what to do with my hair. When it wasn't in a ponytail, it was past my shoulders, perfectly beach-tousled and dirty blond. Mark was sixteen, though, and completely out of my league. But I lived in Coral Bay. I knew how to cast a line.

"They need spoons and fresh app plates for the lava cake." He walked away, shooting me one more look over his shoulder. "Ah, fuck it. Bring a knife, too. Just in case."

I slipped between servers and tourists to the mise en plas and prepared a tray with the app plates and utensils, then weaved toward the four-top nearest the beach. A girl around my age sat there, though she didn't see me. Her eyes were on the ocean, on the kids skimboarding and shouting and splashing: my friends waiting for my shift to end. The breeze poured in from the water and gently mussed her long dark hair, but not a single strand looked out of place or puffed into a frizz. It was as smooth and perfect as her glossy lips and tan skin.

Her parents sat on either side of her like stone gargoyles. Not because they were ugly—all three of them were grippingly gorgeous—because they were so stiff, completely out of place in this laid-back fishing town. Her dad tapped his BlackBerry with thick fingers, and her mother dabbed the corners of her mouth with laser precision. Their clothes were white and crisp, a stark departure from all the Hawaiian shirts. The girl wore a black tank top with a silver chain disappearing into her neckline. Her shoulders mesmerized me. The bones in them.

As I neared the table, she looked up, and the bustling of the bar, the raucous laughter, and clanging of plates and glasses faded. When her eyes met mine, it was quiet, and my stomach felt like it did when I flew off that rope swing last summer in Kaleidoscope Cove. Her gaze mimicked Mark's, and I nearly tripped over my feet. When I caught myself, she smiled as if we were coconspirators, long dimples cutting either cheek. As if somewhere, deep down, she was Coral Bay, too, and had been the best girlfriend I'd never had.

I slid fresh utensils next to her mother. "Excuse me, ma'am," I muttered, trying to remain invisible to the patrons like always. Invisible to everyone except *her*. I could feel her watching as I reached next to her and placed a spoon and knife. She smelled like fifty bucks' worth of Bath & Body Works and fancy salon shampoo, while I smelled like salt and Pantene.

"Thanks," she whispered.

Though her mother had barely registered my presence, her father put down his BlackBerry. "Thank you, dear," he said. His voice was deep and rich. Everything about these people seemed deep and rich. He narrowed his eyes as I pulled back. "Aren't you a little young to be working?"

My cheeks heated, and I straightened, cursing the stupid bikini string curling out of my collar again. His daughter's gaze paused on it before she looked away, seemingly embarrassed by her father. "No, sir," I managed.

"How old are you?" he demanded.

None-of-your-goddamn-business years old.

"Fourteen."

"Fourteen?"

I looked at his daughter, but she was looking anywhere but at me. "That's what I said, yes, sir." Screw this guy. Her mom looked thoroughly disinterested, but she wasn't a man with a savior complex. I had more choice words for him, but this was the only job in town available to me, and I wasn't going to risk pissing off Marge, given I was thirteen and working under the table. Besides, I was off after this and would wash this douchebag off in the ocean. Salt water cured all.

The man scanned my being. "Mm-hmm."

I swallowed my annoyance and gave my most winning smile. "Enjoy your lava cake. It should be right out."

As if on cue, Mark appeared from behind me and slid the chocolate cake in front of the girl with a single candle. The reflection of the flame burnt in her pupils as she ran a hand through her hair and smiled awkwardly. I ignored the way she looked at Mark—the same way I looked at Mark—as if his attention was of the highest value. It *was*. But that didn't matter to me. What mattered was I knew her birthday: May 27.

I took one more look at her, knowing I'd probably never see her again, then slipped away as the singing began, feeling like I'd stolen something. Something I would treasure for a bit. The image of her, the flame in her eyes, her dimples. *Her birthday.*

I ditched my shoes in my employee locker and scribbled my hours in the little notebook Marge gave me. Then I was out of there, sprinting across the beach to meet the boys, the sand I kicked up spraying the backs of my thighs, the sun warm on my face. I didn't have to dodge a million blue resort chairs or lifeguard stands or an army of tourists. Our beaches were still sparse. Still beautiful and open.

"Breezy is free," Oscar shouted, Benny and Austin clapping next to him, wide grins on their freckled faces.

I yanked off my work shirt mid-dash and paused briefly to shimmy out of my shorts. Then I really was free, sprinting to the water. "Serve me up," I yelled to Benny, pointing to his skimboard.

He waited until I was a few feet from the water's edge, then threw his board in front of me, and I jumped on perfectly in stride. Nothing felt better than slicing over the shallow water and cutting through the wind. I did a few switchbacks before a nice little wave swelled toward the shore. It was time to get in the water anyway. I cut toward the ocean and caught the small wave before it broke, launching me into the air as if the wave were a quarter pipe, nailing a flip, and splashing into the cool water.

When I broke the surface, she was the first thing I saw, standing off from the boys, watching. I wiped the sea from my eyes and whipped the water out of my hair before I walked back to shore. The boys shot her glances, but she didn't seem to care. Even through her Ray-Bans, I could tell her focus was on me. I walked straight past my friends, ignoring their compliments and questioning eyes.

I landed in front of her, and to my delight, she pushed her sunglasses on top of her perfect hair. "Hi," I said.

"Hey." Again, her gaze slipped down my wet body, giving me a slight shiver. Or maybe it was the cold water.

I nodded to Crabby's. "Happy birthday."

She shrugged as if she was too cool to acknowledge something so mundane. "Sorry about my dad. He's an asshole."

I broke into a grin. "I don't know…he did get you lava cake."

She chuckled and gave a slight shake of her head, her dimples making a short appearance. "Cool move out there." Her gaze flitted over my shoulder, and I followed it as if expecting to see a replay of my flip.

"Thanks." We stared at each other, and I knew she felt the strange feeling I felt, a curious pull toward one another. "I'm Breezy." I held out my hand.

She raised a brow, and my stomach tightened. "Breezy?"

"My last name is Brees. So, yeah. I go by Breezy."

She shook my hand, and I knew I would never forget this moment. The first time I touched her. The first time she touched me. "What about you?"

"Juliette Peralta."

I took a moment, tasting her name as I pretended to say it behind closed lips. *Juliette. Juliette. Juliette.*

"What's your first name?" she asked, releasing her grip.

I chuckled and looked at my sandy toes before meeting her curious gaze again. Her eyebrows were perfectly arched and her skin perfectly tanned. I couldn't tell if I was jealous of her or attracted to her. But I didn't think I was attracted to girls, so maybe I was jealous.

I shrugged. "For you to find out, Jules." Okay, scratch that. Maybe I was attracted to her.

She grinned, her long dimples deepening as she crossed her arms and pinned me with a glare of feigned distain. "No one calls me Jules." Before I could respond, she said, "Except for you, I guess."

All I could do was smile as I heard the boys approaching from behind.

"Who's the tourist?" Oscar asked. His dark eyes were trained on Juliette, and he ran a hand through his hair, the seawater serving as pomade. He was always cute and basically Coral Bay royalty, the men in his family making up a sizeable chunk of the local government. Most notably, Mayor Westinghouse, Oscar's uncle. But he got his charm and his good looks from his mother, Alejandra.

"Aw, that's cute. The whole tourists versus locals thing. Feels very"—Juliette pressed a finger to her bottom lip and looked to the sky—"authentic beach teen." She smiled and extended a hand. "I'm Juliette."

I nudged Oscar in the shoulder. "Don't be a tool. She's chill." I caught her eye and dropped it just as fast. Oscar finally shook her hand. "And this is Austin and Benny."

"'Sup?" they greeted her in unison.

"Hey," she said, then looked only at me. She fiddled with the ring on her thumb as the boys faded into the background, and it was just us again. "I know this sounds lame, but I have to find a pen pal for my social studies class. It's a summer project. Kind of like summer reading." As I watched her cheeks redden, I couldn't help but grin. She knocked me gently in the shoulder. "Don't laugh," she said through a smile.

"I didn't."

We stood there staring, the breeze blanketing our words in privacy.

"Is that a yes?"

I bit my lip and shrugged. "You never asked."

The way she rolled her eyes made my stomach ache. "Do you want to be my pen pal, Breezy? I promise, I'm nice."

"Yeah. Sounds chill." I nodded.

She pulled a pen from her back pocket and extended her hand, palm up. I held it in mine as I pressed the tip into her skin. "Tickles," she said so softly, it barely reached my ears before the wind stole it. It took a moment to write an entire address neatly on skin.

Finally, I dropped her hand and returned the pen. "Guess you're not swimming, then."

She shook her head. "I gotta get back. My parents, they…" She shook her head and glanced at the ocean.

"When do you leave?" I asked.

"Day after tomorrow. It's a quick trip. My dad just needed to meet with some real estate broker to sign something."

Hope leapt in my chest. I didn't know why, but I wanted her to stay. "Are you moving here?"

"No. Doubt we'd ever leave Atlanta. It's just business."

The disappointment rocketed through me. It shocked me, how much I wanted to see her again. I took a deep breath to make sure I didn't sound desperate. "Will you be back next year?"

"I don't know."

Suddenly, my address on her palm felt so fragile. The only connection we would have once she walked back to Crabby's could vanish if she forgot about it and washed her hands. It was hot out. It could smear from her sweat. Another deep breath. Nothing I could control.

"Well"—I nodded to her hand—"you know where to find me."

She smiled, her dimples deepening, and held up my address. "Yeah, if I can make it home without smudging it." A small laugh escaped her lips, a kind of vulnerability seeping out. Something I had a feeling didn't happen too often.

I grabbed her hand and studied every crisp letter I wrote. "It's still there," I said. Her deep brown eyes flitted from my gaze to my hair to my chest. Until she took her hand back and dropped the sunglasses over her eyes.

"I gotta go." She took a step backward and waved, my address just a black blur. "I'll keep it safe. I promise."

I waved, and that was it. As I watched her walk back to Crabby's, I promised myself I'd remember every word she said to me.

"She was so fucking hot," Austin said, staring after Juliette with his mouth hanging open.

Jealousy bloomed in me, spilling over everything. I was jealous of her. Jealous of Austin, Benny, and Oscar. I groaned. "Shut up. You're never going to see her again anyway."

Benny flipped his bangs out of his eyes. "Still hot."

I rolled my eyes, completely exasperated by them. And by myself. Oscar wrapped an arm around my shoulders, his cool wet skin against mine, his long arm pulling me against his thicker chest. "Don't worry, Breezy. You're hotter."

I shoved him, and he stumbled a couple feet, a wide grin spreading across his face and a mischievous glint in his eye. Oscar was my favorite. My biggest rival. My best friend. Things felt easy with him, and I liked that he found me attractive. More attractive than Juliette Peralta, even. I could feel the blush in my cheeks. "I gotta go help Aunt Pat clean shrimp. Meet y'all at the Meadows tonight."

The Meadows was a middle school that had been abandoned about five years ago. The student population had dipped, and instead of paying for the upkeep, the town had shut it down and moved the students to the only other school in the district. It just sat there abandoned because not only did Coral Bay not have the money to fix it, it also didn't have the money to turn it into anything else.

So we used it for our home base. And the four-wheeler trails ran right into it. Perfect.

❖

I ditched my bike in the garage and ran up the faded wood steps to my small room above the garage. It was my whole world. It felt like a treehouse with its golden wood-panel walls and ceiling, and I even had my own bathroom. It wasn't "nice" by any stretch of the imagination, but it was mine. My private sanctuary. And Aunt Pat and Uncle Trevor always respected that. I owed them everything for taking me in.

I grabbed a quick shower and met Aunt Pat at the cleaning station by the tool shed. The tourists didn't like to clean their own shrimp, so Aunt Pat always had some of her catch peeled and ready for Uncle Trevor to sell at a premium in pre-weighed bags. I got to work next to her, always mesmerized by how quickly her thick fingers could strip the crustaceans.

"Good day, Breezy baby?"

My fingers were already almost numb from the ice-cold shrimp. "Yes, ma'am. Made a lot of tips and got some good beach time with the boys."

"Good. Gotta have them over for gumbo soon. They're always just running through the house for a glass of lemonade and gone as quick as they came. Those little rascals have to sit at my table for a meal every once in a while if they want to keep their barge-right-in privileges."

"I'll let them know. Tomorrow?"

"Tomorrow."

We worked quietly as the sun slipped lower in the horizon, and the evening began to cool. The crickets chirped in the shadows, and the ever-present hum of the ocean shaded in the gaps. "Is Uncle Trevor gonna be home for dinner tonight?"

She swiped the shrimp shells off the work bench into a mostly full, rusty metal pail. It was my job to scatter some of them in the garden when we were done and make a slurry of the rest with the food processor. Good for the soil. "Not tonight. He's staying open a little later this weekend for the big crowds."

We had cornbread and meatloaf that night. Then, I tore up the back roads with the boys on Oscar's four-wheelers because Oscar was Coral Bay rich—just rich enough—and he had nice things. I used to ride on the back of his, my arms wrapped around his waist, his hips sandwiched between my thighs. Until he got a new one for his birthday last year. Now I rode his old one alone, only slightly missing the way his back felt against my chest.

Later, as I lay in my small bed in my small room with the window cracked so the ocean could slip in, I thought of Juliette Peralta. Wondered how she was celebrating her birthday tonight. Her dad probably grilled fancy steaks. I wondered if she got a gift that she especially loved. Wondered if she was thinking of me and if my address had made it home with her safe and sound.

Dear Breezy,

It's fine you won't tell me your first name. I mean, it only makes me want to rip my hair out and yell at you, but whatever. It's fine. Tell Oscar I'm mad at him for refusing to tell me, too. And I won't speak to him when I get back. Only thirty-six days. Can you believe it? Also, Mrs. Dennick said I'm the only one from last year's class who's still in contact with their pen pal. So that's cool. I kind of can't imagine not writing you at this point. I don't know, it feels like you're my best friend.

Speaking of best friends, Beth is still mad at me for texting Jake. It's like she feels entitled to him, and like, it's not my fault I have a cell phone now, and she doesn't. But I know they talk on AIM a little, so she shouldn't be mad. You know, I don't even really like him like that. I mean, he's cute, but I wouldn't be disappointed if I never saw him again. Is that mean? Why can't you just be a boy? You're way better than all the ones I know. I guess Oscar, Benny, and Austin aren't so bad. Everyone at my school is just so... boring.

My parents have been traveling nonstop for work.

It's cool because now I can stay home alone. But things have been really picking up for them, and my dad keeps talking about how I need to be focusing on getting into a good business school so I can be a part of Peralta Inc. one day. I don't know. It's not like I have any other big dreams, but something about working for the family business sounds claustrophobic to me. Kind of thought I'd find something else I'd be excited about at this point. What does it say about me that I don't have a passion?

I do really love kids. Maybe I want to be a teacher. I think I'd be pretty good at that.

What do you want to study in college? What do you want to be?

Sorry I dump these things on you. You're just so easy to talk to.

How's Coral Bay? What have I missed? I know it's not quite season yet, but I hope Aunt Pat catches so much shrimp. Hope the boys are staying out of trouble.

Hope you're happy. But I also kinda hope you miss me as bad as I miss you.

Love,
Jules

CHAPTER TWO

On the day the Peraltas arrived in Coral Bay, I woke up an hour before my alarm and lay in my dark room, listening to the push and pull of the ocean. How could I sleep? My blood was kinetic, my body a buzzing mass of flesh under my quilts. Instead, I daydreamed of her until it was time to get up and shower.

I had met Juliette Peralta on her fourteenth birthday, two years ago almost to the day. *Almost.* It still bummed me out that I'd missed it this year by six days, but I couldn't control the Peraltas' business schedule. We'd never stopped being pen pals even after her social studies class had ended for the semester. Over the last two years, we must have sent around fifty letters apiece. I could count the rubber-banded bundle under my bed, but my energy was a bit paralyzing at the moment.

I didn't know best friends could live in different states, eight hours apart, but what was Jules if not my best friend? Our letters were full of life updates, admissions, secrets. Shit the boys didn't know about. Shit her parents didn't know about. Just between us. With every letter I sent, I worried it would be the one she didn't respond to. But she always came through, and that was the most important thing to me. Showing up. Especially when someone else had bailed.

I finally slid out of bed and closed my window. Aunt Pat was always yelling at me to keep it shut for the AC, but on the cool mornings, I cracked it to let the ocean in. The rhythm of it brought me comfort, like the slow beat of a heart. When I grew up, I was never living in a place where I couldn't hear it. Never leaving Coral Bay.

The hot shower steadied my jumpy nerves. A little. Not much could tame my excitement until I was hugging her in exactly one and a half hours on the beach in front of the empty fourplex her parents had just signed on.

The fact that the Peraltas ran a real estate investment firm worth over thirty million dollars and couldn't keep their hands off Coral Bay property scared the shit out of me. Every time they came down here to scope out parcels or sign contracts, it felt like the building of something we wouldn't be able to stop. They saw something in our town, a different future than what the folks who lived here saw.

I brushed my teeth a little too hard. What could I really do about it? It wasn't Juliette's fault. And honestly, I might have handed Mr. Peralta the deed to the town if it meant I got to hang out with her for a week.

I mean, not really. But I was stoked to see her. I took extra care with my hair and makeup. Slid into one of my newer tank tops. The white one that hit a solid inch above the waistline of my jean shorts. The outfit I'd wear for a cute guy. I just wanted her to think I was as cool as she was.

"Where're you running off to this early? No way any of those boys are awake," Uncle Trevor asked as he poured coffee in the kitchen, then returned to his newspaper at the table.

Water dripped down my neck as I chugged a glass. I wiped it and caught my breath. "Meeting up with Juliette for a beach walk. They got in last night." He raised a bushy gray brow and stared, but I didn't have the patience to answer whatever questions he had. I fished the wad of cash from my back pocket and laid the bills on the table as I counted. "Four hundred and sixty-seven. That's one seventy-seven for the rest of my boat repairs and two-ninety for the trailer." I nodded, pleased to be one step closer.

He double-checked my counting and nodded. "You may be the only person to buy the trailer before the truck."

"I couldn't pass up Mr. Haddock's deal."

He smiled and pushed the cash into his pocket. "I'm proud of you, Tanya. Working hard will take you wherever you want to go."

"I'm staying in Coral Bay forever." I kissed him on the temple and squeezed his shoulder. "Thanks again for fronting me the cash. Love you."

"Be safe," he called as I ran out the door.

I didn't have enough money yet to buy a truck to hitch the boat trailer to. But I wasn't quite sixteen, so really, I was on schedule. And yeah, I had enough money to buy the car, but Marge had helped me set up an investment account, and there was no way in hell I was pulling money out of that to buy a depreciating asset like a beat-up pickup. So I sped down the sleepy roads to East Beach on my beat-up bike instead, the paint and gears in a constant battle with the salty air.

I was racing to be early, the morning wind rushing through my hair. I'd accounted for the wind when I'd gotten ready this morning. Any beach-town girl knew to always account for salt, wind, and humidity while doing her hair. It would only add to my beach-chick vibe. Plus, my skin loved the salt. I found it funny, if not somehow kismet, that the ocean in all its forms healed living things but corroded metal, destroyed paint and chemicals, and eroded anything not born, hatched, or propagated.

The salt seemed to have a goal.

I leaned my bike against a palm tree in the back of the fourplex. I knew this place. I knew every place. It was where the Bowmans used to live before they'd bought a house on Bay Drive two years ago. The fourplex was nice by Coral Bay standards, but something told me the Peraltas intended to knock it down. The lot was big, a little baggy for the modest building.

The worn pathway from the small pool to the beach was just a line of petrified wood. I avoided the most peculiar-looking slabs as the ocean roared louder in my ears, until my toes hit the sand, and I dropped my Vans by the end post.

Instant safety, belonging, happiness. There wasn't a day that slipped by that I didn't set foot on the beach. The pink of the morning was still hazy, sleepy, bruising the ocean below to a soft lilac and dusty indigo. The heat of the day thickened the air. It'd be a slurry of gas and sea by ten. There was just so much—

"Ah. *Fuck.*" Juliette's voice barely reached me over the humming of the water, and I almost tripped, I turned so fast. There she was, her midnight hair waterfalling over her face as she hopped on one foot, holding the other in her hands. She wore the same thing as me: short shorts and a sky blue tank top. Only she wore it better. I jogged over.

"That upset to see me, huh?"

She snapped her head up and smiled, her dimple a shallow canyon in her soft-looking cheek. "Breezy." She dropped her foot, and it hovered over the wooden path as she threw her arms around my neck. Her perfume was floral, spicy—it embodied her somehow—and her hair tickled my face, the fresh smell of her shampoo making my stomach churn.

I gave her a quick squeeze and dropped to a knee. She balanced by gripping my shoulders as I searched for the culprit behind her cursing and hopping. Wasn't hard to find. "Sandspur." I stood, held up the spiky seed, then flicked it into the dunes.

Her hands slipped from my shoulders, down my arms, to mine. "Hi," she said, her smile deepening.

I squeezed her fingers, then let go. Always having to let her go. "Hi."

Her smile faltered, but she recovered quickly. "You never wrote back." She shoved me in the shoulder.

I chuckled as I reached for my back pocket. "Of course I did." The envelope was crumpled and damp from the bike ride and the Florida air. "It might not have made it to you before you left, so I thought I'd hand-deliver it. And careful, your birthday gift is folded up in there. It's special, so don't lose it." She took it. "Read it on the beach?"

We walked together to the edge of the tide and sat in the sand while Juliette carefully unfolded my letter. When she untucked the last corner, the shark tooth fell onto her thigh. She pressed the sharp tip of it to her thumb. "Shark tooth?"

I nodded. "I know it's nothing cool, I just—"

She glared at me, her brows huddled together. "Nothing cool? Are you kidding me?" She laughed as if she found me ridiculous. "It's a literal shark's tooth. What could be cooler?"

I plucked it from her fingers and held it in my palm. It seemed ancient to me. Like it was halfway to fossilization. I liked it because anyone could tell I picked it straight from the sand. We locked eyes over the tooth, and she smiled as if I'd given her the best gift in the world.

"I've been obsessed with finding a shark tooth," I said. She grinned at the high pitch of my excitement. "Everyone finds them. The boys always find them. And a single shark loses thousands and thousands of teeth in its lifetime, so finding one on the beach is common. So the fact that this is the very first one I've ever found is strange." Her eyes were focused on me, and I swallowed down the urge to jump ship. But I promised myself I'd be vulnerable and just *say it*. "Stranger even, since I'm walking on the beach thinking of you and what gift I could possibly give you to show how much you mean to me. Then, boom. This little sucker cuts my pinkie toe."

She grinned as she took the tooth. "So you're bleeding in the sand, bend down to find this little guy, and you thought, what, exactly?"

I took a deep salty breath. "I thought that there are billions of people in this world like the billions of shark teeth. There are hundreds of people in Coral Bay like the hundreds of shark teeth in the sand of this beach. But only one found me, and how lucky that it's the one I was looking for."

It seemed as if she was holding her breath. Until she exhaled an airy word that sounded a lot like "Wow" and squeezed the tooth. "I know the feeling." She cleared her throat, seeming to swallow something dry. "Now, stop distracting me so I can read this letter."

I bit down a chuckle and watched the soft waves crash while she silently read. When she finished, she folded it carefully and tucked it in her front pocket. She stayed quiet for a moment, as if letting my words settle, then gently bumped my shoulder. "Why don't you want to go to college?"

Her question was almost a whisper. I wiped sand from my knees and smiled. "Why do you *want* to go to college?"

She stared at the water. "Guess I haven't really thought about it."

I shrugged. "I don't know. It's not like I want to be a doctor or engineer or anything. Don't see why I need it. Aunt Pat never went. Marge never went. My mom never went. Not that she's a good example."

She flopped back, her back hitting the sand. "What do you want to do when you grow up?"

I peered at her. Looked away when my gaze hit the swell of her chest. "Um." The twisted feeling I always got from her coiled around me. Was it jealousy? Wishing I had her body? And if it was, why the hell did I want to touch her? Just to know what beauty like hers felt like?

No. I knew it was more.

"Aunt Pat wants me to take over for her one day, but I'm not one for shrimping." I swallowed the stickiness in my throat. "I think I want to run my own place. Like Marge."

She tugged me down next to her, our arms pressed together in the soft sand. "I think it's cool you want to stay here." Her pinkie toe brushed mine, and I scooted my foot away. "Every time I come here and hang out with you and the boys, I want to stay."

I chuckled. "You can't stay. You're just a tourist."

"What'd you call me?" She launched upright and looked down with feigned disgust. "Sounded like you called me *just a tourist.*"

Not able to handle her gaze, I threw my arm over my eyes and laughed. "You are a tourist, Jules."

She was on me in a second, tickling my waist, and the weight of her on my hips pressing me into the sand. Until she finally pinned me and her hair dragged over my chest. "The townie and the tourist," she said. But she said it all slow, as if it was the title of an epic, and we were writing the adventure.

"The townie and the tourist," I repeated.

She straightened so her hair was no longer dancing on my skin, but her weight fell heavier on me. I tried not to think about it. "Best friends." She held up her pinkie, and I curled mine around it.

"Forever," I said.

❖

"You know," Juliette whispered as I took a bite of cheese pizza. "Normally, I know my friends' first names." The flickering glow of the patio lights from Mickey's Propane 'n Pizza highlighted her mischievous grin in the dark of the evening. Tourists wouldn't guess it, but the pizza from this gas station was the best in town. A little Coral Bay secret. Something just for the locals.

"Dude. You haven't told her your name yet?" Benny asked.

Austin shoveled another huge bite into his mouth and wiped his greasy lips on the back of his hand. "Aren't y'all, like, best friends or something?"

Oscar's eyes were on me. It made me feel a little hot, especially since they could've been on Jules. The sight of her would be the obvious choice for any guy. I let my gaze linger on him until he gave me one of his signature grins and looked away. His highlighter-pink floral shirt hung unbuttoned almost to his navel, showing off dark skin and trim muscle. He really was cute.

"I don't know," Jules said, knocking my knee under the table and shooting me a side-eye. "Like I said, I don't even know her name."

Benny laughed and tossed his disgusting napkin on the green mesh table. "It's Ta—"

"My name to tell her, Benny." I gave him what I hoped was a glare of disdain.

He shrugged. "What's the big deal anyway? It's just a name. We all know it."

"We've literally known each other since birth, dumbass. Of course we know it. It's none of your business if Breezy wants to tell her or not." Oscar scanned Juliette, his eyes narrow. "It's not like she's Coral Bay."

I yanked my straw from my lips, dribbling Coke down my chin before I could wipe it. "Hey. She's one of us," I said in her defense.

Jules patted my thigh under the table, her fingers cool from her drink. "It's all good. I know I'm just a tourist. It's cool."

Oscar barked a laugh. "Just a tourist? Tourists come to town for a week to dump money in our pockets and leave us with more than we had before. They're annoying, sure. But they buy our catches and rent our rooms at the Inn." He ran a hand through his short black hair and looked at everyone but her. "When are we going to acknowledge that her parents are slowly buying up the entire town?"

Juliette's hand stilled on my thigh. Everyone went quiet. Austin even stopped chewing.

"Oscar," I said, willing him to stop even though his words gave me a stomachache. Even though he was right.

"I'd hardly call a fourplex buying up the town," Juliette said.

Oscar rolled his eyes and picked at his plate. "That's just

the first one this summer. How many did they buy last summer, huh?"

"Who cares?" Benny interjected. "Coral Bay's a piece of shit anyway."

"No, it's not," Oscar and I replied in unison.

"Why do you think the rich people are after it if it's such a piece of shit?" Oscar asked, shaking his head. "Maybe you'll care when your family can't afford to live here anymore and you have to move."

"Stop, Oscar. Enough, okay? It's not like she has anything to do with her parents' business," I said.

Juliette took a deep breath. "I totally get it, I do. Unfortunately, Breezy's right. There's not much I can do about it. My father hardly listens to me talk about my day. He doesn't care about anything besides money." She looked at Oscar. "But I'm not him. So can we just, like, chill out? I missed you guys, and I just got here."

He sucked in his lips and sighed. "Fine."

Austin flipped his rusty brown bangs out of his eyes. "Now that's settled, who's down to crush some beers at the Meadows?"

Benny's smile widened as he gave Austin an obnoxiously loud high five. "Let's fucking roll," he shouted. Benny and Austin were basically brothers. They even kind of looked alike, except for Benny's bright blond hair and lighter skin. But living at the beach kept him nice and tan and on the same level as Austin. The two of them were quintessential teenage boys whose priorities were surfing and skimboarding, pretty girls, and getting their hands on beer, which wasn't hard in this town. There was a strong cord of loyalty among the townies. We helped each other out. And that meant the occasional score for us.

Oscar, on the other hand, had something deeper in him. I could see it in the flash of his eyes. Passion. Purpose. He stood and threw away his trash. "Does that mean you have a shit ton of beer?" he asked.

Austin grinned, his nod slow and big. "Anderson got me a handle of Soco and two twelve packs of Bud Light with the money me and Benny got from helping Mr. Hanson remove that big ol' tree with the rot from his backyard."

Benny sighed. "What the hell, man? Half of that was my money."

Austin rolled his eyes, seemingly annoyed that Benny wasn't thanking him for his epic score. "Yeah, and we used it to buy a shit ton of booze. Now let's go drink it." He walked backward to Oscar's Jeep, not even tripping over the curb. As silly as he was sometimes, the boy had some impressive athleticism.

"We're going *inside* the Meadows?" Juliette whispered as Benny and Austin argued over their shares of the cash. We'd all gone four-wheeling last summer, but I guess we'd never hung out in the building with her. The memory of her arms tightening around my waist and her thighs warm around my hips made the moment hazy. When I'd shared Oscar's old four-wheeler, I'd wondered if he felt how I felt with Jules at my back.

I squeezed her shoulder. "Yeah. It's chill, I promise. We hang out there all the time."

CHAPTER THREE

We piled into Oscar's Jeep Wrangler. Yeah, it technically had five seats, but in no realm was it even remotely big enough for five humans. I sat smashed between Jules and Benny, our sticky thighs fused together on the sticky leather seats. Summer in Florida.

Their shoulders pinned me to the hot leather, and I shimmied forward, uncomfortably glued against a sweaty Benny. There was usually an empty seat between us. "Here." Juliette laid her arm across the seat back, opening a few inches of space between us. I leaned back, and her fingertips skimmed my shoulder. I inched close enough to feel her breast press into my arm, and I was happy again, focusing on how my body filled the curve of hers.

We swung by Austin's trailer to snag the beer and booze and were parking behind the Meadows five minutes later. The car doors slammed, and we walked to the one door we had jimmied open a couple years back. Well, we hadn't so much "jimmied" it as we had shattered a window with a rock to get inside and unlock it. We had boarded up the window with old driftwood and spackle to keep the vibrant Florida wildlife from invading our most treasured hangout.

"You're sure this is, like, safe?" Juliette asked as we trailed behind the boys. In two years of being her friend, I knew her to always be strong and unafraid. She would write to me about the confrontations she had with her other friends, about making the first moves with boys, and I always saw her as my spitfire friend. Jules was *down*. I couldn't tell if something about the Meadows really bothered her that much, or if she was being extra vulnerable tonight.

"Hey," I said, doubling back. "This is Coral Bay, not Atlanta. I personally know every person who lives in this town." I nodded to the faded blue door that looked black in the night. "The scariest thing in there is probably some spiders and Benny's horrible taste in music that he's going to blast on the boombox we found in Mrs. Stile's old classroom." I fingered the shark tooth dangling against her chest. I didn't give it to her as a necklace, but she had made quick work of making one herself. "Plus, if anyone's in there, you can just stab them in the eye with this bad boy."

"You're too much." She chuckled as she pried my fingers from her necklace and gave them a brief squeeze.

"Come on," Austin called, holding the door.

"Ready?" I asked her.

She nodded. "Yeah. Lead the way."

As we walked down the old hallways, the beams of our flashlights bouncing with our gaits, I tried to imagine the Meadows not as a place I hung out at every week of my life but from Juliette's perspective. The walls were grimy and stained, the paint peeling from stagnant humidity and salt. Faint scratching and skittering noises sounded in the distance, and the overall creepiness of a place stuck in time was a bit frightening. A bit eerie.

We turned right into the science wing and walked to our favorite classroom. A dull scraping sound came from behind us. Juliette swallowed loudly and brushed her fingers against mine. It felt like she was asking permission, so I took her hand and laced our fingers. For how warm the evening was, her palm wasn't clammy or sweaty. It was perfectly nice. We locked eyes for a split second, and she gave me a soft smile before she turned away.

Mrs. Stile's classroom never changed, just like the rest of the school. She'd apparently taught biology, and the quintessential educational skeleton stood in the corner next to the chalkboard. We'd hooked him up with some board shorts and cheap shades.

"Juliette, meet Skeeter the skeleton," Benny said.

Jules laughed and shook its plastic hand. "Nice to make your acquaintance, Skeeter." She popped the tab of a Bud Oscar handed her and took another long look at the stack of bones, then shrugged. "Is Skeeter single? He's pretty cute."

"Actually, he's married to the metal rod and string holding him upright. But don't worry, I'm single," Benny said, tossing her an exaggerated wink.

A flare of silly jealousy prickled my ears. It was a feeling I got a lot around Juliette, not wanting to share her, wanting to be the closest one to her. *I* was her best friend. If she dated Benny or Austin, they'd be her focus while she was in town. I couldn't stomach that thought. And I couldn't even begin to conceptualize her and Oscar. It made me sick.

Oscar caught my eye through the skeleton marriage chaos and winked. I guess I didn't have to worry about her and him.

Jules walked to Benny and planted a hand on the pocket of his T-shirt, letting her hair fall just so. She bit her lip and stared into his eyes. "I prefer men to boys." Benny gaped, clearly stuck in her eyes. Maybe her dimples. "And Skeeter"—she nodded to the skeleton—"is all the man I need, baby."

She left him with a slight shove, and he sat in silence, gazing after her.

I loved as much as I hated every second of that. I took a sip of beer. "Okay. Play us some music."

Austin crouched in front of the small CD collection we had amassed and plucked one of Blink 182's. I flipped on the battery-powered purple and green lava lamp that Oscar had gotten for me last year. The room was perfect in its soft glow. It was ours.

It belonged more to us than the past it held. Our games of

Pictionary were smudged on the chalkboard instead of chemical equations or species names. Our music filled the space instead of lectures. Our posters, our lamps, our beanbag chair. *Ours.*

Austin smacked his hands together, grabbing our attention. "Okay. Welcome, Juliette. I hope you like our humble abode." He held up his palms as if giving a sermon. "What's the game of the evening?"

Benny hopped to the front of the classroom next to Austin, a grin wide on his face. "Char—"

"*Not* charades," Oscar barked.

"Fine." Benny shrugged. "Not charades."

"How about Kings?" Austin suggested. It was our go-to drinking game.

"Or we could play a good ol' fashioned round of Truth or Dare," Juliette suggested. "You have to do whatever the dare is or give the truth. If not, you gotta chug a beer and do a shot."

"Shit," I muttered. "That's a lot of drinking."

She shrugged. "Not if you play the game."

The boys exchanged looks of approval as a curious feeling of dread gathered in my stomach. This felt like it wasn't going to end well for me. This felt like I was going to have to watch Jules kiss each of my friends. This felt like maybe I was about to be annoyed at her. Jealous of her. Jealous of them.

Oscar narrowed his eyes as he seemingly considered the option. "Let's do it."

Austin and Benny nodded and clapped. "Yes," Benny said, letting the S slither into itself in his excitement.

"Gather round, children," Juliette said as she pulled desks into a circle at the front of the room. "Class is about to begin."

"What are the rules?" I asked, hating how I could hear the anxiety in my words. I took another quick sip as a small grin played on Juliette's lips.

She raised a brow and held my gaze. "Rules are, there are no rules. Except a pass costs an entire beer and a shot. And we all start with the same dare." She looked to the boys. "Anyone want to kick us off with the group dare? Oh, and you can't skip the first dare. We all do it together."

A lump gathered in my throat as if all my saliva turned to sand. What was wrong with me? I hung out with these people every day of my life, except for Jules. I trusted them. I was safe.

Benny hopped off his chair. "Come on. Everybody up." We all stood, a little hesitant. He ripped off his tank top, exposing his lean, wiry body. "First dare. Everyone drops a piece of clothing."

Everyone shrugged like it was nothing. Oscar unbuttoned his shirt as Austin tugged his off. Juliette had her tank over her head in a second. Only familiar parts of our bodies on display, nothing a bathing suit wouldn't cover. But the white lace detailing of her bra had the sand jamming my lungs. Suddenly, I was the only loser with all my clothes on. And why? I looked like everyone else.

"Come on, Breezy," Jules said as she stepped in front of me. I gasped, hopefully only loud enough for her to hear—because I trusted her like that—when her fingers curled under the hem of my tank, brushing my waist. "You can't quit before we begin." She pulled it gently over my shoulders, careful not to snag it on my earrings. "There," she whispered. Her gaze dropped to my bra before she nodded and stepped away. Of course, she was in some sexy date-night bra while I was in my least sexy one. Soft gray cups. That was what I was rocking. I folded my arms over chest.

Benny clapped obnoxiously. "All right, all right. Now we're cooking with gas. Who's starting us off?"

Oscar looked straight at me, keeping his gaze on my eyes and not my chest. It was appreciated. "Breezy," he started, a smug little smirk on his lips. It made me blush how he said my name. I could feel the heat of it in my chest and cheeks. "Truth or dare?"

I tucked my hair behind my ear and quickly wrapped myself in my arms again. "Truth."

He pouted. "Scared?"

I rolled my eyes. "Just ask the question."

He strutted about, tapping his finger to his bottom lip. "Hmm." He stopped and pointed at me. "Have you ever had a sex dream about any of us?"

Yes. I felt the blood drain from my face. "What? Ew. No, you creep." I'd had a sex dream about him. But whatever, he didn't need to know that, and it didn't mean anything. I'd had one about Benny, too, so it had very much meant *nothing*.

"I think B may need to drink on that one," Jules said, smirking from behind her beer. "You're a terrible liar, love."

I scoffed as she shrugged.

Benny pointed the butt of his can at me. "Come on, B. Tell the truth or drink. But careful if you drink. We've only just begun. And that was probably the easiest truth you're gonna get all night."

I groaned. He was right. I dropped my gaze to my lap and tightened around myself, catching a sudden chill. "I had a dream about Oscar here, in the Meadows, and you in the locker room after gym class. At our real school." I pointed to Benny, whose jaw was basically hanging against his chest. And Jules, in the sand of East Beach on an inky night so black, we could see the Milky Way, but I tried not to remember that dream. When I realized no one was speaking, I dropped my hand and shrugged. "I guess I have a thing for schools."

"Fuck," Austin whined. "I'm literally the only one you haven't dreamt about boning?"

I cringed at his word choice. "Really? Boning?"

Jules patted him on the back and pinned me with a glare. "You're not the *only* one. I don't recall hearing my name in there."

"I think it's my turn, right?" I cleared my throat and looked away, tracking the blobby purple glow of the lava against the chalk board. "Austin, truth or dare?"

He grinned. "Dare, of course."

I took a moment to think of something good. "I dare you to kiss Benny."

"*Pshh.*" He stomped over to Benny and grabbed both his cheeks.

Benny's eyes went wide. "Hey—"

Austin pressed his lips hard against Benny's and ended the kiss with a loud smack. He held my gaze as he strutted back to his spot. "Give me something challenging next time, Brees."

"Dude," Benny complained as he wiped his lips with the back of his hand. "Fuck." He drained half his beer and ran his hand through his hair. "Juliette. Truth or dare?"

Her can hung lazily by her fingertips. "Dare."

Benny grinned. "I dare you to kiss Breezy. Let's even this up."

My entire body imploded. She slid off the desk and took three quick steps to me. "I thought these dares were supposed to be hard," she said as she landed in front of me and pushed my knees gently apart, making space for herself. It felt as if she cracked me open from my core. It felt…oozy. I caught a swallow move down her throat as we stared at each other. A naked moment of hesitancy. A sign that this wasn't nothing to her.

I could smell her skin. It wasn't Coral Bay. It was fresh and vibrant like the city she was from. Not so earthy and briny as ours, being one with the constant saline decay of the sea. I felt the heat of her chest so close to mine. Her fingers dragged on the tops of my thighs as she leaned just a bit closer, her eyes fluttering shut.

Until I stampeded through the thick quiet of Juliette Peralta leaning in to kiss me by cracking open a beer. She straightened, eyes wide, and watched me in shock as I chugged the entire thing, a small stream of it running down to my chest.

I wiped myself clean and crumbled the can. "She passes," I said, a bit out of breath. Everyone looked a little stunned. "I drank for her," I explained.

"Wow." She looked hurt. "The idea of kissing me is that bad, huh?" She stepped away and shrugged. "Noted." Benny handed her the bottle of Soco, which she unscrewed and handed to me. "Don't forget your shot."

Before I could say anything to remedy the situation, she was giving Oscar a dare. What would I say anyway? That it scared me when she leaned in? Not because I thought it'd be bad, but because I knew it'd be good? And then what? I took the hot shot of whiskey with a grimace.

We played Truth or Dare for what felt like ages, half-clothed and more than half-drunk. But Jules felt far away, and I fucking hated it. She never caught my eye or gave me one of her signals that said *I see you*. They always put me at ease.

Juliette laughed at something ridiculous Benny said, and I just couldn't take it anymore. I stood and grabbed my flashlight and the bottle of Soco. "Jules. You and me. Girl talk." I nodded to the door.

"Hey, you can't take all the booze," Austin said.

Juliette considered me for a moment before standing. "Yes, we can. Be back later, losers," she said. A wave of relief soothed me as she followed quietly behind into the dark maze of hallways. "Where are we going?" Her voice had lost all its confidence from moments earlier.

"Um…" I took a right and stopped in front of the media center. "The book fort," I said and shone my light through the window at the small wooden fort with rainbow pillows and reading nooks.

We let ourselves in and lay on a big beanbag we could barely fit on. I flashed the light around to make sure we were alone, then switched it off and let the darkness fall over us. I moved a little closer so our sides were pressed together. Never thought I'd be alone with Juliette Peralta in the reading fort with no shirt on.

"So," she started.

"It's not that I don't want to kiss you," I blurted. And fuck, that wasn't what I'd meant to say.

"Are you saying you want to kiss me?" Her question was slow, as if she was scared of my answer.

I draped my arm over my eyes, the slightest dizziness rumbling through me. The alcohol had caught up to me. "No," I whispered. "I mean, just...felt like a lot of pressure in that moment. A lot of eyes on us. And you're my best friend." I sighed. "I don't know. I panicked. I'm sorry."

Her fingers found my knee, and the dizziness exploded into a kaleidoscope of vertigo. Her hand on my skin felt like spinning endlessly in space. "You know," she whispered, and I heard the nerves in her voice. Which made me even more nervous. "There are no eyes on us now."

She lifted herself, the lack of her weight on the beanbag making me crumple into the middle crevice of it where she lowered herself on me. Over me. She dipped her head so her mouth was so close to my ear. "We should probably make good on that dare," she whispered.

My hand made the unanimous decision for the rest of my body and curled around the back of her neck without permission. "For karma's sake, right?"

She gazed into my eyes. Not in a kiss-you-on-a-dare kind of way, but a kiss-you-like-I've-dreamt-of-it-a-million-times way. A nice way. A nice way that made me ache all over. She leaned in so her Cupid's bow mirrored mine. "For karma's sake. Of course," she murmured. I swore her breath hitched before she ran her knuckles down my cheek and took everything. Everything I had become in my mere fifteen years. Everything I had saved for. My boat, my trailer, my future truck. The ocean in me. It was hers now.

The bare skin of her stomach against mine, the deepening of breath in her chest, built a fire around us as Juliette Peralta closed her eyes and pressed her lips to mine. She was gentle. So gentle. As if she could make up for the crassness of kissing me on a dare with the softness of her mouth. And she absolutely could. Her lips tasted faintly of the vanilla ChapStick she let me use yesterday, and her breath was all Southern Comfort.

Was it possible for a kiss to sink? I was sinking. Under the weight of her lips. Into the deep end, where she was the pressure in my ears and the softened edges of noise.

Her lips left mine, and she filled the space with scattered breaths. The thing about this kiss, besides everything about this kiss, was that it was my first. From her letters, I knew Jules had lost track of how many boys she'd kissed, but something told me she'd hold this one differently. Closer.

I worked up the nerve to touch her. Her lips *were* just on mine. I reached for her, letting my fingertips run over the waves of her ribs. She buried her face in my neck and pushed her hips into me, a pile of hard hemlines and cotton and sweaty thighs between us. Sinking.

None of this was part of the dare.

I pulled her tighter against me, a little scared of the other things I wanted to do with her. "You're my first kiss," I admitted. My words sounded like I was jogging down the beach, a little breathless.

I felt her lips curl into a smile against my neck as she slid to the side and settled next to me again, her arm draped over my abs. "I was hoping for that," she whispered. After a moment, she added, "First kisses always suck. My first kiss was with this guy, Evan, and I swear he was trying to give me a tonsillectomy with his whale of a tongue."

I giggled at her description, then turned to her. It was hard to make out much in the dark except for the fact that her eyes were open, and she was watching me. "I hope I was better," I whispered.

"Of course. But it's like comparing apples and oranges, you know?"

"What do you mean?" I asked.

She drew shapes I couldn't make out on my stomach as I tried not to shiver from her touch. "Kissing you was an apple. No tongue. Evan was an orange. Tongue." Her hand slowed, grazing the top seam of my waistband. I couldn't help but squirm. I wanted her to touch me...everywhere. "In order to compare, we'd have to do it again."

My world froze. I was just trying to digest the fact that I had kissed Jules at all. And that it was my first kiss. And I was just barely beginning to obsess over the question of when I'd be able to kiss her again.

Now. I got to kiss her again now.

"Okay," I barely managed to say. "For science."

"For science." She peeled away from my side and made herself comfortable on her back. She tugged my hand, and I rolled toward her, draping my leg over her thigh, her body half under me.

"Guess you're gonna be my second kiss, too," I said.

She ran her fingers up my shoulder and into my hair. It felt incredible as she gripped the back of my head and pulled me down. "Lucky me," she whispered.

I kissed her with confidence I didn't feel as she moved her hips under mine. Whatever she was doing felt so good. This hot pressure built in me. Between my thighs. It was like she knew it with how she raised to meet me in a rhythm.

Our kiss was all lips again until Jules abandoned my hair and gripped the fabric of my shorts instead, grinding us together until a moan accidently slipped from my throat. I would've been embarrassed if she hadn't used the opportunity to smoothly slip her tongue in my mouth. It was hot and so soft against mine.

And then she moaned, the vibration of it filling my chest, and I lost my fucking mind for her. I gasped—sharp, not at all smooth—as I pulled at her hips and slid completely on top her. Breasts to breasts, hips to hips, tongue brushing tongue. I would have sold my soul to make this kiss last forever. Would've torched Coral Bay to always feel her body effervescent with want for mine.

"Tanya," Austin called. His voice—my name—doused our moment, and I rolled off Jules, trying to catch my breath.

"Seriously, are y'all in here? We've been looking forever." His flashlight jumped from the reference section to the sports section.

"We're over here gossiping about you guys," Jules called. Before she got up, she pressed her lips to my temple. "Tanya. I like it," she whispered.

❖

Jules left four days after the night at the Meadows. The rest of her time here was fun. Normal fun. With absolutely no more kissing, touching, or otherwise more than friendly activity. We didn't speak about what happened. I only hoped that she felt what I felt. Guess it'd be useful to know what I felt. But what I felt was more of a scene than an emotion. I felt like when a storm was gathering over the ocean, and the sky darkened to match the rippling blue water below. That feeling of excitement and a little terror, waiting for the first strike of lightning.

"Breezy baby, you're gonna be late for your shift," Aunt Pat called from the kitchen.

I shoveled another soggy bite of Cinnamon Toast Crunch into my mouth. Aunt Pat always griped about how cereal wasn't a *real breakfast*, but I couldn't care less. Cinnamon Toast Crunch was life. I clicked off the episode of *Hey Arnold!* and drank the last bit of my sugar milk. "I'm never late, Aunt Pat." I tossed my bowl in the dishwasher and planted a kiss on her cheek. I took a step toward the door, but she tugged me back.

"Your momma called last night," she said, her lips tugged to one side in a grimace.

I let out a heavy sigh. Of course she'd called. It was about that time in her never-ending cycle of apologize, come back to prove herself for a week or two, and disappear again for a year or two. I wanted to tell her to just accept it. Don't come back. Or if she did come back, come back to visit. Not under the false hope of staying for good. Well, hope was a strong word. I didn't want that anyway.

My mom was an addict. It had just been alcohol for a while, but in her last visits, we'd seen a new darkness. It seemed to gather under her eyes and even spilled into her mouth and teeth. Gave me the creeps. Addiction was a disease, I knew. Aunt Pat was always warning me that because my mom was an addict, I was predisposed to be one, too. And I was careful.

I wasn't angry at her for it. I was angry at her for coming here and messing up my life for two weeks. Aunt Pat and Uncle Trevor were my parents. They were all I needed. And my mom, Aunt Pat's little sister, was just someone I had to deal with every so often. Didn't mean I didn't love her and hope for the best for her. I just couldn't give her much more than that and a couple breakfast meetups anymore. Aunt Pat had made me go to therapy when I was younger, saying she thought I was repressing my feelings of being abandoned. And maybe I was. But did it matter? When I had her and Uncle Trevor?

"When is she gonna be here?" I asked.

"Saturday."

"Until?"

Aunt Pat dropped her gaze to the sink. "Forever."

I opened the fridge and snagged the orange juice, chuckling. "I give this stint four days."

"Maybe." She shrugged. We were past the pretending part. Past the anger. "Be safe, baby."

Aunt Pat never seemed exasperated by my mom, and I'd like to think it was because my mom gave her me. I knew it was so self-absorbed. But I liked to think it was all worth it to Aunt Pat. It was to me.

"Always." I wiped my mouth with the back of my hand. "Oh, stopping at Ms. Francesca's on the way home. She's gonna let me test-drive her truck."

"This is the F-150?" she asked.

"No, ma'am. It's the Ranger. '91."

She dried her hands on the towel hanging from the cupboard. "Okay. You know what to look for. It's your money, kid." She walked over to me and kissed my forehead. "Love you, Breezy baby."

I smiled, then squeezed her tight, really tight, until she batted me away in a fit of chuckles. "Love you, Aunt Pat."

"Go on. Don't want Marge on your case."

"She's always on my case." I shoved a granola bar in my pocket for later. Marge *was* always on my case. Not because I was a bad employee or anything. I was an exceptional employee, if I said so myself. She just cared about me, so she was hard on me.

"Good. Now get."

As I biked to the Coral Bay Inn, the breeze soft and savory, the ocean in me rumbled with something. Something deep and strong. A riptide pulling me. Coral Bay tugging me tight to its breast. A letter from Juliette that was going to be in my mailbox tomorrow. And that sweet Ford Ranger I was going to buy after work.

Dear Breezy,

I'm sorry your mom is in town. I know you like to
see her, but I also know it's hard. Coral pretty and sticky
sharp. Only to be enjoyed from a distance, right? I don't
exactly know why, but I want to meet her. Three years
of friendship, probably trillions of letters, and at least
twenty skimboard lessons surely earns me the right to
meet the person who produced my best friend.

My shark tooth necklace broke when I was making
out with Travis. The brute basically ripped it from
my neck with his giant hands like a klutz. He's cute,
though, so I forgave him. He actually asked me to be
his girlfriend yesterday, which Rachel was absolutely
pissed about because she dumped Noah for Travis. I
don't care. Rachel was a complete bitch to me all of
last semester, so I said yes to Travis. He's taking me to
prom. We get to have it at the Fox Theater downtown.
So fancy. Can't wait.

Did you take the boat out this week? I'm dying to
get on the water with you after all your hard work fixing
it up.

Speaking of hard work, I don't think I can be a

teacher anymore. My parents have been talking to me more about my position with the company, and I'm starting to get excited about it. I'll be majoring in business now. I know you don't exactly love my parents or what they do, but things are really heating up for them, and I can't pass up the opportunity to build myself into the business. I'm a Peralta, after all.

I don't know. It will be good for me...right?

Only a month until you and me. One month. I keep telling myself I got this. That one month isn't so long at all. And I have fun things to fill it with like prom and finding a roommate for college, but the truth is that I miss you. And I love your letters, but they're not enough. They're not your sunshine hair or ocean eyes. They don't smell like you. They're just one little sliver.

Fuck, I got all mushy. Sorry.

Just miss my bff.

Love,

Your Jules

CHAPTER FOUR

The Coral Bay Inn was completely booked for the weekend, an occurrence that was no longer rare. Marge was eighty percent happy for the accelerated business and twenty percent completely horrified and overwhelmed by it. In the past year, she'd trained me on taking reservations, creating work orders for maintenance, and generally being able to run the day-to-day of the Inn. My shifts at Crabby's were manager shifts now, and lately, I'd been able to sock away a lot of cash.

Today, I was the front of house manager, and it was, to put it mildly, complete fucking chaos. The guest on the phone demanding a surf and turf platter be delivered to his room within twenty minutes during the dinner rush was out of his goddamn mind, but I was able to talk him down by offering him a free drink ticket instead.

I took a deep breath as the restaurant flooded with chatter around me. I had my boat, my truck, my trailer, my job. I had Coral Bay and my aunt and uncle. Ninety percent happy, that was what I was.

The Peraltas sat at their usual table by the sand, dressed in their usual cool elegance, and Juliette sat to her father's right, looking a bit more interested in her parents' words than in years past. Her clothes seemed older now. She'd never fixed the shark tooth necklace. Instead, something shimmery and expensive-looking hung against her chest, and she'd been in town for almost two days and hadn't made it out to meet me.

Meeting me on the beach was normally the very first thing she did when she got here. Now, I felt like I was an intruder. *Me.* In my own town. In my own workplace. We were seventeen years old. She could damn well meet me if she wanted to.

Screw it.

I strolled past a table with a giant fishbowl cocktail, which I wanted so badly to nix from the menu, and walked right up to their table. "Mr. and Mrs. Peralta, what a pleasure to have you dine with us this evening." I shot Jules a quick glance. "Juliette, nice to see you as always." The grimace on her face almost made me feel bad for her. *Almost.*

Her father gripped my shoulder in that condescending way that powerful men did and pulled me close enough to smell his aftershave. Sharp like a pine needle. A smell I wouldn't have hated in a different context. "Breezy, it's always such a pleasure." He smiled at his wife, and she straightened as if she was just now tuning in to her surroundings. "Isn't she growing up into a fine young woman?"

"Dad, please," Juliette begged with a touch of embarrassment. But I was the one who should have been embarrassed. The guy always had a way of cutting me down. Since day one. His disdain for me was palpable.

I cleared my throat and sunk back into business mode. "How is everything tasting tonight? Are we satisfied with the meals and wine selection?"

Mr. Peralta pressed his napkin to his lips and tilted his head. "You know, I keep saying, you need to get some more high-end bottles on your wine list. We drink Dom when we celebrate."

This asshole thought I was going to put Dom Perignon on my wine list so he could drink it once a year, when my regulars were Jack and Coke or tequila types? I smiled through his bullshit. "What are we celebrating today?"

"Well, we just closed a very exciting deal," Mr. Peralta started, but Jules cut him off.

"Dad, I was going to tell her—"

Her mom cleared her throat. "The Meadows, dear. We closed on the Meadows this morning," she said. "You know, that dilapidated old eyesore of a school?"

I swallowed dryly as Jules refused to make eye contact. "Yes, I'm familiar with it," I said through gritted teeth.

"It comes down after the holiday, on Tuesday. The new luxury Sands Living will take its place."

I stared, speechless, as Mrs. Peralta hopped back in. "Oh, I can imagine it now. Coral Bay's finest." She swept a hand over whatever glimpse of nonreality she was dreaming up. "It will have brand-new luxury condos and fine dining and shops underneath. Everything a guest would need to enjoy in one spot."

I swallowed again, but the lump of dread had the staying power of sand in a wet bathing suit.

"Breezy, can we—"

"Sounds lovely, Mrs. Peralta. And congratulations to you all." I waved at a server and most likely confused the hell out of her, pretending someone was flagging me down. "So sorry. I need to attend to something for a moment. I hope you enjoy."

I bowed a good-bye and disappeared into the back galley, my breath hot in my lungs. "I'm taking five," I announced to anyone who was in earshot and jogged to the place that calmed me: the beach. When my feet hit the sand, I didn't stop jogging. I wanted to be out of sight of the restaurant guests in my very recognizable manager's black button-down.

Once I was far enough, I sat on a hunk of driftwood by the dunes and stared at the ocean until my eyes watered. It was easy to shrug at a couple of houses here and there. At a fourplex that was already a vacation home. But the Meadows? It was ridiculous to take this personally, but shit. It felt like things were happening to my town that I couldn't control. That community the Peraltas wanted to build, the Sands Living, sounded like pure commercialized shit. Soulless. And it only took one soulless thing to suck the color out of everything. Like a black fucking hole of capitalism.

And Jules had just sat there, slipping into the grayscale of her parents' joyless existence. She used to have all the color. All the joy. Now she had a stupid necklace, a stupid boyfriend, and a stupid—

"Breezy, hey." Jules walked up slowly as if nervous to talk. She looked beautiful. There was never any denying that.

But the silver heart necklace reflected the sun in my eyes, and that kind of hurt. "I'm just on break. Can we talk later?"

"I didn't know. I promise, I didn't know until we signed on it. It was this big surprise that they wanted to announce." She hovered over me with a needy energy, as if waiting to be released from my hurt. She sighed and sat tentatively next to me.

"Coral Bay may not be, like, the most rich and polished beach town in the world, but that's what makes it perfect to me. That Uncle Trevor inherited the bait shop from his grandfather, and Aunt Pat bought her shrimping boat on the cheap from her old boss. There's roots and community here."

She gently rubbed my back. "I know, Breezy. But the Meadows—"

"I know the Meadows needs to be dealt with. But fancy condos and shops? That doesn't belong here."

"Hey," she said and tugged me by the shoulder into her chest. "I know. I'm on your side, okay? I know it's ridiculous, and the Meadows should be a school again or something. But I can't control it, Breezy. I just can't."

I swayed away from her, frustrated with her excuses. She'd looked happy enough celebrating with her parents when I'd walked up to her table. I tucked a flyaway hair into my bun and stood. "Nice to finally see you, Jules."

She stood and grabbed my hand. I let her for a second. How could I not? I'd been dying to touch her for months. "They wouldn't let me out until the deal was done. Seeing you was the only thing I wanted to do."

We stared at each other. It was the closest thing to a fight we'd had. And I wasn't over it. I slipped my hand from hers and dropped my gaze to her chest. To the silver atrocity on her neck that was the representation of everything I hated and way less cool than a fossilized shark tooth that was ten million years old. But I guess it had never sparkled like that.

"I hate your necklace."

Her hand rose to her chest in one of the most self-conscious moves I'd ever seen from her. Her fingers curled around the pendant like they'd used to curl around the tooth. She held it for a moment longer before gently shaking her head. "It's just more professional."

I stared at her, hoping she could feel the heat of it in her bones. No, in her marrow. But what could I say to that? She'd said it all for me. Instead, I shook my head and started walking. "Gotta get back."

"Wait."

I stopped, wondering if I'd always stop for her, this best friend of mine who stuck in me like coral. *Coral pretty and sticky sharp.*

"Tomorrow. Just you and me. No boys. Pick me up at sunrise, okay?"

The sunlight illuminated the tiny gold flecks in her eyes. There was no way I could say no, though the boys would be pissed to not be hanging with us. I nodded and walked away.

❖

Closing time was blissful. The moment the last guest finally stumbled back to their room, Crabby's returned to us. Someone plugged their iPod into the speaker system, and everyone either took a shot, poured a beer, or made a cheap mixed drink and let them sweat on the bar as we dove into our speedy closing routines. I sipped a Modelo as I counted the till. My eyes were heavy from working so much lately, but my mood had brightened since we closed.

"Seventeen, eighty, eleventy-two." Marge collapsed on the barstool next to me and bumped my shoulder. "Fifty million..."

I groaned and dropped the pile of ones that needed to be recounted now. "I hate when you do that, you know?"

She chuckled her deep chuckle and squeezed the back of my neck with her thick fingers that smelled of Marlboro. She wore her floral Coral Bay Inn work shirt, the red one that matched the blood that seemed to be so close under her skin. "Why do you think I do it, kid?"

I rolled my eyes. "Modelo?"

She freed her gorgeous red mane that was beginning to fade into gray and shook it loose. "Yeah. Why not? I'm feeling young tonight."

I slipped behind the bar and poured a beer, slid it to her, and leaned on my elbows as she took her first sip. Her shoulders relaxed as she wiped the translucent foam from her lips. "The Peraltas bought the Meadows," I said. She nodded as if she already knew. As if she had a superpower and knew all the goings-on before they even happened. "You knew?"

She pushed my beer to me and nodded. "No one had to tell me what was going to happen. Every year, the high-rises creep east. Closer and closer. It was only a matter of time, Breezy girl. The way of the world."

I didn't like how resigned she sounded. *The way of the world* just didn't sit right with me. "You're just, what? Okay with it?"

"Okay with it?" She scoffed. "I'm as okay with it as I am being abducted by aliens. And let me tell you, kid, aliens are creepy little things. I've got no love for 'em. So, no, I'm not okay with it." She gripped her beer with both hands, shaking her head. "You may not think I'm doing enough to fight it, but owning the Inn and Crabby's...it's what I can do to keep Coral Bay what it is. I pour my life into this place. My hours, my creative energy, my back." She chuckled. "There's a lot I can't control, Breezy, but I can make damn sure the Inn stays. And that Crabby's stays. And at the end of the day, that means something to me."

I nodded, slipping my fingers through the condensation on my glass. "It means something to me, too."

"I know, baby." She cleared her throat. "How's your momma?" I drained the last quarter of my beer and turned my back on Marge to refill it. "She's got a good heart. Always did when we were growing up."

"I never said she didn't." I walked around to sit next to her. "Sometimes, you make it sound like I don't show her enough grace or something. I'm always nice. Always there when she wants to crash my life. I literally always—"

Marge laid her hand on my wrist. "Easy. No one's coming for you." She squeezed gently. "I ain't coming for you. Just have a soft spot for Reggie. You know that." She straightened and cleared her throat. "Nothing excuses what she's done, of course. But humans...we're messy and all sorts of fucked-up. Doesn't mean I don't miss her, though."

I knew my mom and Marge were close growing up, but I never asked either of them how close. For some reason, I didn't want to know. Because then, I'd know it wasn't just me she'd hurt, and it wasn't just me she'd lost. It was Marge and this community. "Yeah," I said. "I miss her when she leaves, too." I gripped the edge of the bar and swiveled to face her. "But I don't really like it when she's here. Is that bad?"

"No, Breezy baby. It isn't bad. It's just life." She pulled me in for a quick hug, then stood. "That till ain't gonna count itself." She nodded to the register drawer and cracked her back. "I'll see you tomorrow."

"Night."

She left me to count the drawer and ruminate on everything she'd said. Something nagged me. It was Juliette and the achy, simmering fear that she would turn into someone I used to love. Someone who had a "good heart" underneath it all but had gotten lost along the way. I wondered if I'd be sitting at this bar in ten years like Marge, reminiscing on an old friend.

"No," I grumbled. Jules was not my mom, and I was not giving up on her. I knew she had different dreams than her parents. She wanted to be a teacher and not grind every day to feed a machine of consumption and development. She was different deep down.

❖

The cool thing about a south-facing beach was that the sun set and rose over the water. Okay, the sunrise was kind of over the sand and a bit of land, but its burst of orange always flowed over the ocean like lava. And this morning was no different. As I drove to the Peraltas' vacation home near East Beach, I rolled down the windows and let the salty air calm me. I was anxious to hang out with Juliette and get back to what we'd always been: friends who felt like shelter.

We were always saying how we were each other's protection, worlds apart from reality, where we could rest away from it all. I missed that. Since her last letter, things had felt a bit off. Distant.

I pulled into their driveway and parked next to the Cadillac. It didn't make me feel out of place, seeing my old Ford next to the glossy luxury car as I walked to the door. Didn't make me self-conscious. One of those cars could tow a boat. And it was mine. It wasn't often that I knocked on the Peraltas' door. Never felt quite comfortable with the small talk, especially when Juliette's parents made it so painfully clear they disapproved of our friendship.

But I was feeling a little indignant this morning, looking extra Coral Bay in my jean overalls, red cutoff tank, and wind-tousled hair, hoping to wake up her parents with the doorbell.

I reached for the little white button at the same time the door opened, and Juliette flew into my arms smelling distinctly not like the ocean. But like mountain mist, whatever the hell that was. It was a vibe. *She* was a vibe. She squeezed me tight, and even though I had some mixed feelings about her and her family, she was still my Jules. I tightened her up into me.

She pulled back and gripped the straps of my overalls, giving me a little shake. "You were about to ring the doorbell, weren't you? Trying to wake up Tony and Kathy, huh?"

I groaned. "Ugh. Fine. Maybe I was."

She tugged me so our chests bumped and planted a kiss on my cheek that shouldn't have felt how it felt, like I was a wishing well and she'd just tossed her last coin in my water. We'd full-on made out only a year ago. But time had excused that kiss as normal. We were still friends. Just friends. Who had kissed one time during a silly teenage game. So her kiss on my cheek sinking through me like a wish kind of freaked me out. Especially since I didn't know if her wish was for me.

"You're cute when you're mad, Breezy." She loosened her grip and ran her finger up under the strap, her knuckle brushing my chest. "And when you wear overalls." She had me stuck like gum on a hot sidewalk. "Come on. My parents will be up soon, and they really don't like you."

I unstuck myself and rolled my eyes. "I gathered that."

"And really won't like that I'm bailing on them to ride off in this old truck with you."

I grinned. "No. I don't think they would."

She pulled me by the hand and led me down her front steps. "Especially now that they know I write you every couple of weeks."

I stopped at the door of my truck, a nervous flutter stalling me out. "They...they know about our letters?" It wasn't like I'd said anything damning in them. I hadn't waxed poetic about wishing-well kisses or how it felt to have the weight of their daughter pushing me into a beanbag as she'd made out with me. I hadn't quite processed those feelings myself, much less written them down for someone else. And how could I when I didn't know how Jules felt?

"Yeah." She slid onto the bench seat and motioned for me to get in. "They think you're corrupting me with your Coral Bay manner."

I laughed as I started the engine. "Trying to." The slightest gasp escaped her lips as I reached for her necklace and fingered it against her chest. It was one of the first times I felt like I had power over her. "But it looks like I've failed."

She pushed my hand away and unclasped her necklace, tucking it away in the glove box. "You're no quitter, Breezy. We'll just have to see what happens." She settled into the cracked gray leather and grinned. "I'm very easily influenced."

I pulled onto the sandy road headed east. "No, you're not," I said.

"No. I'm not."

We drove in comfortable quiet until I pulled into the parking lot of the Dolphin Drip, our local coffee shop. Jules ordered a vanilla latte and almond croissant, and I got a black coffee with a slice of banana bread.

"Best banana bread east of the Mississippi, did you know?" I said as we slid into my truck.

Jules balanced her latte on the dash and buckled her seat belt, chuckling. "You're full of shit." Her belt clicked, and she gave me a challenging look. "You've never left the state of Florida to try any other banana breads."

It was a quick little hit to my ego, but what if I didn't want to leave Coral Bay? I was happy here. "Some truths are universal and don't require scientific analysis." I started the car and pulled onto the road.

"Mm-hmm. Is that so?"

"It is. No other banana bread is made at the Dolphin Drip and can be picked up this very morning by you and me and consumed on East Beach as the sun rises, and we chat about how your parents hate me." I shot her a grin. "See? The world's best banana bread."

She shook her head and tried not to spill her latte as I parked in the gravel beach access lot. "Oh, so now it's the best in the entire world, huh?"

I opened my door and grabbed the towels. "Yep. Come on."

We walked through the cool morning sand, west down the beach, past a peaceful tide pool. I laid down the towels, and we sat, watching the early waves roll in and the sun rise higher and higher. We were a little late for my favorite time of day on the beach, when the midnight blues and blacks turned dusty. That was at around five in the morning this time of year. Regardless, it was beautiful.

"I'm sorry you found out about the Meadows from my father. That really sucks," she said.

I stared at the ocean for a moment longer before looking at her. She wore her Coral Bay standard: a navy tank with jean cutoffs and sandals. "Yeah. I don't know. It's not about your family. I think, growing up here, we've always felt this pressure, this inevitable force, creeping up on our town." I nudged her shoulder and nodded down the beach. "Used to not be able to see them when I was growing up." The faint outlines of high-rises were barely visible in the morning haze, but they were there. Always there. The boogeymen of Coral Bay.

"Oh." She fiddled with the lid of her cup.

"And there's nothing—"

"I miss you, Breezy." She stared at me, her brows narrowed against the sun and eyes intense. It was a look she'd never given me before. "I know you and Oscar are basically dating, and I—"

"Whoa. Hold on." I raised my hand to stop her. "We're not dating." A few stolen kisses that felt more like messing around than anything real and a deep friendship was all that was going on. Did I always think I'd marry Oscar? Yes. Was I attracted to him? In some way. He was my one option.

But he wasn't her.

She sighed and shook her head. "Basically dating."

"Well, you're dating Travis. What's your point?" I picked at the sand between our towels, a little frustrated, a little confused.

"I don't know. I just know you're mad, and I'm nervous for the end of this trip because then, I'll be at Penn, and I don't know when I'll be back. And I don't want to lose you. Or your friendship. So I was hoping we could put the Meadows behind us and just enjoy each other."

I chewed my lip. What could one week really solve in terms of the Peraltas, the Meadows, and the future of my town anyway? But Jules was right. I'd had this anxiety in my gut about her going to college and meeting all these new people and falling in love and having a family. Her having a life so full, how would there be space for a Coral Bay townie she used to be pen pals with? How could I ever fit into Juliette Peralta's life? With her charm and her money and her opportunities?

It was hopeless. Might as well give each other one last good trip.

I stood and unhooked the buckles of my overalls, letting them fall around my ankles. Jules stared, her mouth slightly open. "Come on, then," I said, pulling off my tank. I stood in my bra and underwear and nodded to the water. "Let's kick this week off right."

She scoffed. "It's going to be freezing." Her gaze scanned my body, but I had nothing to be ashamed of. Plus, it was nothing she hadn't seen from being in a bathing suit countless times.

"Come on. Take a morning swim with me, and we'll forget about everything but us this week." I held out my hand to help her up. "I promise."

She groaned dramatically but pulled herself up. I watched as she peeled her tank top over her head, revealing all her tanned, smooth skin and purple lacy bra. It looked so good on her and matched her underwear when she kicked off her shorts. The familiar feeling of jealousy and want simmered in my stomach. Juliette was the most beautiful thing I knew. And it was becoming clearer every minute I spent with her, every letter we exchanged, that it was want.

While I was rough and windblown blond with freckled

shoulders, she was glossy and perfect. Her hair always in place and her skin soft and cared for. She took my hand again, and we walked to the water's edge, the cold ocean kissing our toes. Felt like we were facing something together. She gasped when we waded in thigh deep. "Come on. On the count of three," I said.

She bit her lip, shook her head, then grinned. "One," she said.

"Two," I said.

"Three," we said together and plunged into the cold water. My hair flowed weightless as my body went into a bit of shock from the cold, and a menthol numb overtook me. It felt incredible. There must have been millions of endorphins released from jumping into cold water. The whir of the ocean filled my ears, the overflowing sounds of marine life muffled by itself.

Juliette's cursing met me when I broke the surface. "Fuck. Holy fucking fuck. It's freezing." She waded the couple of feet to me as I tried not to look at her drenched bra. But when her eyes dropped to mine, I remembered mine was white.

I crossed my arms over my chest and grimaced. "Sorry. Forgot I was wearing white."

She grinned as she wrapped her arms around me, her skin cold and slippery. "Guess now I know what you look like naked." I tightened her up. We were both freezing our asses off. "What's next in your grand plan for a morning swim, now that we're both ice cubes?"

I shivered in her arms, and she rubbed my back. "It's entirely possible," I started.

"Yes?"

"That I didn't think this far ahead in my plan." We laughed in each other's arms before the most obvious solution popped into my head. I tugged her toward shore. "Come on. We're going to the Inn."

❖

Sometimes, the hot tub at the Coral Bay Inn was suspect as hell. But I knew the cleaning schedule, and the water had just been replaced by yours truly two days ago. The perfect amount of time for the harsh chemicals to fade a bit and the water to be fresh and clean and most importantly, hot. There was a video camera keeping watch of the tucked-away corner that housed the Jacuzzi, but I knew no one watched the film unless there was an incident. I also knew Marge wouldn't give two shits about us using it this early, when all the guests were still asleep.

Jules and I were quiet as we padded barefoot down the cool cement path past the pool and around the corner to the pink-and-mint-green tiled lounge area. I dropped my truck keys on a side table and flipped on the jets as Juliette slipped into the hot water.

She moaned as she waded in front of a jet. "Oh my God. It's so good." I plunged in next to her, displacing enough water to cause a wake in the tub and splash her. She scoffed and swatted me. "My little debutante, so full of grace," she teased but pulled me next to her.

Hot tubs always made me feel so oozy, like a cracked egg. Especially when I was freezing from the ocean. I wiped the chlorine from my eyes and grinned. "I am quite graceful, thank you very much. You, on the other hand"—I nudged her hot shoulder—"have you seen yourself on a skimboard, love?"

She wrapped her arms tightly around my waist and yanked me into her lap, tickling me until I was splashing and thrashing like a fish on a hook. I really was a fish on a hook when it came to her.

"Stop. *Stop*," I begged, breathless, my arms around her neck. "You're the most graceful girl in Coral Bay," I pleaded.

Her tickles stopped, and she held me still. "In Coral Bay?" She stared at me, her dark hair plastered to her cheek and eyes deep and molten. Something had shifted in her tone and her hands, now languid and gentle, one on my hip and one resting in my lap.

I curled my fingers around the back of her neck and gave her a gentle squeeze as we stared at each other, the rumbling of the jets filling any space that would have been awkward. "I haven't really been anywhere," I almost whispered, my fingers playing with her baby hairs. "But I'd bet my boat that you're the most graceful girl in the world. Most beautiful, at the very least."

She squeezed my thigh and leaned in, kissing me hard on the cheek. "That's funny," she said through a grin.

"And why's that?"

She ran her knuckles up and down my thigh. I didn't want to squirm; I wanted to melt all over her. "Because out of the billions of people in the world, there's only one other person I can see right now, and she's way more beautiful than me," she whispered. "Sorry about your boat, babe."

I took a deep breath and pressed my forehead to her temple as she held me close and stroked my thigh. I might have been on fire for her. "Why do you always have to leave?" I mumbled into her ear. "You know it breaks my heart."

I could feel her breath on my shoulder. Until it was her lips I felt just there, on my collarbone. Then against the rim of my ear. Shivers in the heat. "You know it breaks mine, too."

Suddenly, I felt desperate. "Don't disappear on me, Jules. With college and life and everything. Come back to me. You know I'll be here."

"How could I not come back to you?" She stood, and I slid off her lap to my feet. Her gaze dropped to my chest again, but she didn't seem embarrassed about it. Like she knew I was hers, see-through bra and all. She smirked after a moment. "Can we go enjoy your boat before it gets taken by the gods of gambling?"

I nodded. "For sure. Let's go wake the boys."

CHAPTER FIVE

"Can you grab my tacklebox from the truck?" I asked Oscar as everyone piled onto my little aluminum boat. I called him *Silverfish*. Just in my head, though. Wasn't the coolest name in the world. "Should be the only thing left."

He smiled his sharp smile, tan skin radiating in the early afternoon sun, abs like ripples in the water. Handsome as ever. "Sure thing, Breezy."

Benny slid into the seat next to Juliette. "First time on the boat, eh?"

She nodded, pulling her shades from her hair, slipping them over her eyes. "This is a boat? Could've sworn it was a spaceship," she said, completely deadpan.

Benny scrunched his brows. "Rich people are so weird."

"Dumbass," Austin said as he sidled up to Juliette's other side. Every boy seemed to be in love with her, their eyes always dancing over her. Except for Oscar. He was still mine in some sort of innate way. I loved him, wanted him, but there was something in me that didn't fit with him. Didn't really fit with anyone.

Jules caught my eye as I cranked the motor and winked.

Except for her. I fit with her.

Oscar startled me when he hopped back on the boat. "Okay, we've got the rod, the bait, the beer, the boombox. Missing anything?"

Benny groaned. "Let's fucking go already."

These assholes weren't even grateful for my hard work, fixing up the boat and saving for the truck and trailer. *Children.* Oscar helped untie us, and I crawled through the no-wake zone, enjoying the soft morning breeze before it became afternoon stifling. I liked how I controlled the breeze in Juliette's hair as we picked up speed in the open water. I knew exactly where we were going.

Silverfish thunked over waves, graceful as ever, as the smile on Juliette's face grew in accordance with our speed. She liked to go fast. She liked when I cut into a wave and the sea splashed her. Couldn't believe it took me this long to get her on the boat. It wasn't as easy to pry her from her parents' grip these days, so I was thankful for today, at least. The pastries and coffee, the morning swim, the hot tub. And it was only ten. We had all day left of Jules playing hooky. And I was going to milk every minute of it.

When I saw the shore of the small island come into view, I slowed until we were swimming distance, then dropped anchor. Oscar played the Bob Marley CD we'd stolen from Austin's older brother on the boombox. We drank beer and shit talked until the sun heated our skin, and sweat beaded down our backs. Then we jumped in the ocean and swam to shore, wasting time together. Spending it like it'd never run out.

It was what I needed. What we needed, me and Juliette. To clear the storm of the Meadows and the knowledge that everything would probably change after this trip. We weren't thinking about it for now. We were just living it up with bad beer and good music on my yacht and private island. Though *Silverfish* was hardly even a real boat, and the island would probably be gone in the next hurricane, they were perfect today.

❖

We might have never left if we'd packed an appropriate amount of snacks, but beer was prioritized when it came to cooler space, so we left after a couple hours to throw back po'boys at Woody's near East Beach. The fried shrimp and hush puppies filled our growling bellies as we planned what was next in our epic summer day. With every hour that passed, I had a growing feeling that there was some kind of finality to this day. That it would be the last of something. I washed down the simmering anxiety with a long drink of Coke.

"What do you think, Breezy? One last night at the Meadows before the villains tear it down?" Benny asked.

Juliette scoffed. "Rude."

"He's not wrong." Austin smacked him in the shoulder. "But he is rude."

I didn't want to go to the Meadows. Not with Jules. It would only remind me of everything that was about to change. The Meadows was about to be obliterated and turned into some soulless tourist trap, and I was about to lose Juliette. I didn't want to be there. Anywhere but there.

"No," I said, wiping my fingers on my greasy napkin. "I don't feel like being shut inside a dark musty building. I want to be outside, under the stars tonight."

I caught Juliette grin before taking a bite of her grouper sandwich.

"Palmetto Hill pool it is," Osar said.

Palmetto Hill was a shabby old apartment complex with a shabby old pool. But the thing about the pool was that it had a true deep end, unlike new pools that only reached five feet. This pool was deep, and the building was short—only two stories—which was the perfect combination for bored teenagers who wanted to jump off the roof into the water. Which we did probably once a month.

"Sorted," I said.

We went our separate ways until dark to shower off the

sunscreen and salt, making a fresh canvas of skin for the chlorine. Juliette came home with me because there was no way either of us was going to risk dropping her off and her parents not letting her back out. They would be livid enough that she'd been with me all day.

I was clean and lying awkwardly in my bed as Jules showered in my bathroom. I didn't know what to do with my hands. I twiddled my thumbs on my belly, not ready for the sight of her red and warm and in my clothes. My bathing suit and shorts and tank.

The bathroom door cracked open, and steam poured into my room. Jules walked through the threshold like a dream. Her hair was wet and twisted into a messy bun. Her skin was damp and glowing. My T-shirt draped over her curves, and my bikini cupped her breasts.

I stood and slid my phone in my pocket, feeling like if I looked at Juliette for one more second, I'd expose myself. Expose all these feelings that had been slowly building since we were thirteen. And what would be the point of that when she was about to leave for good?

I walked to the door. "Ready when you are," I said.

She tapped the screen of her phone on my dresser. "It's a tad early, don't you think?"

Her eyes looked hopeful, like she wanted this moment together. Just us. Clean and fresh and alone in my room. "No. I, uh, want to get there and make sure the coast is clear."

Her brows raised as she considered me. "Make sure the coast is clear?"

I nodded.

"Okay, Breezy. Whatever you say."

❖

The Palmetto Hill's pool and courtyard were completely deserted. In fact, I was pretty sure we were the only ones who swam in this pool at all. The complex was mostly inhabited by older locals who probably couldn't be bothered with a pool when they had the ocean two blocks away.

"Good thing we made sure the coast is clear," Jules said as she draped her towel over the back of a mildewy, white, plastic chair. It was completely dark except for the rippling light from the bottom of the pool and a dim lamp standing sentry at the gate. Probably a safety hazard, but the darkness was cozy, intimate.

And I was a coward.

It was our last night together before everything changed, and I had just passed up a moment alone in my room with her.

"Actually, Jules, I—"

"Cannonball," Benny yelled as he burst through the gate, ripped off his shirt, and plunged into the deep end with his arms wrapped around his bent knees. An impressive splash wet our toes as Jules and I looked at each other in shock.

"What time is it?" Jules asked.

I pulled my phone from my pocket. "It's almost ten thirty. Why?"

She plucked my phone from my grip, placed it on the table next to her, and shoved me hard and fast in the chest. I stumbled backward until the concrete disappeared beneath my feet, and I plunged into the cool pool water, momentarily cut off from the rest of the world. Everything was muted, and the water held me tight. It always did. The only other time I felt like I did now, at the bottom of the pool, was when Jules was on top of me, her weight sinking into me. When everything faded except for her lips on mine. Her hands on my hips. Tongue running over the sharp edges of my teeth.

Laughter and shouting poured over me when I broke the surface. "How's the water?" Jules asked through a grin. She tucked her purse under the table, and Oscar crept behind her.

"Looks like you're about to find out," I called.

Oscar wrapped his arms around her, and they both plunged into the pool next to me with Austin following quickly behind.

"Fuck, it's cold," Jules said as she wiped the water from her eyes.

"Oh, come on. It's perfect," Austin said.

Oscar splashed her. "It's that city blood of yours."

A flare of jealousy leapt through my chest. He liked her. Of course he liked her. She was Juliette Peralta. But he was supposed to like me, and I was supposed to like him. We were basically dating.

But we weren't dating. We would never be dating.

Because I liked her.

"Where the fuck did Benny go?" Austin asked.

"Let's get this party started," Benny shouted from the roof of the second story. He gyrated to a beat that only he could hear, hips popping and arms flailing, until he tucked his thumbs in his waistband and pushed his trunks down.

"And there's Benny's penis. Jesus," Oscar muttered.

"Ah, my eyes are burning," Austin said, hiding behind his hands.

We had been known to skinny-dip from time to time, and these boys in their birthday suits was nothing I hadn't seen many times before. "Well, go on, then. Jump," I called to him.

He shook his head, his hands barely covering his package. "Not until you losers strip."

I shrugged. "Fine." I had nothing to lose. I wasn't going to jump off the roof tonight, it was dark, and no one could see me underwater anyway. I plucked the string of my bikini and threw my wet top so it slapped on the concrete by our table. Then threw my bottoms to join them. Everyone stripped until all our wet suits were discarded around the pool.

"Excellent," Benny shouted and reared back to jump.

"Jules." I waded to her and pushed her against the wall of the pool before Benny plunged way too close to us. I turned to scold him. "Dude. Fuck. Be more careful. We were literally right where you landed."

"Hey." He splashed us both. "You know better than to linger in the splash zone."

"Prick," Jules muttered from behind me.

All my focus zeroed in on her and me and her hands on me. And us…naked. My entire being buzzed as she gently pulled me by the hips so I was flush against her. I could feel her breasts, her nipples hard from the cool water, pressed against my back. And fuck. I wanted Juliette. Badly.

"Hey. Focus, Breezy," Benny said.

I snapped out of my trance and swam to the center of the pool, treading water. "What?"

"Your turn. Go jump," Austin said.

"No. It's cold." I wrapped my arms over my chest. "And just, no."

"Aw, come on. You're shy now because Jules is here?" Benny chimed in.

I could feel everyone's eyes on me. Well, I couldn't very well admit to that, could I? "Don't look, you creep." I gave him a splash for good measure as I climbed out of the pool. I'd grown up on the beach. I was extremely comfortable naked. But that didn't mean I wanted everyone's eyes on me. Jules averted her gaze as I padded up the stairs. The tricky part about jumping off the roof wasn't actually the jump. It was using the handrail and the sketchy gutter to shimmy up to the roof. Slipping here could have been bad. Like, really bad. But it was just what we did to feel alive. Risk our lives.

Once I had expertly made it to the top, I shook out my arms, took a step back, and went for it. Only, right before I jumped, I heard the distinct *whoop whoop* of a police siren. I splashed hard into the deep end and desperately clawed my way to the surface. Benny and Austin were hopping the fence to the backside of the complex, and Jules and Oscar were rounding the corner to hide in the trees by the parking lot.

"Assholes," I muttered.

I flew out of the pool, scraping my knee on the cement, and grabbed my clothes and phone just as one of the officers banged against the locked gate. Lucky for me, I was seventeen and fast, and he was…not. I was over the fence and around the back of the building before he even saw my face.

I tugged on my shirt and shimmied into my shorts, a feat given I was dripping wet. Benny and Austin had completely vanished, so I crept back around the building to the trees where Oscar and Jules had gone. The dried palms were sharp against my bare feet, but I had my summer skin from hot sand and gravel, so it wasn't too bad. I spotted a flash of Oscar's orange shirt and pulled back a palm frond.

Jules pulled out of his arms and wiped her mouth as Oscar took a step away and buttoned his shirt.

"Breezy," Jules said.

I stepped back as if I'd just run straight into a force field. Seeing her in his arms, her mouth on his, made a thick dread pool in my gut and bile crawl up my throat. I was stuck. Stuck in the inevitable flypaper of heartbreak that was Juliette. "We, uh, better go. They're in the pool…area. In the pool area, so we can get to the truck around back." I pointed over my shoulder. "Unless you wanted to go with Oscar? 'Cause that'd be totally chill, too." So chill. The chillest.

"No, I want to go with you." She gave Oscar a quick hug, then grabbed my hand. "Let's go."

I gave him a searing glare he probably couldn't make out in the dark and followed Jules to my truck. The cops turned at the sound of my doors opening. "Buckle up," I whispered as the two officers jogged toward us.

"Over here, you fuckers!" Oscar shouted from the trees. They turned in his direction as I peeled out of the parking lot.

"Don't worry. They won't catch him," I said a bit sardonically.

She touched my hand, but I pulled away. I felt disgusted. Jules and Oscar…*fuck*. "I wasn't worried," she said.

"Okay."

We drove in silence except for the ocean roaring through my open windows. I turned away from the water onto Lassiter Way, the road that led straight to the Peraltas' beach house.

"Wait. Don't bring me home yet," she said.

I sighed but pulled over. I didn't want to drop her off and never see her again, but what else was I supposed to do after seeing her kiss my best friend, whom I also sometimes kissed? *Ugh.* "Want me to drop you off at Oscar's instead?"

She turned and squeezed my knee. I let her. "Don't be like that. Please."

"It's fine." It wasn't fine. My chest was on fire with rage and pure agony. "If you're jealous of me, don't be. You can have him. We aren't even together like that."

"No, Breezy. You don't get it." She squeezed my knee harder until I looked at her. "I'm not jealous of you. I'm jealous of him."

"What?" I shook my head. "Jealous of…"

"Him." She grabbed my hand. "I'm sorry. Seeing you guys look at each other drove me fucking crazy. I was jealous of him, and I fucked up. I'm so sorry I kissed him. I just couldn't stand the thought of him kissing you."

I pulled my hand from hers, startled by her fervor. By her admission. "What are you trying to say, Jules? That you, what? Have feelings for me?"

She tossed her head back into the seat and groaned. "I can't believe I'm doing this right now," she said with her eyes closed.

"Doing what?"

She leaned forward again, her gaze intense on me. "Yes. Of course I have feelings for you. Friends don't kiss the way we kissed last summer. Friends don't hold each other the way I hold you. Friends don't write each other constantly for years."

"Some friends write—"

"Breezy." Her voice sounded almost pained. "Please. Tell me you feel this." She pointed at me, then at her chest. "I know you do, Tanya. Please."

I shook my head. "But you're leaving tomorrow."

"Exactly. It's kind of my last shot to tell you how I feel." She shrugged. "Well, how I've always felt."

I sat in my truck, speechless, as Juliette Peralta admitted her feelings for me. Feelings I reciprocated, but how could I find the words to tell her that? I couldn't tell her how I hung on every letter she wrote. Or that it devastated me every time she dated some new guy or wore his necklace instead of mine. That every time she left, she broke my heart. And she was leaving tomorrow. *Tomorrow.* I wasn't even sure I'd see her again, and she was begging me to be vulnerable. To lay it all on the line.

Vulnerable was hard. The things I loved had a way of leaving, disappearing, or threatening to. I loved my mom. But when she visited, I couldn't give her more of me; she already had too many pieces, and I knew what I gave would never be returned. I loved Coral Bay, but I knew I'd lose it somehow, too. Lose this version that was so perfect to me. I wished I could preserve it, build a wall around it, and keep it safe from the Peraltas and the hurricanes and the skyscrapers.

My gut told me to build a wall around my heart because the thing about Jules was that she always left. She would leave me. Whether I gave myself to her or not. Either way, my heart was going to be smashed come tomorrow.

Fuck it.

"You had to fucking kiss him?" I faced her. "If it was me you wanted to kiss, you should have kissed *me*." I jabbed myself in the chest with my finger. A little too hard. "That's how we do things down here. We keep it simple. If I like you, then I don't go kissing your cousin instead."

She scrunched her brows. "Wait. Y'all are cousins? But you…"

"No." I rolled my eyes. "We aren't cousins. Gross. It's just a turn of phrase. Like, you know…I don't know."

"I don't think that's an expression," she said.

"*Ugh.* You know what I'm saying."

She chuckled into her hand. "Just to be clear. You and Oscar are or are not cousins?"

"We are not cousins." I clapped with every word just to really drive home my point. And my frustration. "And I'm upset that you kissed him." *Clap. Clap. Clap.*

"Breezy?"

I was grumpy like a petulant little kid because I knew it was hopeless. She had me from day dot. "Hmm?"

She tugged at the hem of my shorts until I looked at her. "Kiss me. Please," she whispered. "I don't want Oscar."

"Benny or Austin?"

She grinned. "I'm pretty sure Benny and Austin want each other. Regardless, no."

I gasped. "Wait. You think they're gay for each other?"

"I think they're gay, period." She nodded. "And they like each other. Yes."

"No."

She scooted across the bench so our wet, cold thighs pressed into each other. "It's you, Tanya. I want you. Ever since that first day at Crabby's and you walked up to our table looking so adorable in your work shirt. Something about the way you looked at me...no." She shook her head and placed a finger to her lips. "No, it wasn't how you looked at me. It was the way the breeze stroked your hair and the way you looked at the ocean. We were what? Thirteen? I'd never seen someone look so soulful." She fingered the hem of my shorts as she chewed her bottom lip.

She sighed. "That's how I see you, you know? You exist on this different plane of life where things matter and where things are beautiful." She shook her head. "Where things are worth protecting and cultivating. Like this town. And everything gets so loud with college applications and my parents breathing down my neck and every stupid guy I try to date." She blinked back what I thought was a tear. I had never seen her this way, so open and a bit desperate. *She* was being vulnerable.

"But with you," she continued, her gaze boring into me, "with you, it feels like plunging into the deep end, it feels like sinking under the waves. So the harsh sun fractures over the water's surface and fades, the laughter and shrieks of the tourists muffle, until I can't hear anything, and the weight of the world literally fades. You're the pressure, the water all around me, holding me tight."

We sat in silence, a thickness weaving between us. One that had never existed until now. Until now, we had held our own threads, keeping them tight to our chests and gripping for dear life. But Jules reached out and made a stitch to mine, connecting us in a new way.

And that was enough for me to let it all go for one night and plunge in. Because that girl was my deep end, too.

I started the engine.

"Wait. What are you doing?" she asked, reaching for her seat belt. Something that seemed odd after skinny-dipping and jumping off roofs.

I pulled onto the main road and drove to the southern public beach access point, the one where the parking lot crept onto the sand. It was the only place cars were allowed on the beach, and at this time of night, it would be empty. Private.

She was quiet as I backed in so my tailgate faced the ocean, far enough away that the tide wouldn't touch us but close enough to be immersed. The sea was alive tonight. It was every night, but on this night, the belly of the ocean roared louder, and the waves crashed harder, as if the moon herself was greedy for the water.

"Is this okay?" I asked as I reached for the blanket behind the seat.

She nodded and opened the door. "I couldn't imagine a better place to be tonight, with you."

We walked around to the back of my truck, the sand cool between our toes. I dropped the tailgate and patted it for her to sit, then hopped up next to her. "Here." I draped the blanket over her shoulders and scooted close. "I know it's chilly in the breeze, being wet and all."

She didn't seem cold, though. She dropped her head back and gazed at the night sky. The stars were the kind of bright that only existed over sand: desert or ocean. And the moonlight spilled onto the black water like cream into coffee. It was all so beautiful. My favorite things.

"This is what I'll miss," I said. I couldn't help it. I waved to the darkness of the road behind us. "When this all gets developed. The stars won't be as bright with the lights from all the condos, the sound of the waves will absorb into the concrete, and it won't be so whole anymore. It will be...fractured, broken somehow."

Her cool fingers wrapped around my hand. "What if I told you I wanted to protect this place? That I loved Coral Bay the way you love Coral Bay, and I wanted to live here?"

I squeezed her hand. "You want to be a townie?"

"I mean, yeah. A townie by association"—she swayed into my shoulder—"then by merit. I'll earn it, I promise."

It wasn't that I didn't believe her. I believed in that moment that it was what she wanted. But she was a Peralta, and she would live a life far away from me. I knew this.

I *knew* this.

"You're going to Penn, Jules. And that's great." I shook my head. "It's a privilege that you shouldn't take for granted."

She groaned. "After college, then. I'll come back, and we can—"

I pulled her into me, and she wrapped her arms around me. Her body felt so good against mine. It always had. I thought that maybe if I were mindful enough, I could memorize how she felt in my arms tonight and carry her with me forever.

Probably not, though.

"Stop, please. I don't want you to say it," I muttered against her ear. "I don't want to talk about the future." I pressed her hand against my chest, flattened it over my heart so she could feel it beat. "You're going to hurt me, Jules. No matter what, you're going to leave tomorrow with your parents, and you're going to hurt me."

"Breezy—"

"And that's okay." I pressed her hand harder into me until I could feel the warmth through my shirt. "But you saying you want to live here and be with me…well, that's only going to make it so much more painful when you don't come back."

She dipped her head and brushed her lips over my neck, right under my ear, making me shiver. "I always come back. I'm coming back for you, Tanya."

I didn't know what it was that made me trust her or if I actually trusted her at all. But in that moment, with her lips on my neck and her hand on my heart, it didn't matter. I was hers. I had been hers for four years. Fear of losing her wouldn't change that. She already had the critical mass of me. And I wanted her to have it all.

Maybe I wanted her to hurt me.

Maybe I wanted the exquisite pain of her leaving to linger.

Maybe then, it would feel like she hadn't left at all.

"Pinkie promise?" I asked.

She locked her pinkie around mine. "Pinkie promise."

"Okay." I pushed her hand under my shirt. "Touch me."

"You're so soft," she whispered in my ear. She stroked from my sternum to my waistline in long, slow drags. With nails, without nails. Gentle and needy. We didn't have time to try to wrangle on a wet bathing suit after the pool; I was bare for her. Dying for her.

"Fuck, Jules." I tried to arch into her hand. Needed her all over me. I wanted her to feel my breasts and how my nipples ached and tightened for her. "Touch me."

I could feel her smile against my neck. "Come here."

She gripped my ass, and I was swinging a leg over, straddling her. We stared at each other, bravado melting away as my weight settled on her thighs, and her hands pushed under my shirt again. I interlaced my fingers behind her neck and pressed my lips to hers.

It was different than how I remembered kissing her in the Meadows. Different but the same. Her lips were a little chapped from the summer sun, and she tasted like salt and chlorine. She groaned and opened her mouth to me, our tongues exploring, teeth nipping, and moans being swallowed. Her mouth was soft and wet and hot, and I wanted it all over my body.

She cupped my breasts, and I jolted into her. My hips bucked against hers in a feeling of complete ecstasy when she brushed her thumbs over my nipples.

"Is this okay?" she asked. "Feel good?"

I crashed into her mouth again as I rocked into her hips, into her touch, and the ocean roared louder in my ears. "Yes," I managed to say. "Please don't stop." I pulled away just long enough to tear my shirt over my head.

She held me at arm's length. "Tanya. Wow." Her eyes pored over me like moonlight. "You are so beautiful."

"Have you seen yourself?" I made a show of eying her. "There isn't a head you can't turn."

"Stop." She gripped my wrists and held my hands firm in my lap so I couldn't touch her. "You are the most beautiful person I've ever met. Period." Her gaze was so intense, I knew she wouldn't drop this until I acknowledged her.

I gave a half nod. "Thank you."

She grinned and released my wrists. "Wasn't so hard, was it?"

I rolled my eyes. "Excruciating."

"Breezy." She looked me up and down again. I didn't feel exposed, just a little naked without her hands on me. "I think I'm in love with you."

I stopped, her words sinking through me. They didn't feel real. They didn't feel *good*. She had to kill the vibe with that bullshit. "Don't be stupid, Jules." I tried to swing off her lap, but she held my hips in place.

"Hey, don't go. Please," she pleaded, her voice gentle.

I sighed. "Why would you say that? In love with me? Don't you literally have a boyfriend right now?" I eyed her chest where I knew a silver Tiffany heart dangled between her breasts. An expensive necklace from whatever rich douchey, flavor-of-the-month boy.

She watched me for a minute before she pulled her shirt over her head and bared herself to me. "This is from Travis." She took my hand and pushed the tiny little heart into it. "And it means literally nothing to me."

"Nothing?"

"Nothing." She raised a brow, dropped her gaze to the pendant, then back to me. "Go on. Rip it clean off. You know as well as I do, I don't care about him. I know what I am, and I know what I do. I know it's wrong. But they get to date Juliette Peralta, and I get to avoid questions. I get to avoid notes in my locker and a million guys trying to touch me. I cut them loose, and they're better off for having 'been with me.' Their stock is raised." She closed my fingers around the charm and whispered, "And I know I love you."

I released a shaky breath and leaned close to her, dropping the necklace. I reached behind her neck, under her damp, cool hair. "I love you, too," I said into her ear as I undid the clasp. I piled the silver chain into her hand. "There. You're free for tonight."

She smiled. "I don't want to be free. I want to be yours." Her smile morphed into a sly grin as she chucked the necklace down the beach, the silver chain catching the moonlight and glittering all the way to the sand like an asteroid burning bright.

I stared at her, both of us half-naked and a little cold. She was always the most gorgeous girl in the world to me, but seeing her like this, naked and needy and vulnerable…she'd never been more beautiful. "Okay," I said as I gently pushed her down. Her skin on mine felt incredible. Combustible. My breasts grazed hers, and she sucked in a sharp breath. The ache between my thighs pulsed like the ocean for her. "You're mine."

She groaned and pushed my shorts over my hips, and I tugged hers down to her ankles, pulling the blanket over us as we explored our sunburnt summer bodies. She pushed my hand between her thighs into warm thick wetness.

"I'm yours," she said.

CHAPTER SIX

S alt heals.
     Salt destroys.

Bears joy and sorrow in equal measure, each revealing the other. At least, that's what Marge always said. But damn. Sometimes, the sorrow drowns. Marge has been dead for three years, and the destruction of Hurricane Sasha is an open wound in Coral Bay. Our town still bleeds a year after landfall. Entire businesses swept away in the wind, roofs ripped from walls, palm fronds sprinkled about like confetti. The Peraltas' Sands Living community has barely been touched since the storm. Salt destroys.

While the Peraltas struggle to secure contractors and laborers for the mass amount of work they need, the rest of the town has begun to heal. Local construction companies have rallied behind the community and their businesses, leaving investment companies and their out-of-state capital for last. It's what we do; protect each other. Salt heals.

I grin as I drive by the once impressive stark white complex of the Sands, now blackened by dirt and grime and ripped open by the ocean. It's the physical manifestation of the Peraltas' greed. Juliette's greed. I roll down the window and let the ocean air cleanse from my system her name and every ounce of pain that woman inflicted on me and my town. She hasn't shown her face in Coral Bay since she left that last summer, even though she's the Southeast asset manager for Peralta Inc., and her assets remain destroyed.

I can't blame her. I wouldn't show my face in Coral Bay if I was her, either.

Once Juliette went to college, everything changed. I knew it would. I was prepared for her to drift away: live her life and get married, start a family, continue her career, slowly forget about me. What I did not expect was for her to write one final letter after we made love, leave it in the visor of my truck, and never speak to me again.

But then, she was never Coral Bay. Just a figment of my heart's desperate imagination. I park in Crabby's sandy lot and grip the hot leather of the steering wheel with both hands. "Shit." Pretty wild how after sixteen years, it still hurts.

I startle at the tapping on my window. "Shit," I say again, as if it's the only word I know anymore. Kinda feels like it. I must mutter it twenty times a day, dealing with the construction and continuing to learn how to run the business Marge left me. I roll down my window instead of getting out. "Scared me."

Oscar dips his head and peers into my truck, his dark brows narrowed in apparent concern. He hasn't changed much since we were seventeen. He's still sickeningly handsome and wicked smart. He wears a starched white guayabera tucked into his pressed navy slacks. Sometimes, it feels like Oscar and I are the Atlases of Coral Bay: him being the mayor and running the government, and me being the owner of the Coral Bay Inn, the biggest hub for business and tourism in the town since the hurricane. Since the Sands.

Tourists don't care that scars from the storm are all around. They don't shy away from the grotesque and mangled homes. They stare and shudder, utterly affected in their hearts, I am sure. Then they sip away their afternoons at the beach bar and try to shrug off whatever hurricane hit them.

And they pay us. Pump money back into our bloodstream.

Mostly through the Coral Bay Inn and Crabby's. And through the locals who work in each. It's a huge responsibility managing the Inn, not to mention the entire repair process. Especially since I used this opportunity to make much-needed renovations to the property. The tourism grant Oscar helped me obtain from the city, a business loan, and the cash Marge left me gave me enough of a budget to not only repair the damage from Sasha and add more rooms to the Inn, but also to renovate the old rooms and Crabby's. We're functioning at half-capacity right now. Just enough.

He taps my door with his keys. "Come on, Breezy. I need a drink."

I follow him into Crabby's, and the new vibe of the restaurant fills me with pride. It looks less like a Cheeseburger in Paradise franchise and more like a "our bartenders use real lime juice in our margaritas" kind of place. The teenage girls huddled in a booth make me chuckle as I slide onto the barstool next to Oscar. They wear the quintessential short shorts and tank tops, a look that is apparently timeless, though I have personally retired the outfit. Now, I wear linen pants and sundresses. Easy, light things.

In case manifestation is real.

"Hi, Mayor Westinghouse. Hey, Breezy. Modelo?" Wren, my bar manager with a sleeve of floral tattoos and a killer smile, tosses a coaster claiming, "A margarita without Cointreau isn't worth its salt," in front of me.

I bend the round chunk of cardboard until it breaks down its soft middle. "I thought we were tossing these. They look cheap and out of place with the new ambiance."

Wren swipes the carboard wreckage into the trash and tightens her blond ponytail. "That's the plan. But everything is on back order right now. Even the black cocktail napkins. So I hung on to these until they arrive."

I nod. "Which is supposed to be?"

"Another week." She cringes.

I slide off my stool. "That's too long. Cancel the order, and I'll go pick some—"

"Sit down, Tanya. Pick some up from where? You think Humbolt's is going to have your fancy little napkins in stock? They can still barely keep water and toilet paper stocked." Oscar tugs me by my hand, and I sigh.

"You're right." I shake my head and look at Wren. "He's right. Don't cancel the order." I pluck a new tacky coaster from the stack and drop it in front of me. "Thank you for hanging on to these until the napkins arrive."

"No problem, boss." She flashes an appreciative smile and places a cold beer on my silly coaster. "And for you, sir?"

"Ugh. Don't call him sir. His ego is big enough," I say, raising the beer to my lips.

"Don't call her boss. Goes straight to that stubborn head of hers." Oscar gives me a light shove and that sharp grin. "A Cuba libre, please. Thanks, Wren." Once Oscar's drink is sweating on the bar next to mine and Wren has busied herself with other guests, he swivels on his stool to face me, his expression hardening into something more serious.

I straighten in preparation. "Oh God. What is it? Out with it, Oscar."

He winces, takes a long pull from his glass, and wipes his mouth. "The Inn doesn't have the capacity for all the tourists who want to come to Coral Bay right now, and the town desperately needs those dollars so we can continue to repair and fortify." His gaze falls into his lap before he meets my eye again. "The Sands Living must be repaired. As soon as possible."

I finger the beads of condensation on my beer. Shake my head. "But—"

"Juliette is coming to Coral Bay to manage the rebuilding."

I feel my mouth open, but no words escape. They're stuck in my throat, choking me. Juliette Peralta is finally coming back to Coral Bay. For years, I dreamed of this moment. I hoped, and I wished, and I tried to manifest her. A letter, a text, a call. Literally anything so I would know what we had was real. That I didn't just make it up every summer. Every letter. But I didn't get a single word from her, and now she's just going to show up in my town after sixteen years.

I swallow hard, hoping to shake loose some of the words stuck in my throat. "When is she…" I nod, hoping he can fill in the blanks of what I just cannot say.

"She arrived this morning." He licks his lips as I press mine to my beer. "We met for coffee at my office and sorted some details of the project and the scope of work to be done."

I roll my eyes. "What? Are there suddenly tons of free construction companies willing to drop their local contracts for the bloodthirsty Peraltas?"

"No one is dropping local contracts. But I've added a nice fee to the contract for whoever takes it on. The city will pay the contractor an extra two percent of the total project cost to sweeten the pot."

"Are you joking, Oscar? You're having the city pay our hard-earned tax dollars to fatten the pockets of those people?" I scoff and grip my beer tighter. "Have you completely lost your mind?"

"Breezy, I know. I know how she hurt you. But you don't get it." He drops a hand on my shoulder, which I shrug off. "Coral Bay needs the Sands. There are more tourists than the Inn can handle. The more people who visit Coral Bay, the better off *our* community is. The more money goes into Coral Bay people's pockets."

"And the more money goes into her pocket."

"It's what's best for the town, and it's my job to do it." He sighs. "I don't want to put money in the Peraltas' pocket as much as you don't."

I take a sip and put my beer down a little too hard. "Well, it sure seems like you can't wait to pump them full of our tax dollars."

He laughs his sardonic chuckle and runs a hand over his smooth black hair. "At least I always knew she wasn't Coral Bay.

Even when she was kissing me, I knew she'd always be a tourist. Knew what her family wanted with this town. Besides, you don't have to see her if you don't want to."

I groan. "This is Coral Bay. We only have two legit grocery stores. There's no avoiding people in this town." The sharp memory of Juliette kissing Oscar that last summer pierces my chest. The pain and jealousy of it. Followed by the achy memory of what happened later that night. The sweetness of her body tangled with mine in the bed of my truck. The same truck now sitting in the parking lot out back. Oscar's right. Only one of us was foolish enough to believe Juliette could be one of us. And it was me.

I drive home annoyed, raw, and staring down every woman walking down the sidewalk. I'm scared to see her. Maybe thrilled to see her. So I can tell her how terrible I think she is. So I can tell her how little I think of her and her parents. I turn onto my street, the same street Aunt Pat and Uncle Trevor still live on, and pull into my driveway. My home is a little, pale yellow beach bungalow with white shutters and a dusty blue front door. The colors don't go well together, but I refuse to paint. It's goofy, and it lightens me.

I stroll under the palm trees that shade the walkway and let myself in. The air-conditioning chills my sweat-sheened skin as I kick off my shoes and walk straight to my bedroom. I dig under my bed for the Nike shoebox I haven't opened in years. I skim over the edge of the old carboard, and I pull it out into the light. It's faded. The orange and black ink is muted, and the brown of the carboard is soft and tired. None of the letters from Juliette matter. None of them except one. It sits on top of the three, rubber-banded stacks. Alone.

This one isn't in an addressed envelope. No stamp. It isn't even written on real paper. It's a napkin from Dolphin Drip, where we went that same morning for one black coffee, a vanilla latte, a slice of banana bread, and an almond croissant. I hold the thin napkin in my palm. It's almost weightless. A piece of trash,

• 92 •

really. Her writing is sloppy, rushed, and tears into the pulpy material at the beginning of each word. Her shortest letter ever:

I'm leaving CB and never coming back. This was a huge mistake. I never want to see you or talk to you again.

CHAPTER SEVEN

Aunt Pat gives the sizzling pan of lemon pepper shrimp a toss as I refresh her glass of pinot grigio. "Oh dear," she says. I hand her the wine and lean against the countertop. It's no surprise Aunt Pat makes the best shrimp in town, and my mouth waters when the tangy, citrusy aroma hits my nose.

"Oh dear, what? What'd I miss?" Uncle Trevor asks. He hangs his truck keys on the hook next to the small whiteboard with their to-do list and slinks into a kitchen chair.

I tilt the bottle of white in his direction. "Wine?"

"You're going to need a glass, honey," Aunt Pat calls over her shoulder.

I place a glass in front of him and pour. When I'm done, he curls his fingers around my wrist and tugs me gently to him, wrapping me in a hug. "Your momma coming to visit?"

I pull away and kiss him on the temple. "No. No, not that." I hadn't heard from my mom since before Marge died. She didn't come to the funeral. Nothing. I don't even know if she's alive. "I met with Oscar for a drink at Crabby's yesterday. He told me Juliette is back in town to manage the reconstruction of the Sands."

His bushy gray eyebrows rise, and he sets his glass back on the table before it even reaches his lips. "Oh dear."

"Exactly," Aunt Pat calls from the stove.

"Want me to feed her to the sharks?" he asks, the twinkle in his eye gleaming with mischief.

I shrug. "It'd be pretty poetic, actually." I fall into the chair next to him. "I haven't seen her yet, but it's only a matter of time until we run into each other."

"Maybe she's changed," he offers. "You two were just kids before. Maybe she's changed and can apologize for—"

I wave him off. "I could forgive someone for doing something dumb when they were seventeen. Of course I could. I could forgive her for the note, for leaving. But she could have reached out at any point after. She never did. Not once." I shake my head, my lip trapped between my teeth so it doesn't tremble. "Every day she didn't is like she left that note in my visor again. So, no, I don't think she will apologize. And, no, I don't think I can forgive her."

He winces at the clear pain my voice. I hate it. "Okay then."

"Okay then," I say and sip my wine.

After dinner, I walk home and daydream of when I see Juliette for the first time. Maybe at Humboldt's or at Mickey's Propane 'n Pizza, or maybe she's feeling bold and struts right into Crabby's. I imagine her trying to get my attention and me ignoring her, turning away the way she ignored me for all these years. I wonder if she'll have a spouse with her. Or maybe even a kid. I shudder at the thought. Not about the kid. Just everything.

The katydids sing in harmony as I let myself in the house. The night sounds make me feel less alone, so I snag the thriller I'm reading and make a cup of tea. My back porch is screened in for the mosquitos, but I still light a citronella candle. The smell brings me back to childhood, when I used to run around this town with no worries, not stopping until someone's mom got ahold of us and demanded we come in for dinner. We always ate outside like this, under the moonlight, with citronella shields and katydid songs.

Now, Benny and Austin call their two kids home for dinner

every night, and they eat outside just like this. I sip my hot tea in the hot night. I want what they have. The love. The family.

It never did work out with Oscar. After Jules left, he went off to college to study history and political science to put himself in a position to run for local office. He was successful, of course. He was always going to be successful. He asked me on a date after he won the race for mayor. "A proper date," he said. "Come on, Tanya, let's see if this thing that's always been between us has legs."

By the end of the night, he was calling me Breezy, and I was glancing at my watch. "Oscar—"

"We're always just going to be bros, aren't we?" he asked, a smile playing on his lips. There was a sadness in his eyes. I felt it, too. Some kind of final loss of possibility between us.

I smiled gently. "I don't know why, Oscar. I thought it could be us, too. But, yes, I think we're always going to be bros."

He chuckled and loosened his tie. The seriousness of him melting a little, as if we'd been playing house, and now we were back to being kids. "Can't believe of the four of us, Benny and Austin were the ones to find it."

"They didn't have to find it. They just always were." I pulled out my credit card, and he protested. "Come on. Let's split this and go crush some beers at Crabby's. On me."

He shook his head and grinned. "Sounds good, bro."

❖

The morning crowd buzzes around Dolphin Drip. I scan the usual goods for sale: mugs and bags of beans, all with the logo of a dolphin sipping from a giant steaming cup. The air is hazy with coffee and steamed milk, and it makes me sleepy. Doesn't help that I hardly slept last night. But I have to be sharp today. I have a meeting with my contractor and need to make some big decisions about the budget and scope of work for the next phase of construction. Something about knowing repairs has started on the Sands makes me feel like there's a fire under my ass. I have some big competition now.

"Morning, Breezy. The usual?" Peter asks. He went to high school with all of us and took over ownership of the Dolphin after Mr. French retired and moved to Atlanta to be closer to his grandkids. Flashes of gray pepper Peter's black curls now, but it looks good.

"Please."

He hits a few buttons on the screen and bags a slice of banana bread. "How's construction been going? On schedule still?"

A teenager I can never remember the name of slides my coffee in front of Peter, and I chuckle. "Has any construction project ever finished on time? Ever?"

"Fair point." He hands me my coffee and smiles. "As long as it's finished before the Sands grabs every worker they can get their hands on, am I right?"

"Oh. You heard about that, huh?" I feel the customers behind me growing anxious to order, so I step aside, but I want Peter to tell me every detail he knows.

He smiles softly and nods for the next guest to step up and order. "It's Coral Bay, Breezy. Everyone has heard about it."

"Right." I hold up my coffee and bread. "Thanks, Peter. See you tomorrow."

He waves as I push the door open with my elbow and my shades down with my knuckle. It's a balancing act, the banana bread, the coffee, the door, the glare of sun, and not falling off the curb.

A car horn blares next to me, and I jump. A splash of coffee escapes through the hole in the plastic lid and burns my hand. "Watch it," I shout at the sleek Range Rover that has no business being in Coral Bay. When I don't get a response from behind the tinted windshield, I raise my arms in exasperation and call, "Excuse me. A little fast for a small parking lot, don't you think?"

Nothing.

I shake my head, annoyed with the Range Rover and annoyed at my salty attitude. But I can't help it. Word spreading about the Sands getting repaired makes me grumpy. After one more second of staring down the dark windshield, I sigh and turn to—

Hot coffee burns my hands. Or is it the gravel stuck in my palms that feels like fire? My knees ache, and I already know I've ripped my favorite sundress. I faintly register the sound of the Range Rover's door opening, but everything is bright and glaring. The sun off the shiny black paint and the burning of my knees and hands.

I fell, and holy mother of dolphins, it's embarrassing. Especially after my stare-down with this guy. I wipe the gravel from my palms and try to pull myself together.

"Breezy."

No.

I slowly raise my eyes to meet the owner of the voice I haven't heard for sixteen years. It sounds the same. Only the last time I heard it, we were tangled up in the bed of my truck. Juliette Peralta stands next to her glossy tank, her black dress and heels matching the tint of her car. She looks like money. I don't miss the pop of red on the soles of her heels. I have quite the view of her Louboutins from the hot gravel pit of hell I am currently in.

She takes a hesitant step toward me and stops, as if she thinks she'll get shocked if she comes any closer. "Can I give you a hand? Please?" Her sunglasses are too dark for me to see her eyes, and her hair is twisted in the most professional-looking bun I've ever seen. I'd bet she smells like a magazine perfume ad. Expensive, rich, and fake. Who she's always been, no matter how hard she tried to hide it from us. From me.

I scramble to my feet and dust myself off, trying to ignore the very distinct feeling of blood trickling down my knee. Not exactly how I imagined this moment, but here we are.

"Please?" she repeats. When I don't respond, she nods to the half-squished bag in my hand. "Banana bread?"

That's it. "No."

"No?"

I shake my head. "I mean, yes. Obviously."

"Some things don't—"

"Everything changes," I blurt.

She takes a definite step toward me. "Breezy, can we maybe talk about what happened sometime?"

"I know what happened. I don't need to talk about it." She watches me in silence as I pat my bloody knee with a napkin. My coffee soaks into the fabric of my dress and the dusty gravel of the parking lot, but stubborn pride prevents me from going inside to order another. Now I'm just angry. "I can't believe you, Juliette." Her name feels foreign on my tongue.

Peter flies out of the coffee shop and hands me a large coffee. "Shit, Breezy. You okay? That was quite the spill. I have bandages and ointment and—"

I clear my throat. "No. I'm okay. Thank you for the refill. I can pay you."

"On the house," he says and squeezes my shoulder before he leaves Juliette and me alone again.

I tap the lid of my new coffee. "You should be more careful. This isn't Atlanta or New York. It's Coral Bay. We have different values down here. I know that doesn't mean anything to you, but it does to us." It's hard to remain coolly indignant with a bloody knee and coffee down my white sundress.

"Breezy."

I ignore her, get into my truck, and watch in my rearview as she seemingly steadies herself before climbing into her Range Rover and parking. "Wow," I mutter to myself. "Just...wow." She's exactly how I expected her to be. A giant bitch with too much money. "She really leaned into it, huh?" I mutter and throw it in gear.

It doesn't take me long to get to the Inn. I'm annoyed and have a surge of caffeine rushing through my veins. I nod at a few employees on my way into Crabby's. No matter what I have going on, I make it a point to be polite—even if I did just live my worst nightmare—because I know what it's like to work hard for someone else and how important it is to feel valued.

"Oh. Nuh-uh. Nope to whatever this is." I wave a dismissive finger at Oscar, who leans against the bar looking like a young Benjamin Bratt. The restaurant inventory sits next to the register, and I grab it, hoping he takes the hint.

The ocean breeze ruffles his perfect hair before he smooths it back down. "Breezy, I understand this isn't your favorite—"

I smack the clipboard against the wood of the bar and make him jump. "Isn't my favorite? We're not talking about ice cream flavors, Oscar. I almost got run over by some city slicker at the Dolphin, and I ripped my dress and skinned my knee, and guess what?" I give him my most agitated raised brows.

He shrugs.

"Would you like to know who almost hit me?"

"To be fair, you fell on your own." I jump at the sound of her voice. Juliette strides into Crabby's like she owns the place. *I own the place.* "Into the middle of the parking lot. Without looking." Her tone is playful but cool.

We all stare at one another. Until Oscar speaks. "Jules—"

"Don't 'Jules' her," I complain. "She's only here for the money." A flash of hurt passes over her face, and it's the sweetest feeling. Like pie. "Did she call any of us to check up after the hurricane? No. Nothing. Guess you stick to your word, at least." I slow clap because I'm petty. And my knee is throbbing. And Jules—Juliette—looks just as gorgeous as she did when we were seventeen. Even more gorgeous, if that's possible. Her dark brown eyes hold the same intensity.

Oscar clears his throat. "I asked Juliette to meet us here, okay? I have something I want to discuss with both of you."

I pick up the clipboard again and pretend to look busy. "You should have scheduled this. I'm too busy. Absolutely swamped," I say.

"You wouldn't have agreed," he says.

"I can come back," Juliette offers.

I shake my head, completely annoyed by the two of them. "No. You're here already, and I'd rather not have to see you twice. What do you want, Oscar?"

"The mayor's office is throwing a festival. A weeklong festival. And we want Coral Bay Inn and the Sands to be sponsors. Not only will your establishments be sponsors, but they will be collaborators."

"Collaborators? What are you talking about?" I ask.

Juliette shakes her head, also clearly shocked. "Peralta Inc. doesn't collaborate like that. We are the sole proprietors of our properties and intend to keep it that way."

Oscar rolls his eyes like we're being a problem. *He's* being a problem. "I understand you two didn't end things on the best terms."

"That's an understatement," I say under my breath.

He flashes me a scolding look. "*Regardless*, you each own one of the most important businesses in our local economy, and my staff has come up with a way to boost exposure and advertisement for both of them."

He looks far too satisfied with himself. I sigh. "Come on, Oscar. I don't have all day, and I'm sure Ms. Peralta needs to get back to her soulless endeavors soon."

Pure pain flashes across her face before she catches it and calms her features. I was hoping "soulless" would cut her. It did. "Actually," she says, eyes on me. "It's *Mrs. Halloway.*"

My chest implodes. Stomach sinks. I catch the glint of the giant diamond on her left ring finger. "Oh, of course," I say, and I hope she can hear every bit of sarcasm in my words. "Halloway as in Halloway Homes?" Halloway Homes is one of the biggest builders in the Southeast, propagating mediocre townhomes like rows of corn.

She nodded. "Yes, as in Halloway Homes."

I shrugged. "Glad you married for the love and not the strategic industry alliance."

"Breezy, please," Oscar says. "I need you two to work this

out and be able to work together. Just for a few months, until Coral Bay get its tourism dollars pumping again."

"I don't see the issue. The Inn has been at capacity for months," I mutter.

"Half-capacity." Oscar shoots me a sharp look. "And I imagine you're going to want to up the rates after construction is done to recoup your cost? I also imagine being booked out from the influx of tourism after the Sands is also complete will only increase *your* demand and *your* ability to raise rates."

"Damn, Oscar," Juliette chimes in. "Still in charge, I see."

I can't tell if she's flirting or teasing or what, but I hate it. "Fine." I groan. "Tell us your idea."

He shakes his head as if annoyed with his kid sisters, but he can shove it where the sun don't shine because he is pushing it. I don't owe him a damn thing. Juliette, on the other hand, with her favors from the mayor and her—

"So Coral Bay Inn and the Sands are sponsors *and* collaborators. The Sands doesn't have direct beach access since it's a couple blocks up from East Beach. The town is going to fund a trolley that runs continuously from the Sands to the Inn's private access point—"

"Absolutely not." I scoff, hands up in frustration. "Oscar, you have no right and no authority to access my private property for the benefit of another private and *not local* business. I will not allow it." I can feel the blood pool in my cheeks. The anger.

He runs a hand through his black hair and sighs. "You're right. I don't have the authority. But if you grant the trolley access, the Inn will be making a steep flat rental fee for every day the trolley runs."

I cross my arms. "How steep?"

"Steep," he says. "On top of the fee you collect, we will zone the beach in front of the Inn as private. Meaning, you can do whatever you want with it, firepits, tables, cabanas, whatever, and the Sands tourists will branch off to the west a little down the beach. We'll build a fork in the boardwalk."

I shake my head, confused. "And why the hell doesn't the trolley just drop them down the beach, and the Sands can build their own boardwalk?"

"The dunes, Breezy. You know we can't touch those dunes. The Inn has the only access point for a mile. And it just makes sense since the Sands is literally blocks behind you."

Juliette stays quiet. As she should. She doesn't look shocked. She and Oscar have obviously already discussed this plan. It's not a bad plan. In fact, I've been wanting to expand Crabby's onto the beach and run service to cabanas. Oscar, the son of a bitch, knows this. And the fees we collect from the trolley would be a nice boost to our income.

I look at the two of them, their faces hopeful but cocky, as if they know I'll say yes. I lift a finger and cock a hip. "I am highly annoyed with both of you."

Juliette clears her throat and takes a small step forward. "Tanya, I—"

"Fine," I say, not letting her speak. I don't want to hear it. It's a good deal, and whatever comes out of her mouth will only make me more resistant to accepting it. "Fine. Make me an offer I can't refuse on the trolley."

Oscar grins. "There's one more thing."

CHAPTER EIGHT

I cannot believe this is what you meant by 'collaborators.' Are you out of your damn mind, Oscar?" I try not to shout, but it's always been difficult to be heard over these boys, and I just cannot with Oscar right now. Benny and Austin exchange grins across their long kitchen table as we drink their famous spicy margs, and the kiddos keep themselves entertained in the backyard.

The huge sign splayed across the table will soon read, "Dunk a boss, spend a night, post a review." It's Oscar's ridiculous master plan to invite travel bloggers to the festival to try to dunk me and Jules for additional nights on their already comped one-night stay in each hotel. *Ridiculous.* Yet here I am. And she will also be here soon. I fought Oscar tooth and nail. Told him I could more than handle painting a sign on my own, but he said it would be good for us all to work together for the community. Especially since we would have to work together to plan the trolley.

I am all for the community, but she—Juliette Peralta—is *not* our community.

This is my literal nightmare. Hanging out with my family and *her*. After she left me high and dry. After she tried to run me over. After everything, I'm expected to have a casual margarita with the woman and *finger paint*? The nerve of this man.

"Still can't believe Jules is going to be here in our home," Benny says, stroking his red beard and grinning, the margaritas widening his smile.

Austin squeezes his shoulder and peeks at the clock in the kitchen. "Yep. Any minute now."

There's a knock on the door as if on cue, and my entire body stiffens.

"Well," Benny says. "Here goes nothing." He walks to the front door.

I hear the lock clunk free and the door open. Then, "Benny? Oh my God, how long has it been?"

Sixteen years.

"At least a decade," his voice booms through the house. "Look at you, Jules. You were always beautiful, but wow. Gorgeous. Simply gorgeous."

I think I liked Benny better when he was trying to get in her pants instead of this super reverent, compliment-giving gorgeous gay man. The sound of footsteps gets louder, and I take a deep breath. I am an adult. I can do this.

The chorus of welcome from Austin and Oscar sends a small shiver of rage down my spine. Okay, fine, a big shiver of rage. Giant, really.

"Hey, Breezy. Good to see you again," she says. There's a hint of hesitancy in her voice.

She wears a simple but expensive-looking light green sweater and black jeans. Her hair looks effortlessly perfect as always. Glossy and oak brown with the silkiest waves. Fancy waves, not beach waves.

I give her a small wave. "Hey."

"Juliette. Wow," Austin exclaims. "Look at you. All grown and fancy."

She laughs and takes a seat next to Oscar. If she wasn't married, I'd wonder if they would try to pick up where they left off because she and I are certainly not going to pick up where we left off. "Your darling husband just said almost the exact same thing," she says. Benny fills her glass from the pitcher. "It's lovely, by the way, seeing you two finally happy and together. It seriously warms my brittle little heart."

I bark an involuntary laugh, and all eyes fall on me. "Sorry." I take a long sip of my margarita. "Sorry. That wasn't supposed to"—I shrug—"you know, escape my body."

Austin widens his eyes as if to say, "Get it together, you silly woman."

I clear my throat and try again. "I can't believe I was the only one who couldn't see it."

"I think everyone kind of saw us as the same person," Benny says.

Austin pulls Benny's hand into his lap. "When really, we've been in love since we were ten years old. We weren't like twins."

"We were inseparable, sure. But for other reasons," Benny says, looking lovingly at his husband.

"True," Juliette pipes up. And it annoys me. It annoys me that she saw my best friends, my Coral Bay family, clearer than I could. And it annoys me how damn beautiful she is. I tear my gaze from her lightly glossed lips as she speaks. "Still beach bros. But amazingly beautiful fathers and husbands. Cheers, and thank you for having me in your home." Everyone raises their glasses, so I do, too. I have manners.

"It's kind of surreal, isn't it?" Austin says.

Juliette smiles softly. "It really is."

The ice in my cup clunks as I take the last sip of my margarita. "So you have a husband. A builder husband. How fascinating. Congratulations."

"Um. Thank you." She fiddles with the soggy napkin under her drink, her eyes refusing to meet mine.

"Any kids?" I ask.

She exhales a long breath of relief. "God, no."

Her answer surprises me. Not that the things we want as teenagers should never change, but Jules always wanted to be a mom and a teacher. It stuck with me because kids don't usually say things like that unless they feel it deeply. When I was a teenager, my response to the same question would have been, "I have no clue if I want kids." But Jules always did.

It could be that they've tried, and it hasn't panned out, but by the tone of her answer, it's like she's relieved. While I, on the other hand, want them more each day. I want to foster, specifically. Give someone a safe, loving home the same way Aunt Pat and Uncle Trevor did for me.

An awkward quiet takes over the table, then Austin clears his throat. "Well, wouldn't recommend them anyhow." The kitchen door flies open, and the two little ones race each other into the living room. "They're pure evil and chaos," he shouts so the kids can hear him.

"Sorry, Pop," and "Love you," sound from the living room, and we all melt into soft laughter. That's what I want.

We spend the next half hour bent over the sign, painting and shading and putting a weird amount of effort into something that could have easily been hired out. But I have a sneaking suspicion that Oscar is up to something. That for some reason, he wanted us all to get together over this little project with Juliette. Maybe he's taking his final shot with her, and I just happen to be getting dragged into it. But she's married. To a builder in Atlanta.

When all the paint is put away and the sign is drying in the garage, I grab my purse from the counter and hug everyone good-bye. Everyone except for Juliette.

"Yeah, I have an early meeting tomorrow at the Sands." Juliette jiggles her keys. "Better follow Breezy out." She kisses everyone on the cheek except for me and follows me outside.

We stroll silently down the driveway. There's her black Range Rover parked behind my old truck. The perfect analogy for me and her. I flash back to picking her up that last day and how my truck looked next to her parents' Cadillac. Jules loved my truck. She loved my down-home vibe. And I thought she loved me.

I open my car door.

"Breezy, one second." She steps next to me and gently closes my door. I can smell her perfume on the sleeve of her sweater. It smells like lavender and something musky. It smells like money. It smells good.

She leans against the hood and crosses her arms, staring at her boots. "I know things are weird between us, but—"

"No," I say, waving in front of my face. "No, no. Things aren't weird between us. There are *no things* between us. Nothing." I shake my head. "You made sure of that. Or do you not remember?"

She pushes off the hood and steps right next to me. I can feel her calm breath tickle the hair framing my face. And that perfume. The soft fuzz of her sweater brushes against my arm. She squeezes my wrist, and the anger leaps in my chest, but I let her.

"I was a kid making the best decision that I could at the time. I thought I was doing the right thing. I'm so sorry I hurt you, Breezy."

Her voice is sincere. But none of this makes sense. Why did she have to make a decision at all? Doesn't matter. "Well, I guess you made the right choice, Juliette. You've got your money, your car, your cashmere sweater, your rich husband. Congratulations." I nudge her arm out of the way and grab the door handle. "Now, if you'll excuse me, I've got to get going." I open the door, but she grabs it before I can close it.

"Not everything."

"Can you…" I pluck her fingers from my door, annoyed at her wasting my time. I slide into my truck and start the engine. "Don't worry, Jules. You're taking tax dollars for your own benefit. You always get what you want. The Sands will be back in action soon." I end the conversation by slamming the door.

She doesn't look hurt or shocked. She only bites her lip and nods. Of course she understands why I couldn't do this with her. She knows what she did. What she didn't do. She knows.

❖

Aunt Pat shells a bucket of shrimp as I pluck herbs from the garden. My loft is still here, mostly untouched and "ready for the next teenager," as my aunt puts it. I don't know who she thinks will fill it, but she refuses to turn it into a gym or more storage space or one of those "she-sheds." I told her if she wants someone to use it, she should post it online. It'd be perfect for someone just starting on their own. A bartender, scuba instructor, boat guide. Anyone.

"Breezy baby, you mind taking over? Damn arthritis is acting up."

"Course." I drop my wicker basket of herbs and walk over to the worktable to start shelling. "Been acting up a lot lately. That medicine that Dr. Thorvald gave you stop working?"

She rinses her hands under the spigot and dries them in the towel tucked in the waistline of her trousers. "Getting old ain't for sissies."

I'm faster at peeling shrimp than she is now. Which makes me proud but also concerned. "Didn't answer my question," I say.

"Fine." She squeezes my shoulder. "I'll make an appointment on Monday. If you tell me why you couldn't let me be polite and invite Juliette tonight."

I groan. "You know why."

She sighs. "Because she's big business. Because she's not Coral Bay. But she's eaten at my table, and like it or not, baby, that makes her our people."

"Because she hurt me," I mutter.

"People are weird. They make mistakes. But she's trying to talk to you. Maybe she's even trying to apologize. You'll never find out if you don't let her talk to you."

I wipe my eye with the back of my hand a push a stray hair behind my ear. "She broke my heart in the cruelest way imaginable and ran off to marry a sleazy builder. And you expect me to just up and forgive the woman?"

"Really seems like this being angry thing is working out for ya, kid. You're right. You should keep doing that instead of trying to be friends again." She grabs the bucket of shrimp. "You've got no choice but to work with her, anyhow."

CHAPTER NINE

A nd then, this wave completely took him out," our neighbor, Mr. Sanders, says.

I chuckle politely into my glass of zesty dry white that Oscar brought. "You, uh, mean the two-year-old who was getting water for his sandcastle?" I wince.

"Yes." He wheezes a laugh and slaps his belly. "The little nugget squatted down with his bucket, and *boom*." He slaps his hands together, and I jump. "That wave toppled him like a domino."

I smile and nod, slightly horrified at the amount of joy he seems to get from this mildly tragic story. Mr. Sanders cornered me the minute he walked into Aunt Pat's house. Out of all the guests—maybe fifty people—at this shrimp boil, he finds me in the first second. I search over his shoulder for Oscar, Benny, or Austin. Anyone who could pull me away and save me. Aunt Pat with a request for help in the kitchen, maybe. But no one comes to rescue me. Mr. Sanders is getting old, so I give him the benefit of the doubt with this story. "Well, we all have to learn the strength of the ocean the hard way," I say.

"Exactly, Breezy girl." He squeezes my arm, nodding enthusiastically. "I remember one of those learning moments for you." He lifts his brows as if what's on the tip of his tongue is a national secret. It's not my favorite story, but it's not exactly a secret, either. In fact, it's one of Aunt Pat's favorite memories to share whenever more than me and the boys are seated around her table.

"You were just a girl. Just a little thing," he starts and holds out a hand level to my elbow. "Maybe this tall. And you were playing on the beach during a purple flag."

I sip my wine and grimace. "I have a feeling I know where this is going, Mr. Sanders," I say in my best cheery voice.

Juliette appears on my left out of nowhere, and I jump again, my hand pressed to my chest. "*Jesus.* What are you doing here?"

"Sure are jumpy tonight, Breezy," Mr. Sanders says.

"Oscar invited me." Juliette grins as her gaze drops down my body. It feels like she's taking stock of me, and I hate it. Her opinion of me holds no weight. None. "Sounds like the beginning of a juicy story to me," she says.

"Oh no." I wave in refusal. "We don't have to tell—"

"So," Mr. Sanders says, barreling over my words. "Breezy was just a little thing about up to here." He holds his hand at my elbow again. And as he describes the purple flag conditions and the unusual number of jellyfish in the water that day, I feel Juliette lean just a little closer to me. Her fancy lavender perfume softly wafts into my nose as if the way it travels through the air is elegant, too.

"And then, she came running out of the water with three of them damn jellyfish hanging from her arms," he exclaims, the stale cigarettes on his breath stinging my nostrils and beating the scent of lavender dead. Jules leans away from Mr. Sanders almost imperceptibly. I notice, though. "Aunt Pat is trying to calm her, but she's wailing because them damn things hurt when they sting ya. Little Breezy girl wasn't having it no more, so she yanked off her trunk shorts and squatted all funny and pissed all over her own arms." His eyes are wide, and his lips are curled up as if he thought he was making me proud.

Juliette's brows scrunch in a vee, and she pops her lips. "Wow."

I hold up a hand and close my eyes. "Don't," I say. "Don't you even—"

"Them jellies really do sting ya good. I'd have peed on myself, too," he adds.

Juliette bursts into uncontrollable laughter to the point where I'm concerned she'll spill her Modelo all over her nice white dress.

"Nice," I say. "Thank you for that, Mr. Sanders." I pat him on the shoulder and nod. "Another beautiful retelling of my favorite story."

"Oh no," Austin calls as he rounds the corner with a fresh pot of shrimp. "Did I miss the Breezy peeing on herself story? It's my favorite," he whines.

"Oh my God," Juliette wheezes between laughing fits, her free hand holding her stomach. "I cannot. I cannot. This is too funny."

I almost smile watching her be so silly, watching her seem so free, beer bottle dangling from her fingers. She looks good like this. Relaxed. Like when we were teenagers, before she joined her family's business and took the blood oath to the Peralta throne. She looks like someone I recognize. Someone who never left that note in the visor of my truck. Someone who loves me. *Loved* me.

"Thank you." I smile and nod, accepting the shame. "Thank you all, I'll be here all week." I shrug and take a sip of wine. It's making me feel good tonight. A little buzzed, a little brave, a little happy. "Actually, forever. I'll be here forever."

Mr. Sanders, seemingly content with his storytelling, smiles into his cup. "Oh, wow. What a time. We do it 'cause we love ya, Breezy."

"Oh, is that so?" I say through a smile.

"It is." He gives me another pat on the shoulder. "I'm going to serve myself some of Pat's famous shrimp. Enjoy, ladies." Mr. Sanders walks to the long table spread with garlic bread, boiled shrimp, corn, collards, and banana pudding. It's almost as Southern as Southern gets.

Then it's just me and Juliette, standing side by side in the sea of people.

"Gotta love Mr. Sanders," Austin says.

Oh, and Austin is here.

Juliette sways toward me until her shoulder gently bumps mine. "Any chance we could talk for a moment outside?" she asks.

"Look." I stare at her, then drop her gaze. Focus on my wineglass instead. "There's nothing you can say that will make up for what you did or how you left. Nothing you can say that would make up for not reaching out, ever. And there's nothing you could say to explain how on God's green earth you made those decisions."

She nods. Then, her lips pluck apart as if she's snapping out of a trance. "I know," she says. "That's why I was going to start with an apology. See what kind of reaction that got. Then maybe, we could go from there."

My eyes drop to her glossy lips. *No.* I raise my gaze, but it falls again to her full breasts pressing against her tight white bodice. *No*, I repeat to myself, as if I have a choice here. And I don't. Not at all. Never did.

I cross my arms and give her an intimidating stare. "Fine, but I don't have all night. Uncle Trevor and I need to win back our money in dominoes."

She grins and drops her eyes to her pretty brown leather sandals. "I promise, I'll make it brief." She holds up a pinkie. It seems like a simple gesture. But she's made many pinkie promises to me before. And the last one…well, the last one she broke in a very major way.

I push her hand down, refusing her silly promise. "Yeah, we'll see about that." I walk to the back patio. "Come on. Dominoes, remember?"

"Right. Dominoes."

She follows me to the backyard as we weave through most of my family's colleagues and friends in Coral Bay to find a bit of privacy. I lead her to the back corner of the garden where no one is lingering. The long palm leaves flop lazily above us, lending a bit of privacy from the other party guests. The late afternoon breeze rustles the trees, and the saline scent of oyster and crab shells surrounds us. To me, it's a clean smell. Fresh and salty and full of nutrients and life.

"I'm sorry," she blurts, her fingers softly tapping the top of her bottle.

I roll my eyes. "Wow. That was quite the apology." I lean in a little closer so she can feel my arm against hers. So she can feel *me*. "You seriously show up in Coral Bay without so much as a word. After sixteen years. *Sixteen years*, Juliette. Just because no one wants to work on your precious family property, so you had to come running to Oscar to fix your own problem with Coral Bay tax dollars." I wait for her to respond, my breathing loud between us.

"Yes."

I scoff and step back, but she grabs my wrist.

"Please. All that is true. You're right, but—"

"But what?" I shake my head, letting the anger that has built in my chest for over a decade and a half spill onto her. I am completely valid. "But now you're bored and over your life in Atlanta, so you thought you'd just show up and fuck with me?"

"That is so far from—"

"You are the Southeast asset manager for Peralta Inc. Surely, you have underlings to do these types of things for you. Surely, you do not have to live in Coral Bay. I'm sure you could jet down on a Monday, fly back on a Friday, and not have to disturb your perfect little life in Atlanta." I shake my head and laugh. "Sorry, perfect *big* life in Atlanta. Being Mrs. Halloway and all..." I roll my eyes. Maybe I'm beginning to feel the wine just a little.

"Mrs. Halloway." She barks a laugh. "I have attained the highest form of woman, haven't I?"

I squint in the growing dusk. "Is this a joke to you?"

"No." She taps her bottle again. "It's not a joke. It's just, I know you have the complete wrong idea of what my relationship is like with Jim. Or what it *was* like with Jim. We are in the final stages of getting divorced."

"Oh." I lean back, a little shocked. "I'm...sorry?"

She chuckles and shakes her head. "Nope. No apologies necessary. I thought I could make it work, but I couldn't stay in a passionless marriage."

"Fizzled out?" I ask with a hint of snark.

"It never had *fizz* to begin with." She shrugs as if it doesn't hurt. "It was a career move for both of us. An alliance of sorts that brought in a lot of business. He understands my life, and I understand his. He's smart and stable, someone I could start a family with." True pain crosses her face, and things become just a bit clearer. "But, yeah, I just...*can't*. Can't start a family in a loveless home."

"I'm sorry it didn't work out how you hoped." And this I say with sincerity.

She nods, her lip trapped between her teeth. She has this look on her face, one I only saw a few times when we were teenagers. When it was just us at the end of the night: Jules, me, and the ocean. When we talked about our hopes and dreams. She told me how badly she wanted to be a teacher. She always loved kids so much. She'd get this exact look, as if she knew her dreams would never come true.

"It's okay. There's more than one way to have a child. I think we both know blood's not so thick." She sucks in a deep breath and lets it out slowly. "Anyway, I adore Jim. One of the best men I know, but with that off the table, I feel empty. I don't need him. We have already cemented the business relationship between our families, and we both deserve something more." She shakes her head.

I nod. I'm not really sure what I'm supposed to say to all this. "Okay. That's okay to feel." I sip my wine awkwardly, unsure of how Juliette got me worried about her. "Look, I know life is hard and weird, and I am sorry it didn't work out with Jim." I take a deep breath. "But you hurt me. Deeply. You prioritized everything in your life over me. I don't know why you're here. I don't know why you're suddenly in my life. Like, you're everywhere," I say, frustrated.

"I know I hurt you, Breezy. I was young and didn't know—"

"Stop." I hold up a hand. "I don't want to hear it. You were young, yes. But you grew up. You grew up, and you never reached out."

"I thought it was best for both of us." Her eyes seem heavy. "It was a different time back then, Tanya. And I had my career to chase, and I wasn't going to stay in Coral Bay. We would've drained each other. Fought through college and—"

"I didn't go to college," I say, a little indignant. I don't know why, other than to draw a stark difference between us.

"I know, I just meant that time in our lives." She shakes her head. "It doesn't matter. I thought what I was doing was the best thing for us both. And as the years passed, no matter how much I wanted to reach out, it became harder and harder. Like, I'd dug my hole too deep, and there was no climbing out. Then Hurricane Sasha changed everything."

"How?" I ask, surprised I'm indulging this weird conversation at all.

"The Sands is more important than you know. It's the cornerstone property of our Southeast portfolio, a blueprint of how projects should be managed and grown, given how quickly we were able to tear down the school and—"

"The Meadows. You tore down the Meadows."

She looks down, and I hope she's thinking of our nights in the cobwebbed hallways and abandoned library. I hope she thinks of me on the beanbag and her lips on mine. I know it's a silly thing to harp on. An abandoned school can only stand untouched, except for by the local kids breaking and entering, for so long. But it mattered to me. The end of the Meadows was the end of me and Juliette. Years of friendship, countless letters, obliterated just like the rotted drywall when the wrecking ball hit it.

I can never forget the plumes. Me and the boys scored a bottle of Southern Comfort, and we watched from atop the monkey bars on the playground as it fell. We were silent. It was the first time we'd ever seen it happen before our eyes. It wasn't just the shadow of the skyscrapers lurking up the coastline, it was *here*. The boogeyman had crawled through our window.

Oscar was the first to jump to the ground. He looked up at us and said, "I know the Meadows had to end, but you'd think they'd replace a school with a fucking school."

Which is why it bothers me no end that he's so gung ho about bending over backward to help the Peraltas repair it. Now he has the power, and it's like he's lost sight of everything he used to care about, the soul of Coral Bay.

"Right," Juliette says and snaps me back to reality. "The Meadows. And it doesn't look good to investors when your crown property is in disrepair, and rebuilding efforts haven't even started. Turns out it's a huge fucking problem, actually, and I'm in huge fucking trouble. Almost as much trouble as the morning after our last night together." She shakes her head. "Never going to be VP," she mutters.

"Juliette—"

"I got a text." She winces. "From my father. Early that morning." She touches my wrist, and I let her. "It's not an excuse, just what happened." I nod for her to continue. "He said if I planned to continue interacting with you to not bother coming home. There would be no position for me at Peralta Inc., and I'd need to secure my own funding for college. I was seventeen, scared, and out of time to make a very big decision."

We stand quietly, the hum of the shrimp boil a faint white noise as I think about what happened that morning. How I woke up half-naked in the bed of my truck, alone on the beach, my nipples aching from her mouth. Everything aching from her. For her. How the scent of her was everywhere. Not the perfume. Not the chlorine. *Her.*

I rub my eye, trying to get the image of us out of my head, but it flashes through my brain in quick spurts. Juliette on me, under me, all over me. Drowning me in her deep end. "I understand," I finally say. "But I can't go back. I can't do this again."

She taps her bottle. It's cute. "I'm not asking you to. I just wanted you to know." She clears her throat, and I could swear she's fighting tears. It's weird to see her so vulnerable. "Anyway, there's a lot of pressure to get this project done, obviously. And I have the divorce. There's a lot on my plate, but I want us to be good. I'll be here until the end of construction, and I could use a friend."

I basically growl.

She chuckles. "Yes?"

"I can be your casual friend. I'm stuck with you anyway. But I'm still mad at you."

"That's okay. I can work with that." She smiles, her perfect white teeth glowing like her perfect white sundress, softly in the night. She is and always will be breathtaking to me. My breathtaking, casual friend, Juliette Peralta.

"You've got yourself a friend." I pat her shoulder a little too hard. "Should we get back to the party?"

She runs a hand through her perfect waves as if relieved, then gives them a quick bounce with the palm of her hand. "Yes. Let's jump back in."

The glow of the citronella tiki torches and the string lights cast a warm light over everyone I've ever loved. These parties Aunt Pat throws are adored and looked forward to by the entire community. They happen once every couple of months, and everyone is welcome. Including Juliette, apparently.

We spy Benny by the grilled lemon pepper shrimp, a broad smile on his face as he raises his beer. "Aunt Pat never misses," he says in pure bliss, his paper plate stacked high with grilled shrimp and garlic bread.

Juliette grins in the firelight, and it makes my stomach buzz the way it used to when we were young. "Benny doesn't like to peel his own shrimp, but the Cajun boiled shrimp is the way to go," I say and reach for the ladle in the steel pot.

"I just like the lemon pepper the best," he says. "Excuse me, it's not about the shell. I'm from Coral Bay. I don't mind peeling shrimp."

"Sure, Benny. Whatever you say." I hand Juliette a small plate of the boiled shrimp and eye her white dress. She eyes her dress, too. "Oh, I should've asked if *you* mind peeling shrimp. It can be a little messy." I chuckle at the image her splotching her fancy dress into a tie-dye of shrimp juice and Creole seasoning.

She comes to some unknown decision, probably that she could buy a hundred more of the same dress if she stained it, and takes the plate. "I like messy."

"Oh, damn," Benny hollers. "We see you, Jules."

He claps as she sets the plate on the deck railing and masterfully peels a shrimp and drops it into her mouth. She drops her head back and moans. "Praise all that is holy, that is the best shrimp I've ever had."

"Damn well better be." Aunt Pat appears at Juliette's side and steals a shrimp from her plate, shelling it almost imperceptibly fast and popping it in her mouth. She snags a napkin from the table and wipes her fingers. "Though my past self is very offended. I know you ate plenty of my shrimp when you were a little girl, Jules."

"Aunt Pat." Juliette sets down her plate and wipes her hands before she accepts my aunt's hug. "You know your shrimp is the best in the world. Future, past, and present. Hands down."

Aunt Pat gives her a big squeeze and holds her at arm's length. I wonder if Juliette feels fifteen again getting hugged that way. "You look good, Juliette. Nice and strong."

This is exactly the compliment my aunt would give. Not beautiful or gorgeous or lovely. *Strong.*

Juliette chuckles, and a hint of blush colors her cheeks. Or maybe it's just the candlelight. "Thank you, Aunt Pat. Gotta be, dealing with all these foremen and contractors."

"It's nice that the Sands is finally being looked after," she says. "It was quite the eyesore for some time."

Juliette stiffens and morphs straight into business mode like a Transformer. "Yes, we did not anticipate the difficulty in obtaining a crew to begin repairs. But we are well on our way now and have hopes of completing the construction within two years."

I choke on my beer, and everyone turns to stare as I thump my chest and cough in the corner.

"You okay, Breezy?" Juliette asks.

"Sorry." I nod and continue to thump. "I could've sworn you just said two years."

Her brows rise, and she shakes her head. "Two? No, no. Not two. My apologies. The Sands repair should be completed within a year if everything goes remotely according to plan."

I breathe a sigh of relief, the beer finally dislodged from my lungs. "Good. 'Cause I could not imagine you in Coral Bay for that long."

Benny laughs. "Yep. Think of how much Coral Bay rubbed off on you the first time. I heard the second time is worse." He gives her a look of serious concern that we all chuckle at.

Austin appears at his side and wraps an arm around his shoulder. "Second time for what?" he asks.

I shake my head. "It doesn't matter. It's never going to happen."

CHAPTER TEN

I love the hustle and bustle of the Inn when it's busy. It doesn't sound like stress or work or chaos; it sounds like the rumble of a well-oiled machine. Like a sturdy truck that won't let me down. The Coral Bay Inn has stood in this very spot for decades. Its old-school construction withstood Sasha way better than some newer buildings around. It has staying power. The Sands, on the other hand, is like a luxury car: fast and not good for much. Hit a pothole in that thing, and the wheels are sure to fall out of alignment. May even bottom out. Looks. Places like the Sands are all about looks.

I sit in the small office of the Inn. It holds a handful of desks, one for each department head, a computer on each, and a few whiteboards. Marge was very big into brainstorming. I smack the edge of the envelope I'm holding against my desktop. It's the first check from the mayor's office for the future trolley. Construction started smoothly today on the new boardwalk.

I grimace. It can't end soon enough. The construction is a huge deterrent and bother to my guests. This better be worth it. I slide my thumb under the adhesive and pull out the paper. It's a short letter with a check slipped inside:

For the headache of the construction, an initial one-time courtesy payment. The agreed upon rates for

use of the trolley will follow in accordance...yes, this is
mostly from the Peraltas. Just accept it, Breezy.

I flip the check over so I can see the amount. "Holy shit," I mutter. I look up to see if anyone is around. "Holy shit, that's a lot of money. Hell, yeah, I'm accepting it." I make a mental note to head to the bank after work and deposit this before it disappears in the wind. I don't feel weird about accepting their money. I'm stuck with them, and they are using my property for their own gain, and I place an extremely high value on it. I blow over the top of my coffee, take a small sip, and moan.

"Ah, the coffee moans. Good cup?" Mark asks.

We were servers in Crabby's together when we were younger. Then bartenders, bar managers, and Marge trained me to run the entire show. I trained Mark to manage the entire restaurant. We have always worked well together, at least after I got over my massive teenage crush on him. Juliette might have had something to do with that.

"Yep. We got our first check from the Peraltas."

He eyes the check in my hand and grins. "Big holiday bonuses this year?" He's only kidding.

I grin. "What did Marge always say?"

"If there's a thing you want, don't buy it with capital. Buy an investment that will pay for it with profits," he recites.

"Exactly." I lean back in my chair and consider the projects I want to pursue now that I have a chunk of change to invest. I hear Mark, though; times have been hard, and people are still looking for relief in the form of raises or bonuses. Anything that can give them a little more breathing room. "What about beach gear rental? We can easily use this money to convert the old umbrella shack into a place that does rentals by the hour. I'm thinking bikes, skimboards, kayaks, the whole shebang."

He looks excited and disappointed at the same time.

"I hear you, Mark. But this money must be invested into the business first, then used to boost income for employees. I will write into the plan that the first year's profits from gear rental will go straight into the pockets of the employees in the form of a bonus. Deal?"

His grin widens, and he nods. "Yes. Deal."

I wonder if the Peraltas would ever do that for their employees. It's probably why they struggled to keep their megacomplex staffed before the hurricane. Sure, they can rebuild, but that's just half the battle.

After Mark leaves, I spend the rest of the afternoon going over next month's general budget and the construction budget. It still feels like there's a lot to do, but it's manageable and should be finished before the Sands, within the year.

I check in with each of my department managers before I walk to my truck. The breeze is warm, and it feels like the perfect night for wine on the boat. I draft a text to the boys:

It's gorgeous out. Gonna gas up Silverfish *and drink some wine, cruising under the sunset. Who's in?*

My thumb hovers over the send button, but before I can chicken out, I add Juliette's name to the group. Send. "Fuck, fuck, fuck." I climb into my truck and start the engine. "Shit, shit, shit. What the fuck?" My phone buzzes in my pocket as I drive home cursing all the way. When I get there, I throw it in park and fish out my phone, anxious to see the responses.

Oscar: *No can do. Prepping with the team tonight for a press conference on the new high school curriculum changes.*

Benny: *Oh! Will there be snackies?*

Austin: *Ben, babe, Kyle has that play date with Dash, the new kid at school with the hippie parents, remember? The parents have good friend potential, so we're having dinner all together.*

Benny: *Not being homophobic is a low bar for friend potential...*

Austin: *...*

Juliette: *Sounds perfect. I'm wrapping up at the office just now. What can I bring?*

I throw my phone in the passenger seat. "Oh my God, what have I done?"

❖

Sometimes, life throws a curveball. Like sabotaging yourself and ending up on what turns out to be a pretty romantic date with the woman who shattered your heart and works for an evil empire.

But she walks through the marina looking like a dream. A floppy-brimmed green hat keeps the sinking sun off her cheeks, and her dark shades keep it out of her eyes. She wears a beautiful purple sundress with a delicate floral print and three-quarter sleeves. In one hand, she carries a wooden board covered in plastic wrap, and in the other, a bottle of wine.

"Hi," she says as she hands me the wine, then the charcuterie board. "Looks like it's just us, huh?"

She's only been on my boat once, but when I take her hand and help her in, she's not clumsy. She hikes up her dress and steps in with confidence, showing off the sliver of herself that belonged to Coral Bay at some point.

I avert my gaze from her beauty and pull a wine key from my overall pocket. "You didn't need to bring wine. I have plenty," I say.

She unwraps the charcuterie and plucks a piece of cheese. "I don't like to arrive empty-handed."

"Fair enough." I open the sauvignon blanc and pour us each a glass in my reusable plastic cups. They're not fancy, but they don't break. All I need for the boat. My hand trembles as I hand her a cup. I'm nervous as hell.

"Are those the same overalls you had back in the day?"

"Oh my God." I look at myself, slightly horrified. "Yes. These are literally the same overalls I wore on our last day together." I take a long sip, the splash of lemon curd and gooseberry zipping across my tongue. "Just last month, I was going through some of my old things at Aunt Pat and Uncle Trevor's and came across this box of clothing. The overalls still fit, and at this point are kind of cool and vintage-y, so I snagged them."

She lifts a brow and eyes me over her cup. "So you're not trying to take me back to those days by wearing my favorite outfit?"

"Favorite?"

"Of course." She takes a step toward me and runs a finger down my strap. I stand motionless while every nerve ending in my body goes completely haywire. "I'll never forget you standing outside our beach house, about to wake up everyone with the doorbell, looking so damn cute and indignant." She drops her hand but eyes the strap. "Wearing these adorably Coral Bay overalls."

I take a slow breath and nod. "Okay, then."

She quirks a brow and grins. "Okay, then?"

"Mm-hmm." I sip my wine and walk to the captain's chair. "Better cover up that nice charcuterie board. From what I remember, you like to go fast."

A grin spreads over her face, and just as she's tucking away the snacks, I make it out of the no-wake zone and hit the throttle. *Silverfish* jolts forward, and Juliette lets out an excited laugh, holding her hat so it doesn't blow away. I cut through the waves in a silly zigzag so ocean spray mists us. The sun is just starting to set, casting a soft orange glow over everything: the water, Juliette's skin, the sand on the distant beach, the clouds. Everything.

After I've had my fun, I crawl *Silverfish* to the island we used to waste our days on as teenagers. It too is bathed in the sunset and looking spectacular. I don't drop anchor; instead, I walk to Juliette with the bottle of wine and splash a little more in her cup. "You're not supposed to drink and boat, but this is Coral Bay, and no one cares. Wanna learn?" I nod to the captain's chair.

She smiles and nods. "Hell, yeah, I wanna learn. You're really going to let me drive *Silverfish*? Oscar is the only other person you let touch the wheel."

I shrug. "I guess age has softened me." I tug her by the hand until she sits in the chair and grabs the wheel. "Okay." I point to the lever on the right side of the helm. "This is the throttle. To go faster, we advance like this." I push it gently forward until the boat starts to move slowly. "And steering is just like you would a car, only the currents and the waves are going to give it a very different feel."

"Hold on," she says and stashes her hat in a compartment at the stern. She sits back down and looks over her shoulder. "I'm ready."

The wind catches her hair and blows it in my face, wrapping me in the scent of her. It's not the super-fancy perfume I'd begun to associate with her; it's something more subtle. Closer to how she smelled when we were kids. She steers the boat carefully. "Let's give her some gas. Advance the throttle." She gently nudges it, and we pick up a bit of speed. The smell of her hair is low-key intoxicating as I cover her hand with mine. "Never thought you'd be afraid of going fast, Jules." I push her hand, and *Silverfish* gallops forward through the waves. "Remember, boats don't have brakes," I call through the whipping air.

She squeals as we fly over a wave. "You're telling me that now?"

I lean just a bit closer so I don't have to yell. "I'm right here. Nothing's gonna happen."

She turns into my ear, and I make sure to take over steering. "Promise?"

"I promise." I put her hand back on the wheel. "We're going to trim up a little now." I hit the button up, and the bow rises. "Feel the difference?"

She nods. "Yeah. It's, like, lighter or something."

"We've raised the bow, so it's like we're skimming over the water instead of fighting through it."

After another ten minutes of zooming through the ocean, Juliette says, "Can we go back to the island and anchor?"

I pull back the throttle and slow us. "Of course. Turn her around."

We drift along the coast of our island, and I drop anchor as Juliette lounges on the long seat along the bow of the boat. I take my wine and sit next to her. "It's so beautiful," she says, sipping her wine and gazing at the island in the sunset.

Coral Bay is beautiful. Special. It exists in a world apart from the typical vacation towns around Florida. The island hasn't been developed. Not that it should or probably could, but beautiful things are allowed to merely exist here without a dollar being made from them, and that's okay.

"It really is so gorgeous." Something about being on the boat with her feels easy, as if the years of pain and hurt between us are beginning to melt away. That scares me, the idea of letting go of my anger. It has become part of me. But enjoying Juliette's company and the wine feels so much better. I knock her shoulder. "Did you ever come back here without me knowing?"

She doesn't look at me, but I catch the corner of her mouth twitch. "Once," she admits. She takes a deep breath, then pulls off her sunglasses. The gentle light from the sunset turns the gold flecks in her eyes iridescent. "I was a junior in college on spring break. Was meeting up with a bunch of friends down the coast in Panama City Beach." She winces. "As you know, I did not have to drive through Coral Bay. In fact, it added almost two hours to my trip, but I couldn't resist."

I scratch at an evaporating drop of seawater on my arm. "I wish you would've told me."

"I couldn't." She bites her lip. Shakes her head. "You have no idea the misery I was in, Breezy. I…I—"

"What?"

"I drove by your house. I drove by the Inn. I drove by the Drip, Austin's, Benny's, Oscar's, East Beach. I drove by anyplace I could think of that you might be, desperate to catch even a glimpse of you. Just needed to see you, to know you were real." Tears gather in her eyes and turn them molten. "I thought it was all I needed to tide me over, but I never saw you. Ridiculous of me." She wipes at her eyes. "You were probably on shift or reading at home or on a date, for all I know."

I laugh at the last image. "Date? Please." I sip my wine and chuckle. "It was always you for me."

"And a little bit of Oscar?" She knocks my shoulder, and I push back against it.

"You know I never felt it all the way with him." I shake my head. "It's confusing being young. He was my best friend besides you. He was handsome, passionate, and so smart that it irritated me. Still does." I chuckle into my cup. "All those things attracted me to him, of course. He was supposed to be the one for me, but it just"—I rub my hand over my heart—"wasn't in here, you know? He's perfect on paper, but my heart never raced for him."

She stays quiet for a moment, seemingly considering her next words. I sip my wine and wait. "Did you keep my letters?"

I swallow my sip and nod. "Yeah. I kept your letters." There's only one that matters at this point, though. "All of them."

She squeezes my knee, sending currents of electricity up and down my leg. "That last letter was a lie."

I shake my head. "Was it?"

"I'm here now, aren't I? Talking to you again, seeing you again." She squeezes harder, and I can feel a little desperation in it. I like it, but it also annoys me.

I swing my leg away. "You literally have to be here living in Coral Bay for months. Of course we're going to see each other. You're building on to my property. Kind of need me, don't you?"

She shakes her head, a look of defeat on her face, as if she knows she can't convince me today. "I do need you. In more ways than you know." She clears her throat and tucks a loose strand of hair behind her ear. "Can you take me back? Have a busy day tomorrow and emails I still need to respond to tonight."

"Sure."

CHAPTER ELEVEN

"At least things have been cordial between you two," Oscar says. His fatherly attitude about this is really starting to piss me off, acting like Juliette and I are just bickering and should pull it together for the good of the town. I don't owe him anything, and I don't owe Juliette or the Sands anything. My responsibilities are to my family, the Inn, and this town. And I know Oscar thinks somehow this will save the town, but the Sands isn't Coral Bay. The Inn is Coral Bay and has been the beating heart of the local economy for decades, right along with the fishing industry.

The sun reflects off his white hard hat, making him look almost heavenly in his matching white guayabera. Sand has gotten in my heels, and I feel a trickle of sweat down the back of my sundress. I am cranky, I am tired, and I am hot. "Whatever, Oscar. Sure. Can you just tell me what you need approved so I can get back to my job?"

He lifts his perfectly thick brow. "Did you eat lunch?"

I sigh in frustration. "The hell does that have to do with anything?"

"You just seem a little hangry."

"That is so inappropriate." I smack his shoulder.

"I just know you is all." He chuckles and slides off his hard hat, running a hand through his jet-black hair, which looks supermodel sleek with the sheen of sweat in it. He toes the boardwalk under our feet. "We're going to build the fork for the Sands's guests here."

I look back toward Coral Bay Inn, then to the ocean. "Seems like a good spot. Close enough to the lot and the trolley that we'll split foot traffic early on and keep my side less crowded."

"Exactly. You'll hardly notice it's here."

I scoff. "Don't patronize me."

His mouth falls open, and he presses a hand to his chest. "Patronizing? Me? I would never."

"It's like I know you or something." I take off my hard hat. Didn't think we needed one anyway, given the one piece of construction equipment. I shove it in his chest, and he lets out a little *oof.* "It was fun playing construction worker with you. Now, I really must get back to work." I spin and walk back to the patio of Crabby's.

"But I want to talk about the festival."

"If you need more of my time, feel free to schedule another meeting," I call over my shoulder. If he responds, it's muffled by the early afternoon ocean and breeze.

The patio is nice and full for a Wednesday afternoon, and the general vibe seems relaxed and happy. It's perfect. I hope the influx of tourists walking by on the boardwalk won't disturb my dining guests. But hey, it will be a treat to be able to offer beach supply rentals and maybe some other fun things with the new surplus in the budget. With that will come vouchers and a little added flexibility in keeping guests feeling special and happy.

It almost feels like it can't possibly be worth it to the Peraltas to pay this much for my beach access. That's their decision, though. I'm happy to collect the checks.

It's difficult to not think about Juliette every minute of every day. If I'm not replaying the intimate moments of our boat excursion, I'm thinking about work and the Sands and the construction. And right now, I'm thinking I'd like to see her again soon.

"Get it together, Breezy," I mutter into the wind. It's not like I'm rushing to trust her again or have any feelings other than friendship, I just...maybe it'll be nice to have a close friend who's a woman. It's always been me and three men. Lovely, beautiful, amazing men, but *men*. It was always just a bit more with Juliette. In every way.

"How are sales looking compared to last week?" I ask Wren as she shakes a margarita.

She smacks the metal shaker against the bar, and it cracks open. She was never one to use a strainer. Instead, she angles half the shaker into its partner and pours. It's not my favorite technique. Not the nicest-looking technique. But as the boss, some things you let slide. Light green liquid splashes into the salted rocks glass. She hangs a lime on the rim and floats a slice of fresh jalapeño on the drink. "Up," she says. "Up, up, up. Always up."

I see a small pile of drink tickets and slide behind the bar to knock a few out. "I know you don't need my help. I'm just avoiding my own job right now." I dry shake a guava gin fizz, my favorite cocktail on the menu right now, and reminisce about when making drinks and serving food were my only responsibilities. But when I was just the bartender, I would shake cocktails and imagine owning the place.

I pour the guava fizz into a chilled coupe glass and grin at the perfectly foamy egg white top, then garnish it with a beautiful twist of lemon. It's perfect. I rinse my hands and dry them on a fresh bar rag. "Be thinking about what kind of support you need going into the busy season. Staff, equipment, changes to the menu, anything. We have that meeting next week, okay?" I slip back to the guest side of the bar.

Wren wipes her hands and takes a breath, seemingly noticing her pile of drink tickets has mostly disappeared. "Thanks for the little boost, Breezy." She rinses out the shakers and strainers—my strainers—and starts on the next order as the small printer spits out a new ticket. It's a triggering noise, the sound of tickets printing. But Wren isn't stressed. It's what makes her so good and fast. "Want anything?"

Normally, I'd say no. Professionalism is important to me, and while I understand restaurant and service industry culture, I cannot set the example of drinking on the job. So if I want a delicious guava gin fizz, I need to decide to be done for the day at—I peek at my watch—half past three. I groan. "Fine. You're too convincing, Wren."

"Good. You deserve to cut out early and relax a little. Guava fizz?"

I nod. There's nothing pressing on the agenda today, and I saw Oscar walk to his car a few minutes ago, so he won't be bothering me anymore. It's a busy stressful week, but for today, it's over.

"Hi."

I look over my shoulder, slightly startled. "Juliette. What are you doing here?"

She clearly just came from the Sands. She's wearing all black. Black jacket, silky black blouse, black trousers, black heels—except for the red bottoms—and a black watch. "I just had to get out of there." Wren slides the pretty pink fizz in front of me. "Oh, are we drinking already? I'll have one. Thank you." Wren nods and starts another of the same.

"If you're here to talk business, I'm off for the day," I say and take a sip of the decadent cocktail. Damn, it's good. The guava is sweet and ripe, but the lemon is sharp and acidic, then the egg white makes it so smooth and creamy. "Fuck, that's good."

Juliette chuckles. "You've got a little…" She touches the shoulder of my sundress where a small pink stain sinks into the cotton.

"Shit. Wren, could I have a clean rag and some soda water, please?"

She hands me a cup and a rag, and I try to dab at the small spot, but it's hard to see, given its location right under my ear.

"Let me get it." Jules takes the rag and dips it in the soda water, then dabs it on the stain. It feels intimate. I can smell her perfume, her shampoo. She gently dabs the stain, and I stay still until she's finished and rubs her thumb over it. "There. That's better." She pushes the rag and cup back across the bar.

"Wren, this is my friend, Juliette Halloway."

Wren smiles and shakes Juliette's hand. "Nice to meet you, Juliette."

"You as well, Wren. And it's Peralta, really. Juliette Peralta."

"Juliette is managing the repair of the Sands," I explain. But it sounds like I'm leaving out crucial information. "Also, she kind of owns the Sands," I add. "Anyway, she's a good person to know." What am I even doing?

Juliette chuckles, and Wren looks between us as she polishes a glass. "You trying to pawn me off on the fancy hotel down the road?" she asks through a grin.

"Never." I gasp, hand to heart. "I would cry forever if you left for the Sands, but you know I'd still love you and completely understand."

"Not to fear," Juliette says. "I wouldn't dream of stealing your amazing bar manager." Wren places the guava fizz in front of her, and she takes a sip. Her eyes widen as she licks the froth from her lips. "Damn, that's delicious. I take it back. I'm definitely stealing you."

"We'll see about that." I shake my head and laugh, and Wren busies herself with another drink order. "It's good to see you, Jules."

She tilts her head like she never expected those words to come from my mouth. I guess *I* never expected those words to come from my mouth. "Really?"

I sip my cocktail and nod. "Really. What's up? Did you have a question about the boardwalk or something? Oscar was here showing me the spot where they want to build your side in."

"Did it work for you? Everything still looks okay?" Her eyes are narrow, and she looks like she sincerely cares about my opinion. It's not how I imagined her after all these years. I thought she'd be exactly like her parents, a heartless business executive.

"Yeah, it looks good to me. I like that it splits early. So thanks for that."

"To be fair, it has to split early."

"Oh. And here I was thinking you were being considerate." I put my drink down and angle toward her. "Why does it have to branch off early?"

She smiles. "I want to be considerate, too. Don't get me wrong. Ideally, the boardwalk should be perpendicular to the ocean, so you feel like you're walking straight to the water. But there's some lateral distance we need covered, and if the offshoot was closer to the water, we'd need to build parallel to the beach instead of perpendicular, and that'd be all wrong. So the sooner we can offshoot, the better."

"Hmm," I say, unimpressed. "Should've just lied. You were about to get so many points with me."

A mischievous look crosses her face, and her brow arches. "Was I?" I nod. "Too bad I can't lie to you, then."

I roll my eyes. "Oh, come off it. Maybe you didn't lie, but you did...*something*."

She tilts her head back and forth as if considering if she did lie or *something*. "That's fair. Completely fair."

Wren is busy at the other end of the bar, and it feels like we have a moment of privacy, so I take advantage of it. "I know it's petty of me to keep bringing up a decision you made when you were seventeen. It's just a lot. Everything. The Sands, you being back, the boardwalk. And I was so angry with you for so long, it's hard to let go of."

"I understand, Breezy. Completely." She turns her gaze to her drink, her long fingers fiddling with the stem. "I actually didn't come here for business."

"No?"

She shakes her head. "I wanted to ask if maybe you wanted to come by this weekend and catch up some more. I'll make us something tasty, and we can drink wine and just hang out together as friends. I really enjoyed our time on the water the other day, and you definitely promised to be my friend while I'm in town, so…"

"Mmm. I don't recall promising anything," I say, smiling.

She scoffs. "I am so disappointed in you."

"No, you're not," I say.

"No, I'm not."

I take a moment and wonder if in any alternate universe, I ever say no to this woman. It feels utterly impossible. "Yes. I'd like that."

A smile spreads across her face, a splash of color among her all-black seriousness. "Really?"

I smile, too. I can't help it. I like to make her happy. "Really."

❖

"No. Absolutely not. What are you? A nun?" Benny says as he and Austin lounge on my bed and watch me sort through outfits for dinner at Juliette's tonight. They decided that drinking wine and helping me pick out what to wear was reason enough to have Austin's mom watch the kids tonight.

I look at the sweater I'm holding up. "A nun? It's just a nice light sweater. Practical and slightly business-y."

"Business-y? Honey, this is a date," Austin says.

I hang the rejected sweater back in my closet. "This is the farthest thing from a date. We're just catching up."

"The farthest thing from a date?" Benny asks, and I can basically feel them roll their eyes. "Going over to her house for wine and a home-cooked meal is the *farthest* thing from a date? Really?"

I flop on the bed between them and groan. "Oh my God, what am I doing?"

"It's a date," Austin adds.

"You're not helping," Benny says over my head.

"But it's really not a date," I say. "I agree, I shouldn't wear that sweater, and I agree that it's more intimate than your typical hangout, but we specifically decided to be friends. *Friends.*"

"Yeah," Austin says. "Kinda like you were 'just friends' when we were kids, too."

"But she—"

"Listen," Benny interrupts. "You're always in a sundress. Wear a sundress. Maybe that light green one with the flowers. It's a little booby and sexy in a casual way. In a Breezy way."

"Oh yes. Good idea, babe. That would be perfect," Austin says.

I go to my closet and slide hangers down the rail until I find the green dress. I present it to the boys. "This one?"

"Oh my God, yes," Benny says, clapping.

"Yes. Love it. Do it," Austin adds.

I lay it on my bed. "Okay, what about my hair?"

Benny twirls the ends of it between his fingers. "Okay, go shower and maybe, like, put some product in it?"

Austin smacks him on the shoulder. "Put some product in it? That's so mean, Ben."

"Hey," he complains, rubbing his shoulder. "How am I supposed to know what to do with her long wavy hair? I've had the same haircut since middle school. I am not that kind of gay."

"To be fair, everyone uses something in their hair. I put detangler in this mane after every shower. So don't worry, it wasn't mean," I assure him.

"Still. Your hair is gorgeous no matter what you do with it." Benny sips his wine and stares. "Well, go get ready. You only have an hour until you need to drive over."

"*Walk* over, actually," I amend.

"Walk?" Austin asks. "She's that close? Is she stalking you? That's kind of creepy, just saying."

I roll my eyes. "She's not stalking me, Austin, she doesn't know where I live. Just where Aunt Pat and Uncle Trevor live." I shrug. "It's a coincidence."

"Hmm. I'm still skeptical."

It really is a strange coincidence that Juliette is renting a place a mere fifteen-minute stroll from my house. But then again, Coral Bay is a pretty small town, and I live in one of the cutest neighborhoods. Jules just has good taste. My stomach swirls with nerves, and I clutch it, mildly worried I'm going to throw up. "Okay. I'm going to get ready."

The water is scalding hot, just how I like it, but I cool it down a touch. I don't want my skin to be so red and angry when I see Jules. It feels like how it felt to get ready as a teenager before seeing her again for the first time in months. Eager. Anxious. Excited. Scared. Except this time, I'm in the shower shaving my legs, wondering if there is any possibility she'll see me naked.

"Ah, fuck." I nick myself with the razor, and a thin trail of watery blood races into the drain. "Ouch."

No. The answer is no, Juliette will not be seeing what's under my dress. *Get it together, Breezy.*

I dry off and, taking Benny's suggestion to heart, put some nicer product in my hair. I grab the pink tube of Curl Angel I bought on a whim two years ago. It was one of those moments when I splurged on an iced coffee and walked around Target feeling fancy. I had to pick up a new juicer from a restaurant supply store in Panama City and thought I'd pop in. And here I am, being fancy.

I squirt a small amount in my hands and work it into my damp hair. It smells weird but good. Just different. My hair feels instantly amazing, though. As it should. This bottle of goo cost more than my shampoo, conditioner, and detangler combined. And I buy the big bottles.

"Okay, fellas." I strut out of the bathroom, feeling pretty good about myself. My hair is mostly dry and has some extra volume and curl to it. My dress is comfortable but fits nice and snug, showing off more cleavage than I'm used to. I don't know why I'm leaning into this evening with Juliette so hard. It's not even a date, and I'm acting like it's prom. Maybe because I don't date much. Ever. And even though she hurt me, Juliette is the only person I've ever felt that connection with.

Benny and Austin whistle and catcall, clapping and cheering. "Hot damn, Breezy, you are a babe," Austin says.

"You look gorgeous," Benny adds.

"Thank you." I can't help but grin. "It's this expensive hair product. So really, thanks for the tip." I wink.

He laughs and gives Austin a sly smile. "See? Hair product is always the answer."

"Oh, sweetie." Austin leans in and gives him a peck on the lips.

"Okay, finish your wine and be on your way, boys. Thank you for the help, but I have to get going. Have a great dinner and enjoy your night off from kids. Love you two."

"Good luck," they say in unison as we all leave.

CHAPTER TWELVE

The walk to Juliette's is lovely. The air is cool and calm and prevents me from breaking a sweat while also keeping my hair looking nice. The evening is clear, and the moon is almost full, only missing a sliver from the top left. I can hear the ocean in the distance, and it sounds peaceful, too, as if the universe is at ease with my decision to go see Juliette tonight. All systems go.

As I near, I spot her Range Rover shining under the streetlight next to her driveway. I hate that car. It represents all the things I hate about the Peraltas and all the things that Juliette values over community. But people are different, complex. Juliette is not her parents, and I'm sure it's a nice car.

I take a deep breath and knock on the door. It doesn't take long for her to answer. I'm hit with a waft of something delicious and savory and the scent of burning candles. The aroma, the lighting, everything is warm and bright, including Juliette herself. She steps to the side to let me in.

"Welcome. Don't judge me for the décor, it came furnished." She gives me a quick hug, and tonight, she smells like home. Like she's been cooking and baking all day, but her fresh shampoo still shines through it all. "You look amazing, by the way."

"Thanks. You look good, too."

She wears a boxy navy tee that hits right at the waistband of her jeans. Her hair is free and gorgeous as ever, luscious and shiny and soft-looking. She's barefoot, and her toes are painted a deep burgundy that matches her fingers. She's stunning and casual. It's interesting getting to know her style as an adult. I like it.

She drops her gaze to her toes before she meets my eye again. Is she nervous? Whatever she is, it's cute. "Thank you. Come on. Let me show you around."

I follow her a few steps into the living room. It's small but with tall ceilings and a fan with wide wicker blades that resemble palm fronds. The room is full of kitschy beach decorations; pristine fishing nets, giant conch shells, and endless adages about how life is better at the beach. Something about it is nice, though. Homey.

I stop in front of a sign that reads, "Drink in my hand. Toes in the sand." I point to it, its egregious font highlighted by the glow of a candle. "Did you make sure to bring this one down from Atlanta with you?"

She chuckles, her shoulder brushing against mine. It feels good. "Oh yes. When my mother gifted it to me for Christmas, I knew I'd be bringing it down to Coral Bay with me."

I laugh hard into my hand. The thought of Mrs. Peralta buying a printed beach poster one could probably get from Target to give to her only daughter on Christmas is ludicrous. Something as common as that is far beneath her. "I love how you placed the candle just so. Really makes it pop." I pop my lips for emphasis.

"Shut up," she says through her laughter. "Come to the kitchen with me. Let's get you something to drink."

I follow her around the corner to the kitchen. It's *shockingly* also beach-themed, with pale, sand-colored cabinets and dusty blue walls. But with only one light on and more candles, it feels very cozy and warm. The Bluetooth speaker in one of the open-faced cabinets plays a mellow tune as Jules checks under the lid of a pan.

"What can I get you?" she asks.

"What are you having?"

She snags a glass of red wine I hadn't noticed and takes a sip. "Virgin blood."

My eyes widen, and I let out a small gasp. "Ew, Jules. What?" I chuckle at her weird joke, a little shocked she made it.

Her cheeks turn red, and I don't think I've ever seen something so adorable as Juliette Peralta blushing. "*Ugh.* I know. Terrible joke. I'm just a little nervous. I can't help it. Tanya Brees is in my house." She tilts her head back and forth. "*Rental* house. My house is much more me."

I would have imagined Juliette's house as cold. Lots of stainless steel and brushed metal and fancy technology. But seeing how she's made this space as cozy as possible, I think I could be wrong. Maybe it's full of earth tones and reclaimed wood and more candles. I hope it is. Not that I'll ever see it, but it makes me happy thinking she lives in a warm home.

"Right. Um. I will also have red wine, thank you."

I sit on a stool by the island as she pours me a glass. "Let me know what you think. I got it last week from Big Carl's Liquor on a recommendation from Big Carl himself. No big deal." She brushes her shoulder as if she just name-dropped the president.

I sip cautiously. I know Big Carl, and I don't peg him as a sophisticated wine connoisseur, but I'm hoping to be wrong. The wine is smooth but still strong and spicy. I don't know much about wine, but this red is delicious. "*Mm.* It's tasty." I hold it up to the candlelight as if I have any idea what I'm looking for. "Okay, Big Carl, I see you. Now I know who to ask for wine recs."

She smiles and leans on the counter across from me. "I'm glad you like it. I bought six."

"Damn, Jules. I mean, we'll probably get through one, but six?"

She chuckles and reaches for my wrist. Gives it a squeeze. I want her to linger, but she doesn't. "They're not all for tonight, you know. I'm gonna be here awhile."

"Right." I shake my head. "Sorry, maybe I'm a little nervous, too."

"I know it's a lot." She nibbles her bottom lip, another show of nerves I'm not used to seeing from her, someone so put together and confident. "But I really appreciate you coming over and giving me a chance."

I nod, swirling my wine. "A chance at what?"

She shrugs, then meets my gaze. "A chance to be in your life again, Breezy. In whatever capacity you're comfortable with. I miss you. I miss feeling so deeply connected to someone. I missed the boys, too. And even though I didn't want to come back here, I'm so glad I did."

We look at each other in silence as I take in her words. "I'm glad you did, too."

"Good." She takes a deep breath through her nose, then pushes off the counter. "I hope you like mushroom risotto. I probably should've asked."

"I do like it very much."

She takes the lid off the pan and gives it a stir. "There's salad as well."

I walk behind her and peek over her shoulder. "Aren't you, like, notoriously supposed to *not* cook risotto with the lid?"

She looks back at me, and we feel very close. If only she leaned back a little, or I leaned forward, we'd be touching. I feel her breath as she gives me an unamused look. "You offend me," she says.

I chuckle and throw my hands up. "Just saying. Everyone knows you gotta let the steam—"

She whirls around and pins me with a fierce challenge in her eyes, brow raised and arms crossed. We are very close now. Her hips are just at my fingertips.

"You think I, Juliette Maria Peralta, one hundred percent of Italian descent, don't know how to properly cook risotto?"

I double down because she's absolutely adorable when she's

fired up. Adorable and sexy. "I don't know what goes on in the Peraltas' kitchen. Kind of thought you all had a personal chef or something."

"What?" She scoffs and pops a hip to the side. "A personal chef? What a ludicrous, silly notion." Her offended and shocked facade slips, and a smile tugs her lips.

"Oh my gosh." I laugh and squeeze her arm. "You totally did have a chef, didn't you?"

"Yes. We totally did." She laughs, too. A hard belly laugh that shakes my hand from her. "What do you think I did all day after school while my parents were God knows where, and I was avoiding my boyfriend of the month? I was annoying Chaz, our chef, and making him teach me to cook, or I was writing you a letter. That's how I spent my days."

Something about the thought of Jules clinging to her family's chef to learn classic Italian cooking instead of being able to learn it from her parents makes me ache for her. "What made you want to learn?"

"Thought it would impress my parents." She grimaces. "But as it turned out, only money-making ability and dating fine young men impressed them." She reaches for her glass and takes a sip, seemingly lost in thought. "But, hey," she says, snapping back to the present. "Now I can cook a mean risotto for my date."

"*Date?*"

She chokes on her wine and sets it down before she spills it. "*Friend* date. Oh my gosh. Friend date. Sorry." Her cheeks are adorably pink as she stammers. If only she saw me and the boys preparing for this *date*. "Friends," she repeats.

"You're kind of cute, you know that?"

Her blush deepens. "Oh yeah?"

"In a friendly way, of course," I add.

"Of course." She rolls her eyes and turns back to the stove. "I was just keeping it warm and moist, for the record."

I burst into laughter. I can't help it. It's like my teenage self emerges when I'm with Jules. But it feels nice, laughing at such a stupid thing. It feels good. Light. "Keeping it warm and moist, are you?"

She turns and shakes her head, but she's smiling. "Wow, Breezy. Very mature." She points the wooden spoon at me. "Ms. Brees, everyone. Business owner and pillar of the Coral Bay community."

"Oh man." I wipe a tear of laughter from the corner of my eye. "I haven't laughed like this since we were kids."

Her face shifts, eyes soften, and smile fades. "Really?"

I take a small step back, the vulnerability of the moment taking me off guard. I always fell into her gravity when we were young, and I can feel myself slipping now. But would it be so bad? Apart from her being technically married, being the person who broke my heart, and living in another state? Concern shadows her face, and before she can ask me what's wrong, I decide to let go. Just a little.

"Yes," I say. I look at the floor, a bit of shame tugging my gaze from hers, but the smell of something burning pulls my attention back. "Jules, the risotto."

"Shit." She whips around and shuts off the stove, knocking the wooden spoon to the floor in her haste. With a dish towel, she lifts the lid, and a plume of acrid smoke fills our nostrils. "*Ugh.* Nope. Nope. Nope." She drops the pan in the sink and runs water until the sizzling stops, then turns back to me, eyes wide and arms crossed. "I cannot believe I just ruined the risotto."

I blink, a little shocked from the whole ordeal. "Was it because you were trying to cover up the fact that you actually have no idea how to cook?"

A grin replaces her scowl as she leans against the counter. "I don't remember you being so sassy." I shrug. "I kind of like it."

"All I'm saying is, you didn't even taste it. It could have been fine." I snatch my wine and take sip. "Total cover-up job. You're not fooling me."

"Oh my gosh. You smelled the smoke. There's no way it

wasn't ruined. Now, if you'll just excuse me…" She gently hip checks me out of her way and opens the drawer behind me, pulling out a takeout menu for Mickey's Propane 'n Pizza. "The only place I know of that still has paper takeout menus."

I snatch the menu from her hands and scan it, even though I know it by heart. I lean on the counter and concentrate. "Everywhere in Coral Bay still has paper menus. You just haven't been here in years."

"I suppose that's fair." She leans next to me, her arm warm against mine. "What are you craving?"

It's an impossible question, really. I'm not one for casual sex, and I haven't dated in a very long time. So what I'm craving is to run my hands up Juliette's shirt and feel her soft skin against mine. I'm craving her mouth, her teeth, her tongue. I'm craving her.

I clear my throat and straighten. "Right. Um. You still like Hawaiian?"

"Hell, yeah, I do." She grins and nods, pulling the menu from my hands. "Do they still deliver?"

"Hell, yeah, they do."

"Perfect." She calls and orders one medium Hawaiian pizza with a side of cinnamon bun bites. "I've been craving them," she whispers with her hand covering the receiver. She recites her credit card information and hangs up. "Just forty minutes till it arrives. Can you last that long?"

"Yes. I think I'll survive." I take both our glasses and walk to the sliding door that leads to the backyard. "Come on." I nod to the door. "Let's sit outside. It's so nice out tonight, and the moon is almost full."

She gets the door and follows me onto her back porch. Two Adirondack chairs sit side by side with a table made from an old wine barrel between them. We each slide into a chair and sip our wine. The crickets sing a constant tune, fighting the ocean for first chair. It's peaceful, being with Jules out here.

"I missed it here," she says softly.

Though I'm not sure if she's looking at me, I nod.

"I never thought I was cut out to be a Peralta, you know?" she admits.

This catches me slightly off guard. Growing up, Jules was always on about kids and being a teacher or something that wasn't a heartless real estate empress. But she always valued her parents and the family business. It was always assumed she'd grow into her position with Peralta Inc. And though she had other dreams, I didn't think she saw it as a sacrifice but as a privilege to be a Peralta.

"What do you mean?" I sip my delicious wine and sink into the chair, enjoying the soft breeze and Juliette's soft words.

She blows out a deep breath and taps the arm of her chair. "Guess I never really thought I'd be enough. My parents, they made it very clear what their expectations were for me, and it's not like they were going to throw me out if I didn't choose to follow their path, but they were so good at wielding that quiet power of theirs." She sighed. "When they threatened to not pay for my college at the last minute, it scared the shit out of me. But the truth is, I'd rather be drowning in student loans than be at their beck and call every minute of every day forever."

I can understand her feelings. I can understand why she was afraid to be bold for herself, but there's one thing I can't let slide. "You were never not enough," I say.

She turns in her chair, sitting on one leg, to face me. So I do the same. "What do you mean?"

"Why you felt like you might not fit into the role with Peralta Inc…you were never not enough. You were too much, Jules. Too much fun, too much joy, too much passion and heart. Too many dreams and desires to fit into that small little position of a big-time real estate developer." I stop for a moment and enjoy another sip of wine, revisiting every word I just said. I nod. "You were lovely."

"Am I not now?" Her voice is soft. She doesn't sound angry; she sounds worried.

"You don't overflow the way you used to. You're lovely still but trying to live within the small means of your big budget." I shrug. "I don't know. It's weird how rich you are and how trapped you feel."

She chuckles softly, and I think it's meant to be sardonic. "At least I'm divorcing Jim."

I shake my head. "Makes no sense to me still."

"I don't know, Breezy. It's like I walked so far down one path, turning around felt worthless. Impossible."

"Ironic you ended up here, then," I say.

"Yes." She laughs. "I love a good joke from the universe."

We're quiet for a few beats before I decide to slip into her a little more. "I missed you, Jules." I finger the rim of my glass until it makes a low-pitched whistle. "You have no idea how much I've missed you."

She stands and walks in front of me, the lights from the porch highlighting every perfect feature. Her dark brows and sharp jawline shadowed and prominent. She reaches for my mostly empty glass. "I'm here now. Let's just be here together."

I hand her my glass and nod as she walks back inside. *Let's just be here together.* How much time of Jules being here with me will I waste because I can't get over the past? Will I blow all my time with her because she was young and scared and trying to appease her parents?

I walk inside and find her pouring me another glass of wine at the counter. I approach her quietly and slip my hands up under her arms. She jumps, then relaxes into me. The weight of her leaning against me feels amazing, and I tug her tightly to me, my belly pressed to her back so I can feel her breath deepen.

"Tanya," she murmurs and drops her head backward against my shoulder.

I melt.

I completely melt into her. I'm seventeen again, and Jules is on top of me in the beanbag chair in the library of the Meadows. Her weight, her breath, her lips, her tongue. She corks the bottle of wine and spins in my arms to face me. Her eyes are so dark. So molten.

She melts.

When she strokes my cheek, I shudder until her thumb brushes my bottom lip, and I feel it in my entire being. "All this time, and I never once stopped," she whispers.

"Never stopped what?"

"I never stopped loving you, Breezy."

I lean my forehead against her shoulder. "Fuck you, Juliette Peralta, and fuck the Range Rover you drove in on."

I can feel her chuckles rumble in her chest as she laughs and runs her fingers under my chin, gently lifting my head to stare into my eyes. "And I will never stop."

She leans in slowly, and I freeze, anticipating her lips pressed to mine, but instead, she presses a chaste kiss to my cheek and leans away. But her kiss, it sinks through me. "Like a wishing well." The words spill from my lips on accident.

"Like a what?" she whispers.

Her lips are so soft-looking. I know what it would feel like to lean in and just—

The doorbell rings, and we jump away from each other as if caught by her parents. I press my hand to my chest, a nervous chuckle escaping. "Just in time."

She runs a shaky hand through her dark waves and exhales. "For what?"

I shove her gently in the shoulder. "Just get the pizza, Jules."

While we eat, we turn on *Friends* and revert to our teenage selves, laughing and reminiscing on all the dumb shit we did with a drink in our hands. But now, it's nice wine instead of cheap whiskey and even cheaper beer. It's comfortable. Jules laughs as she wipes the grease from her fingers with her napkin. Feels like she never left.

"Casual looks good on you," I can't help but say.

"Oh yeah?" She smiles, the tail of a fresh piece of sloppy

pizza dangling from her hand. She holds it higher on display. "This, uh, this does it for you, huh?" She opens her mouth wide and lifts the pizza, a piece of pineapple falling into her lap before she gets it in her mouth.

"You're a mess." I laugh and move her plate to the coffee table, grabbing her hand. "Come on. Let's treat this spot before it stains."

She follows me into the kitchen, her hand still warm in mine. I pull her in front of the sink and wet a paper towel with dish soap and warm water. "It should come out okay with just some gentle dabbing." I dab around the edges of the oil stain, then squirt a little more soap on my towel for the middle. "Don't want to rub it," I say, just to fill the silence. I can feel her eyes on me. On my hands as I work on the bottom of her shirt.

"Remember playing Truth or Dare at the Meadows that one night?"

How could I ever forget that night? "Mm-hmm." I keep my head down and stay focused on the oil stain. Stay focused on anything other than the coiling in my gut and the want gathering in my chest.

"Almost done?" she whispers.

I suppose I can't stay hunched over her shirt forever. "Um. Yeah." I give it one final dab. "It should be okay. Just try to get it in the laundry tonight if you can."

She grazes her fingers up my forearm, and it makes me shiver. "Breezy…"

It feels too good. I close my eyes and a take a step into her, shaking my head. "Jules, I can't. I just can't. You…you disappeared, and I can't lose you again."

"I know. It's scary. I'm scared, too." Her hands find my waist, and she gently pushes me against the sink, her hips falling against mine. I can't help but groan. It's been so long since anyone has touched me this way. And she's the only one who I want to touch me this way.

"Jules…"

"I dare you," she whispers in my ear. "I dare you to kiss me, Breezy."

Her breath is warm, and I know she'd taste like red wine and pizza. She grazes the shell of my ear with her lips as I grab fistfuls of her shirt. I need to do something with my hands before they go rogue and explore her skin. "I want to so badly."

I groan and drop my hands to her front pockets. Give them a tug. Something jagged pushes against the tip of my finger. "What do you have in there? Are you collecting arrowheads or something?" I chuckle, relieved for the small distraction from my desire to kiss her. "It'd be pretty cute if you were."

She smiles softly. "No. Not arrowheads." She fishes a hand in her pocket. "Something I've had for a very long time, though. I carry it with me always. Kind of like a worry stone, I guess."

It hits me just as she's uncurling her fingers to show me. "The shark tooth," I whisper. "You kept it."

She grins and fingers the tip of it. "Of course I kept it. It's only my most prized possession."

I tug her belt loops until her hips crash back into me, and she reaches for the counter behind me for balance. "You kept it," I repeat. I can feel the heat from her lips. Can feel her warm breath on my cheek. I skim my lips over hers until I feel her body shudder against mine, then I press them gently to hers.

"Fuck," she mutters. She kisses me back hard, as if she's been waiting years for this exact moment. The way I have. Her tongue is needy, and we clash teeth like eager teenagers, our heavy breathing and moans filling the air around us. I hear a clattering in the sink and pull away, a little out of breath.

"Where's the tooth?" I ask. She tugs at my dress, seemingly not ready to let go of our kiss. "Jules, focus. The tooth, do you have it?"

She peeks around me at the countertop and pats her pockets. "Oh my God." Gently nudging me out of the way, she scans the countertop and the floor in front of the sink. "It must have fallen down the sink." A look of terror flashes across her face. "My shark tooth. What do we do?"

Squeezing her arm, I can't help but grin. She's being ridiculous and adorable. Ridiculously adorable. "What do you think is at the bottom of a sink, Jules? A black hole?"

"Don't joke. Please." She worries her lip, eyes glued to the drain. "I don't think you know what it means to me. I even had it tucked in my bra on my wedding day. Fucking hurt."

"Your wedding day? Really?"

"Yeah." She shrugs. "It was a hard day. Needed you with me."

Her admission shatters my heart. How she sought comfort in me through all these years... "I'm sorry your wedding day wasn't blissful. I wanted that for you. Even though I was upset with you, I always wanted you to find your joy."

"Thank you. I always wanted you to find yours, too." She leans in and kisses me on the cheek. It feels familiar, almost normal, at this point. "So can you get it out?"

"You're a real estate mogul, and you don't even know how to empty a drain trap?" I sink to my knees in front of her. I don't mean for it to be sexy, but it feels kind of sexy. And given the look in Juliette's eyes, I'd bet the farm that she thinks it's sexy, too. I look up and smirk. "Can you stop staring and make yourself useful? I need a pot to catch any excess water and a dish towel for grip."

"I was not staring." She crosses her arms, but I wait her out until she groans. "Fine." She rummages in a cabinet for a pot and hands it to me with a dish towel.

The plastic trap is easy to unscrew, and I tip it into the pot. A bit of murky water splashes, followed by the unmistakable *ping* of something hard hitting the metal. I pluck it from the water and hold it up for her. "And that's how you save a million-year-old shark tooth from the black hole that is the kitchen sink."

She takes the tooth and deposits it safely in her pocket, then helps me off the ground. "You're my hero, Breezy."

I situate my dress and wash my hands. "I'm seriously concerned about your lack of basic house knowledge."

"Come back here," she says, pulling me into her.

I wrap my arms around her waist and allow myself to feel her. To really feel her hold me. Tonight was a huge step forward for us, but I need to be careful. Just a little careful. Some mistakes shouldn't be made twice. I squeeze her tight before I let her go. "Thank you for this evening. It meant a lot to me."

Her pout cuts right to my quick. "Leaving so soon?"

I nod, so full of regret, but I have to go slow. "I think it's best." I lift her hand to my lips and kiss it softly, savoring the taste of her skin. "But I'd love to see you again like this. If that's something you think you'd want…"

"Yes. Please."

I nod. "Okay, then. Walk me out?"

Jules follows me to the front door, and on a whim, I whirl around and peck her on the lips, hopefully leaving her wanting more of me. Because I certainly want more of her.

"Good night, Breezy."

After a few paces down her driveway, I turn and say, "Good night, Jules. Thank you for dinner."

"Thank you for saving my shark tooth." She looks so effortlessly cool and casual, leaning against the door frame, her figure bathed in the low light from the sconce lamp. "Walk safe."

When I get home, I slip into my pajamas and fall into bed, replaying our kiss over and over and over. I can feel her lips on my mouth. Her tongue running over my teeth. I imagine her kissing my neck, nipping at my skin, grabbing my ass.

I come to the thought of Juliette Peralta making love to me on her kitchen counter, under the sign that says, "If life gives you limes, make margaritas." And I sleep soundly.

CHAPTER THIRTEEN

For a family who lives at the beach, we don't have many beach days together. Maybe once a month, Aunt Pat, Uncle Trevor, and I will pack the coolers, beach chairs, volleyball net, and umbrellas and have a proper beach day. Of course, we invite the boys, and of course, they almost always say yes. They bring the beer and the Frisbee. And the cute kiddos with sandcastle supplies.

I situate the umbrella so it shades Aunt Pat and Uncle Trevor. She says she spends enough time in the sun and on the water, so when she goes to the beach, she wants to be pampered: a glass of icy white wine and shade. She likes to drink and doze while we play around her.

"Still think you got it, Breezy?" Oscar asks, producing his old skimboard from his beach trolley.

"Of course I still have it. I'm in my thirties, not dead." I top off Aunt Pat and strip down to my bathing suit.

He raises a brow. "All right. Prove it."

I grab the board and march to the ocean with the kids, Joey and Layla, on my heels. Benny and Austin haven't taught them how to skimboard yet. It will be another year or two before they graduate from sandcastles to water sports. But they watch eagerly as I begin to jog alongside the water. Though it's been a few years, it all rushes back to me. The tide hits my toes, and I throw the board, jumping on and riding it down the beach until the perfect little wave approaches, and I cut toward it.

Some things feel like freedom. And youth. Like nothing in the world is actually so important. Owning a business, fighting for Coral Bay to remain intact, reconnecting with a childhood love? *Kissing* the childhood love who broke my heart and wants to take over the town that I love? None of it feels so important when I launch through the sea air and flip, cradling my knees as if I'm fourteen again and made of nothing but sunshine and rubber.

It feels like freedom when I splash into the sea. Wiping my eyes, I feel the dull burn of the salt water mixed with the heat of the sun, a summer simmer. It ignites something deep in me, something buried and dormant, as if I've been asleep for so long, and the adrenaline of doing something so lighthearted and thrilling as skimboarding was all I needed to wake again.

And maybe kissing Jules.

I fish the board from the water's surface and march to the beach, Joey's cheers bringing me back to focus.

"That was amazing," Layla squeals, completely thrilled.

I stand the skimboard next to her and pretend to measure her, holding my hand flat against her head. "You're so close," I say. "Maybe next year, we can get you on here."

"Please, please, please?"

I smile and muss up her hair. "Definitely."

"Looking like a teenager out there, Breezy," Austin says as I reach for my towel. "Still got it."

Wiping my face in the warm dry fabric feels incredible. "Water's great, you know. Why don't you get out there and recapture your youth, too?"

"Maybe next year." He eyes his slight beer belly and gives it a loving rub. "I gotta do some yoga in preparation, or I may break something."

Benny chuckles and plants a kiss on his cheek. "Here, babe. Have another margarita and be old with me."

They laugh and sip their drinks, seeming so at ease and happy together. It's what I want, what I've been missing. If I'm honest with myself, maybe what I've been avoiding, using excuses like *I want to meet someone the old-fashioned way*, or *online dating just isn't for me*. Which is all well and good, but when you live in a town where the population is counted by the hundreds and you basically know every single person, saying no to online dating is saying no to dating, period.

Oscar pushes his sunglasses up his nose, his cheeks reddening from the booze and the sun. "Tanya, love. When are you going to marry me already?" He busts into laughter, and if I didn't know him better, I'd think he'd snuck something special into those cookies he's been munching. "What?" He laughs again. "We could have what these two have."

I roll my eyes and hold out my hand. "You kill me, babe. Now give me a cookie, please."

"Maybe if y'all had a lick of chemistry, you could have what these beautiful boys have," Aunt Pat heckles from her chair and sips her wine.

Uncle Trevor leans on his knees, laughing. "But you ain't got a lick," he shouts.

"Sorry, Mr. Mayor, but we ain't got a lick of chemistry," I say, smiling down at him.

He pops open his cooler and pulls out the big thermos of margaritas he mixed up for us. He scoffs as he pours me a drink, garnishing it with a fresh-cut lime. "Nope. No chemistry but a shit ton of love."

I take my drink, knocking it against his. "Here's to a shit ton of platonic love."

He gives me a wide grin and sips his drink. Oscar buzzed is adorable. He's always so put together and serious. It's good to see him relax and let it go. *Get loose, Oscar.*

"Is everyone sufficiently buzzed?" I ask, looking around at my family.

"Oh, oh, Aunt Pat," Benny says, sounding like a child himself. "Can we come over for boiled shrimp after the beach? Please?"

I roll my eyes. "I gather the answer to my question is yes," I mutter.

Aunt Pat peeks at him over the rim of her sunglasses. "Yes, Benny babe. But you boys bring a salad, and Oscar, you and Breezy make that garlic bread I love."

"Yes, ma'am," Oscar shouts.

"Y'all," I say, gathering the focus back to me. I don't know why I'm announcing this to everyone, but I feel so good and light. I want to share it. "I kissed Jules."

Benny and Austin smile quietly while Oscar, Aunt Pat, and Uncle Trevor lose their damn minds.

"Excuse me?" Uncle Trevor asks, sounding scandalized. "You kissed who now?"

"You heard the girl." Aunt Pat smacks his shoulder, sloshing his drink over his arm. "Breezy, what in the hell happened? I thought you hated her still. Certainly gave me enough crap for inviting her to the party, then you go kissing her? Fill us in."

Oscar's jaw hangs open as I begin to explain how we ended up on *Silverfish* alone and how she invited me over for dinner in the spirit of comradery. "It just felt like it did when we were kids." I close my eyes, briefly lost in the memory. "I don't know what it means, but it felt good. And I haven't felt that kind of good in so long."

"Since she left?" Oscar asks. I don't think he's trying to be mean, but the question is sharp. It hurts because it's true. Jules is the only person I've met who could pull me under, and I love the water. But Oscar is right...she drowned me.

I nod. "Yes. I almost forgot about that. Thanks, Oscar."

"Sorry." He grimaces and sloshes the ice in his drink. "I didn't mean for it to sting, and I obviously want you two to be friends and work together, but..." He drops his gaze to his margarita.

"But what?" I ask, a little frustrated. I'm finally getting over this thing with Jules—what Oscar has been begging me to do for months—and now he's acting like I'm doing something wrong.

He looks up and smiles softly at me. "Nothing. Just be careful, okay?"

"Yeah, okay." I kick sand at his feet, trying to lighten things up. "Now stop being a weirdo, and let's get this volleyball tournament started."

Oscar and Benny set up our net and draw a messy court in the sand with their heels while Austin and I finish our drinks. The makeshift court is a little wonky, but that's what makes it fun. Aunt Pat and Uncle Trevor are the line judges—*harsh* line judges—and Austin and I are teammates. We hardly ever win. Oscar and Benny are over-the-top competitive and extremely athletic, while Austin and I have heart and a lot of fun. But my athletic prowess is more suited for swimming and skimboarding.

We play for about an hour, then cool off in the ocean together, tossing the little orange squishy water ball that we've collectively had for almost five years now. It's a miracle we haven't lost or destroyed it.

That evening, I get home and shower, feeling at peace. Feeling happy. I walk down the familiar streets to Aunt Pat and Uncle Trevor's for family dinner. I pull my phone from my purse when I'm a block away and stop at the small playground on the corner. I sit in the swing and text Jules:

Family dinner with the boys at Aunt Pat's tonight. Would love for you to join if you're available.

She responds within the minute: *I'll walk over in ten. Bringing wine.*

CHAPTER FOURTEEN

We sit in the backyard, the sun setting over the palms and the strung lights glowing soft orange over our heads. We sip our drinks of choice: white wine for Aunt Pat, a nice mezcal on the rocks for Oscar, red wine for Uncle Trevor, and more margaritas for me and the boys. Buena Vista Social Club plays in the background, and we chat while we drink and snack on cheese and crackers, enjoying each other and the pleasant ache in our muscles from our day at the beach and the tiredness that comes from playing in the sun.

"Your mother is too kind to babysit on short notice," Aunt Pat says, pouring herself another glass.

Benny laughs, squeezing Austin's shoulder. "Well, she was desperate for grandkids, wasn't she, babe?"

"Yes." Austin nods, wiping margarita from his lips. "So desperate. I honestly don't think we ask my mom to babysit enough. If it was up to her, she'd be over every day watching them."

There's a soft knock on the patio door, and Juliette walks out to join us, a bottle of white wine in hand. "Hi, everyone," she says. She looks gorgeous and casual with her feet in a pair of strappy sandals, her hair in adorable messy waves, the same jeans as when we had dinner together, and a faded Wharton School of Business sweatshirt. It's pretty ironic.

"Jules, welcome," Aunt Pat says. "Pull up a chair. We missed you at the beach today."

"Oh? I could use a beach day. Let me know next time you all get out there." She walks up behind me and lays a hand on my shoulder. "Hi," she says just to me.

"Hey." I squeeze her wrist and give her a gentle tug, eager for her to be near. "Come sit next to me."

She settles in the chair, and all I can feel is her. Conversation continues, and I reply with various acknowledgments. Jules jumps in with some anecdotes about how construction is going at the Sands, but all I can focus on is her knee against mine under the table. It's as if my entire universe revolves around that one point of contact, her jeans against my skin.

I almost choke on my margarita when she lays her hand on my knee and leans close to my ear. "I like your dress," she whispers.

Her words slip over my body and warm my skin. I feel the beat of my heart quicken. I feel alive. I take another sip and reach under the table, looking at my family, nodding and smiling as I curl my fingers around hers and pull her hand into my lap. Then I gain the courage to look at her. She watches me, the flame from the tiki torch swimming in her eyes. She looks alive, too.

"I'm glad." I smile and break eye contact just for a second before I gain back my confidence. "I wore it for you, Jules."

Her eyes widen in surprise, then narrow in what I swear is want. It could be hopeful wishing, but when she bites the corner of her lip, it sends shivers down my body and straight to my core. She leans even closer, her lips so close, I can feel her breath on my ear. On my neck. "Lavender really is your color," she whispers and squeezes my hand.

She clears her throat and turns her attention to the rest of the table, leaving me to digest her words alone. I swallow, my tongue feeling thick and hot. My stomach is in knots as I unlace our fingers and cover her hand with mine. She slowly slips her hand down from my lap to my inner thigh, shooting me a questioning glance. I nod, giving her the consent she needs.

She softly strokes my thigh, and I try not to combust. A hot ache gathers low in my belly, and I shift in my chair, my panties uncomfortably damp.

She responds to some question Austin asks and slips her hand an inch higher. I grip the arm of my chair tighter, desperately trying to keep my cool. But how can I be cool when Juliette Peralta is inching her hand closer to my wet panties devastatingly slowly?

I clear my throat and place both hands on the table. Everyone stares, but I look at Jules. "Can you help me in the kitchen for a second?"

She lifts a brow and nods. "Sure."

"What are you doing in there?" Aunt Pat asks. "Everything is sorted and ready to go. The shrimp will take two minutes once we're ready to eat."

I stand and smooth my dress, feeling like everyone can see right through me. "I just need to…" I have no idea what I need to do. Not be standing, red as a tomato, I'm sure, in front of all my family, feeling drunk on desire for Jules.

"Breezy was going to help me open the wine." She stands and snags the bottle she brought from the table. Holds it up as evidence. "Can I get anyone anything while we're inside?"

"Bring out some more of that cheese Benny and Austin brought, please," Uncle Trevor says. He leans on the table and smiles. "It's very tasty, boys. Thank you."

"You got it." I grab Juliette's hand and tug her inside.

She places the bottle on the counter and reaches for the wine key. "That was some pretty quick thinking on my part, just saying—"

"Shut up." I push her against the counter and kiss her hard, my hands buried in her soft, messy waves. She groans into my mouth, teeth nipping at my lips, her warm tongue gliding over mine. I want to drink her in. I want her to consume me. Her hands are firm on my hips, and she pulls me against her, the heat building between us until Benny's bellowing laugh cuts through the moment and makes me jump away.

I wipe my lips with the back of my shaky hand as Jules stares at me with wide eyes and a grin playing on her lips. "The wine," I say.

"What?"

"The wine." I sigh in annoyance, hiding my shaky hands behind my back. "Open the wine, please. Like you said. I'll get the cheese."

I turn away from her, feeling far too vulnerable in my naked want. I can feel how obvious it is. My cheeks burn, my limbs wobble, my breathing is heavy. I open the fridge and let the cool air calm me. Ease all the fire in my nerves.

Jules walks behind me and grips my hips again. I do my best to not melt into her. She pulls my hair back off my shoulder and drags her teeth over my skin where shoulder meets neck. My hands fall to hers as I groan in uninhibited pleasure from the pressure of her sucking my neck. I push my ass into her and drop my head back. "Fuck," I whisper. "Jules."

She releases me in an instant, my neck cold where her lips used to be, my body unsteady without her holding me. "The wine," she says in my ear.

I watch her walk to the other side of the kitchen and slowly cut the foil from the neck of the bottle. "You're the literal worst," I say, my eyes glued to her hands, wishing they were on my body.

She winks, a sly grin on her lips. "You started it, kissing me like that."

"I started it?" I snag the cheese, closing the fridge door with my hip. "I recall you getting quite handsy with me under the table."

She pours herself a glass and gives it a swirl, then a taste. She moans softly in approval, then gives her attention back to me. "What? Are you saying you didn't like it? Because I can refrain from touching you in the future."

I walk straight past her to the door, expertly nudging it open with my hip. "Just don't start things you can't finish," I say over my shoulder and walk outside, leaving her alone in the kitchen.

"Did you kick her out already?" Uncle Trevor asks in a loud voice, obviously wanting Juliette to hear his joke.

She emerges from the kitchen, wine in hand. "Not quite yet." She laughs and sits next to me. "I'm feeling hopeful that I'll make it through dinner before Breezy kicks me out."

"Oh good. I have to admit, I'm growing quite fond of having you back, Juliette," he says.

She smiles and swirls her wine. "I have to admit, I'm growing quite fond of being back. I missed it here," she says, and I feel the sincerity in her voice. I find her hand under the table and pull it into my lap. She looks at me and smiles. "And I missed all of you. It feels good to be back." She looks at my aunt and uncle. "Thank you for being so welcoming. I don't deserve it."

Aunt Pat waves a dismissive hand. "Don't be silly, Juliette. Everyone deserves it."

"You may have lived in Atlanta, but we saw what Coral Bay meant to you. This is your home, too. And you are always welcome here with our family," Uncle Trevor says, looking around the big cedar table at all of us. The amount of love my aunt and uncle have is incredible, and we are so lucky to receive it.

Oscar stands, wiping his hands in his napkin. "Excuse me. I'm just going to use the bathroom real quick." He knocks the table as he moves his chair out of the way to get by. "Sorry," he murmurs.

"You okay?" I ask after him.

He nods. "Just gotta break the seal."

"Gross."

"You're gross," he says and disappears inside.

The evening continues in a comfortable coziness with long

conversation and more drinks. We swap stories and memories and laugh our asses off at all the silly things we did as kids. But more than all of the laughter, there's a heavy gratitude. All of the people I love—all of my family—are together loving each other. And Juliette's hand is in mine. It's a moment I couldn't possibly imagine being real. But I've spent my life protecting myself. From my mom, from change in my heart and my town, from Jules. And now I'm a little older and a little lonelier, and for the life of me, I don't see the benefit of playing it safe anymore. Not when Jules looks at me the way she looks at me tonight.

"I should get going," I whisper to Jules, squeezing her hand. "Do you want to walk home together?"

Her brows twitch upward, and she smiles. "Yes. Please."

We say our good-byes and wish everyone a good night, then walk out the front door together. Once we're out of view, Jules takes my hand. Somehow, it feels more intimate now that we're alone. Neither of us speaks, but the breeze and the breathing of the ocean fills the quiet for us.

Finally, I ask, "Did you enjoy your night?"

"Yes." She says it quick, automatic. She stops walking when we approach the playground on the corner. "Swing with me?"

The swings sway gently with the wind, creaking in that spooky way that swings do. I grew up swinging on this play-ground, skinning knees and climbing up the slide while Benny barreled down it and sent me to the hospital with a broken wrist. I don't have any memories of Jules here, though. Not until now.

I sit in a swing and dangle my feet as Jules walks behind me and pulls me back by the hips. "I don't need help," I say sarcastically.

"Shh," she says into my hair. She doesn't release me but holds me close against her chest as her mouth explores the shell of my ear, my neck. It makes me shiver.

"Jules, please…"

She kisses my neck, then pushes, and I swing away from her.

She sits in the other swing and pumps her legs. We're quiet as we get going, enjoying how the wind feels the faster we go. Higher and higher. I forgot how good it feels to swing. The swing set whines as we continue to rocket to the sky, then fall back down to earth. Over and over.

Until Jules launches off her swing and lands on the sandy ground in front of us. Well, almost lands. She stumbles a few feet before falling on her hands and knees.

"Oh my God. Are you okay?" I shout.

All I hear is laughter as she flips over onto her ass and watches me. "Yes," she calls back. "Yes. I'm okay." She shakes her head, still laughing. "Even if I'm clearly not as young as I used to be, that felt amazing. You're next."

I slow my swinging, hit lower and lower in the sky with each ascent. "I am not flying through the sky like that," I say, adamant about not hurting or embarrassing myself.

"Well, you're definitely not going to fly at that rate. You're hardly moving."

I scoff. "You have no idea who you're up against, Ms. Peralta." I pump harder and get my swing going higher.

She grins, her elbows on her knees. She looks seventeen again. "I think I know exactly who I'm up against."

I take a deep breath and fling myself off at the crest of the swing. My stomach sinks through the air, but it feels amazing to soar. No matter how brief. I thud in the sand next to Jules, stumble, then topple over just like she did, chuckles overcoming me.

"You okay?" she asks.

I can't respond because I'm laughing so hard. The adrenaline of flying through the air, falling in the sand next to Jules, feeling so damn young and free, and being completely alone on this playground during this quiet night...

"More," I say once I can manage to speak. "More than okay."

I lie back and look at the stars, and Jules does the same. I reach for her hand, and she must reach for mine because it's right there. We interlace our fingers and take it all in.

"The stars are always so bright here," she says.

Normally, I would go on a rant about how it's because Coral Bay hasn't been developed within an inch of its life like every other beach town, so there's less light pollution. Instead, I squeeze her hand. "They really are. They're beautiful."

"I don't want this place to change, you know. I never cared about real estate or development. I just wanted to live here with you and be a teacher."

I know she means well, but it hurts to hear that there was this entire other life that could have happened. It hurts to know how little she cared for the business but how much value she put in obtaining a position within it. Leaving me so painfully, marrying a random man she didn't love, keeping herself from the things that would make her happy.

"You live here for now," I say, rubbing her knuckles. "And maybe in a different life, that's what happened. You stayed and became a teacher. But in this life, you're here with me now, holding my hand. And it feels pretty damn good."

"It really does."

"Plus, you can always become a teacher."

She rolls onto her shoulder and stares at me. "Breezy?"

"Yes?"

"You're my favorite human. I knew it from the day we met that I wanted you in my life always. I'm so sorry I left like that. I wish I could change it."

I reach for her face, cup her cheek. She leans into my touch, and it completely melts me. Her eyes go soft and vulnerable, and she kisses my palm. "I know you do, Jules. It's okay. It doesn't matter anymore. I forgive you." I prop myself on an elbow to reach her lips and kiss her softly. Softly so she knows I have soft feelings for her. So she knows my words are true. I forgive her.

She breaks our kiss and stands, brushing sand from her thighs and arms, then helps me up.

"Are you okay?" I ask.

"Yes." She smiles and nods. "This night is so lovely. I just want to make sure I get in some monkey bars before it's over."

"Monkey bars, eh?" I grin and walk over to the yellow bars. "They're a lot harder to swing across as an adult, you know?"

She presses her hand to her chest in a dramatic display of shock. "You don't think I can handle monkey bars? I'm in okay shape."

I give her a once-over and shrug.

She gasps.

"I'm just kidding," I assure her. "You're clearly in amazing shape, but I still don't think you'll make it across without dropping."

She walks to the other side and climbs to the first bar, ready to swing. "If I make it, you have to kiss me. With tongue."

I laugh at her silliness. "Jules…"

"Yes?"

"I've been kissing you with tongue."

She grins. "Second base, then."

I roll my eyes. "Oh my God. Are we actually fourteen right now?" She just stares with that grin plastered to her lips. "Fine. Over or under the bra?" I can't help but giggle. She brings out my silly and my calm.

"We'll start with over. Don't want to get too carried away, now."

"Okay. Over."

Jules nods and swings to the first bar, then the second. The third. I'm already impressed with the three, but she continues, bar by bar, until she gets close to where I'm standing by the end. She groans, and I expect her to drop right in front of me, but she powers through, and I have to step out of the way as she swings by to the end. The small of her back is exposed from her shirt riding up. I want to touch her there.

She lets go and falls on both feet. "Made it." She turns to me and grins.

I'm like a magnet to her, my feet on their way to her before I even realize I'm moving. "I suppose you win, then."

She spreads her arms for me and says, "I suppose I do."

I wrap my arms around her waist and hug her tight, spinning us so my back is against the stack of yellow bars. I take her hand and tuck it under the hem of my dress. "Your prize," I whisper.

Her hand is soft against the outside of my thigh. It doesn't move. She doesn't push up my dress or go straight for my chest. She leans into my ear. "You feel so amazing. Where are my boundaries, love?"

"For you, there are none." I push her hand up my thigh, over my belly. She cups my breast through my bra. I gasp and push my hips into her. "Under."

"What?" Her question is breathy and deep.

"Fuck." I pull down the cup of my bra so my breast falls into her hand. "Under. Please. I need to feel your skin on mine."

"Oh my God, Breezy." She kneads my breast, my nipple hardening under her thumb. It feels exquisite, and I am already so wet for her. "You feel so fucking good."

I pant against her neck as she feels me up, her hands more demanding now, squeezing and stroking. "I need you, babe," I say into her ear.

"You need me to…"

"I need you. Need your fingers inside me. Please, Jules."

She kisses me hard, her tongue bruising mine, our gasps tangling together in our throats. She spins me away from her, and I grab the bar in front me, slightly bent over. I know it's dark out, and no one could see us behind the cover of all these palms. Wouldn't care if they could.

She pushes my sundress up and pulls my panties down. I wonder if she can feel how wet they are. How just touching my breast made me ruin them for her. She grips the back of my shoulder with one hand and explores me with the other, running her finger through me. Over my wet pussy. She groans. "You need me, don't you?"

I grip the bar tighter and cry when she runs her thumb over my clit. I'm so turned on that things are hazy. "Yes. I need you inside me. Right now."

Her mouth is on my neck as she pushes into me, and I can't help but drop my head back and moan into the rushing breeze. I meet her every thrust, greedy for her, as she tries to slow me down by gripping my shoulder and setting the pace.

But how can I possibly go slow when Juliette Peralta is fucking me in my nice purple sundress against the monkey bars outside my aunt's house? My body begins to hum in unison, and I feel my orgasm building. It reaches from my clit and extends to every tip of my body. The buzzing. She strokes me right each time. A finger rubbing over my clit each time.

"I'm going to come," I say against the crook of my arm. I don't know why I warn her. She can surely feel it. Feel me tightening around her slippery fingers.

"I know," she says like she can't quite catch her breath. "Come then, love. Come for me."

Her words make me lose control. All the buzzing in my body implodes in a burst of energy. I shudder in her arms, shivering with aftershocks.

"I've got you," she whispers against my neck. She eases her fingers out of me, and I feel so empty without her. "Wow."

I turn in her arms and bury my face in her chest. "Holy shit." My words are raspy against the cotton of her sweatshirt.

She tightens me against her, and it feels for the first time in a very long time like she's my home. It feels like she would protect me from the storm. Start a fire to keep me warm. It feels as if being in her arms is the safest place in the world. I know she hurt me in the past, but she was seventeen and scared. She grew into the woman holding me now. The woman who kept my shark tooth for a worry stone.

"Come on." I peel myself from the warmth of her embrace, fix my clothing, and lead her down the sidewalk, a little unsteady on my feet. "Walk me home."

We walk hand in hand in a comfortable quiet, me occasionally catching her staring with a goofy smile until we arrive at my front door. She hangs back, probably not wanting to assume an invitation. I slide my key in the lock and look back at her. "Stay if you want. We can have a nightcap."

"Are you sure? I don't want to intrude on your night." She looks adorable with her hands tucked in her pockets, bouncing on the balls of her feet.

"I'm sure." I open the door and nod for her to come in.

I follow in the wake of her, wanting to be submerged in her again. In that cool fresh scent and the warmth of her skin. Being with her always felt like sinking in the best way. I don't care about a nightcap. I don't care about talking. I just want to be in her arms again.

"So," I say, looking through the bottles on my bar cart. "What are you feeling? Wine? A nip of whiskey?"

I hear her walk up behind me. And when she speaks, her breath tickles my neck. "Um, I don't really—"

Abandoning the drink options altogether, I face her. "I don't want a drink," I declare.

Her eyes are heavy, and there's the slightest arch in her brow. "No?"

I shake my head, trying not to bite my lip. Trying not to be so completely obvious in my want of her. But have I ever not been obvious?

She reaches for my hand and strokes my knuckles. "Maybe we could just go to bed?"

"Yeah." I nod, staring at her hands on mine. "Yeah, that sounds like a good idea to me."

I lead her down the small hallway and into my bedroom. She takes a moment to look around, fingering the glass rim of a candle and reading the framed news clipping about the Inn. "It's different now," she says softly. "Everything is different." She sits on the edge of my bed, the same sadness from earlier seeming to weigh her down.

I go to her and take her face in my hands. "Of course everything is different. It's been over a decade. We grew up, I bought a house, and my bedroom isn't over Aunt Pat's garage anymore." She sighs, but I tilt her chin upward so she's looking at me. "But it's not a bad thing. We don't need to hide in my truck for privacy or hope that my aunt doesn't barge in on us."

She grins, and it makes me happy to see the sadness melt away from her. "We didn't seem to care much about privacy earlier."

I step back, maintaining her eye contact, and reach behind my back, undoing the zipper of my dress like an expert. "Well, we were fully clothed then..." I let my dress fall to my feet and puddle around my ankles. I feel no shame standing in front of Juliette in my bra and panties. The woman just fucked me against the monkey bars.

Her mouth falls open as she stares, her eyes flitting over my exposed skin. I curl my fingers under the hem of her sweatshirt and peel it over her head. She lifts her arms to help me, and I drop it next to my dress. I run my fingers over her shoulders and down her ribs. "Jules...you're so beautiful, it hurts," I whisper. "Can I take off your bra?"

She grips my hips and pulls me closer. "Please."

I reach around her back and flick open the clasp. The fabric loosens, and I slide it down her arms, adding it to the pile of discarded clothes. "Fuck," I mutter, closing my hands over her perfect breasts, so full and soft. Her nipples harden against my palms, and I can feel myself grow wet for her again. So ready again.

She moans and leans back on her elbows, clearly indulging in my touch and having her breasts rubbed. I lose my own bra and climb over her, straddling her thighs. I let my breasts drag over her stomach and barely skim over her nipples. She lets out a sharp inhale and squeezes my ass. "Fuck, Breezy. Please."

"Please what?" I pepper her chest with kisses before I lean down and tug one of her nipples into my mouth. I suck gently at first. She buries her hand in my hair and pulls my mouth tighter against her, so I suck harder until it sets her hips in motion underneath me, spurring me on. I groan against her nipple when her hips hit a particularly sensitive spot between my thighs.

"I need you," I say and slide from her lap to my knees on the floor. She stares down the length of her body at me, completely entranced as I work on the buckle of her jeans. When I get them unbuttoned and unzipped, I pull them down her thighs to her ankles, and she pulls them off the rest of the way, never breaking eye contact. Her underwear is visibly wet as I spread her thighs. "My poor girl," I whisper, leaning close enough to skim my lips over the saturated fabric. I lick the cotton the entire length of her pussy.

"Oh my God." She bucks and squirms, her hand draped over her eyes. "Tanya, please."

I slide her panties down her smooth legs and drink in the sight of her, wet and ready for me. I kiss up her thighs and indulge in every inch. And though I've tasted her once, nothing prepares me for her warmth and her wetness on my tongue. Nothing prepares me for how she moves her hips against me, sliding over my mouth, finding her pleasure. Nothing prepares me for how it feels to make love to Juliette, even when I've made love to her once before. It's all different now.

I drown in her deep end. And as always, nothing else matters when I plunge into her waters. There's no noise from the outside world, just me under her gentle pressure. We make love all night, until we begin to drift to sleep in each other's arms, completely satiated.

"Don't go. Please," I hear myself say. But it sounds muffled and far away. It could have been a dream, but she squeezes me and kisses the top of my head.

"I'm not going anywhere."

❖

I wake to the sound of my front door closing. Or opening. I don't even need to open my eyes to know she's gone. I feel the empty sheets next to me and sigh. Rub my eyelids until they can hold their own weight. It doesn't surprise me that she slipped away after making love to me all night. It has happened before, after all. But damn, it makes my chest ache.

I pull the covers over my head and cocoon myself. Leaving is the standard thing to do when sleeping over for the first time. Get on with the day. Avoid the awkward light where everything we did together in the night comes rushing back in startling clarity. Of course she left. I don't blame her, but waking up alone after giving myself to her over and over is triggering. I feel completely abandoned.

I groan into my pillow, then force myself to get out of bed. I will not wallow. This was expected. *This was expected.* It's the kind of groggy morning that requires a cup of coffee for the shower, a shower coffee. I pull on my favorite hoodie and grab a pair of clean boxers from my dresser, then head to the kitchen to put on a pot.

"Good morning, sleepyhead."

I jump, shocked to see Jules sitting at my counter with two cups from the Dolphin Drip and two pastry bags. "I thought you'd gone home."

"You asked me not to, and I didn't want to." She stands to give me a hug, nuzzling my neck and kissing me under my ear. "I didn't want to wake you up, but maybe I should have let you know I was grabbing the goods. I just woke up so early."

I give her a quick peck on the cheek. "It's okay. Thank you." I reach for the cup closest to me. "I'm dying for a cup of coffee."

"I got you banana bread, too." She holds up the brown bag and gives it a gentle shake. "I hope you still like it."

"Like it?" I snag the bag and peek inside. "You know I love it."

She smiles. "I do."

We eat our goodies and sip our coffee as I slowly become

more human again. The disappointment of thinking she'd bailed still simmers in my stomach, but she's right here next to me. I take another sip and let the dark-roasted goodness anchor me back in reality. And my reality is that it feels cozy and easy with her. As if this could be the kind of morning we share every day. It's a thought that scares me. The fact that I let all of my walls crumble for her and now I'm dreaming of waking up next to her and sharing morning coffee? Terrifying. But it's a little late to go back now.

She throws her empty bag in the garbage and drapes her arms over my shoulders, kissing my cheek. "I wish I could stay, but I have to head to the Sands and meet with my project manager." She sighs. "Thrilling stuff."

"Okay." I'm hit with disappointment, but she's right. I need to go to work, too. I spin on my stool and pop a kiss on her lips. "I should get going, too." I rub up and down her arms, struggling to let go. "Thank you for last night. It was—"

"Amazing," she supplies. "Everything I've been dreaming of. You and me."

"Yeah. Exactly."

She smiles and kisses the top of my head. "I'll text you. Maybe we can link up tomorrow?"

"Link up?" I raise my brow and smirk. "You really are such a businesswoman."

"Oh my gosh." She rolls her eyes and gives me a light shove. "I will not stand for this abuse. I am leaving."

"Text me," I call after her.

CHAPTER FIFTEEN

The construction of the Sands's segment of the boardwalk was admittedly quick and relatively painless. Leaning on the bar, I have the perfect view of their guests hopping off the trolley and dragging their beach gear down the wooden path, quietly and without disturbing the patrons of my restaurant. One of them points to our bar and says something to their friend. I finish signing off on the subpar repair work we just received from the dishwasher tech and sigh. Maybe the Sands patrons using our boardwalk will bring extra business on top of the fee we make from the deal.

I hand the tech his paperwork and send him on his way.

"Did he fix it?" Wren asks.

I shrug. "For now."

She gives me a look of disappointment. It truly is a pain in the ass to have a less than perfectly functional dishwasher when our bartender is already busy and in the weeds and needs clean glassware without having to run the damn thing three times. "Next time it breaks, I'm buying a new one. I promise."

She nods. "Thank you. It will make a huge difference."

It feels good knowing the business can easily afford a new dishwasher. We could afford it before, but with the extra chunk of money we make from the Sands each week, it's well within our monetary comfort range.

"I think I'm going to call it a day," I say. I mentally go through my checklist of to-dos and nod. Everything is taken care of and on track. The construction is actually ahead of schedule and should be finished within the month. The fact that the Coral Bay Inn will be complete so soon makes it easier to accept that the Sands is getting help from the mayor's office and our tax dollars. But again, it doesn't seem like such a negative for our business anymore.

"Time for a Modelo?"

I sink onto a stool at the end of the bar and nod. "Please." I unclip my name tag from my shirt and tuck it in my purse.

She pours me a cold one, and I take a sip. It always hits the same, cold and crisp and perfect. I look over my shoulder and take in Crabby's. It's casual but nice. The kind of place where someone can enjoy a lovely meal and quality cocktail but still have their toes in the sand if they want. The new decor fits that vibe perfectly.

It's moments like these when I miss Marge the most. When I wonder if she'd be proud seeing the changes I've made. Each unit has been upgraded, and with the new additions, I'll have earned back our entire renovation budget within two years. And that's not even including what we get from the Sands.

I make one more mental note to thank Oscar. For the personal and the professional. For Juliette in my bed and for the Sands's money in my pocket.

My phone buzzes in my jeans, and I pull it out. It's Jules asking if I want to come by after work and do a walkthrough of the Sands. *It's not so terrible. I think you may even like it just a little.*

I chuckle and type, *While I highly doubt that, I do like* you. *So yeah, I can pop over. What time?*

I'm just finishing up here, so any time will do. Just let me know when you're on your way.

I wipe the bit of foam from my lips. *I'll be over in a half hour.*

❖

The Sands is…impressive. Even in the midst of all its construction and repairs, it stands out in its beauty. There really is no denying that. The completed sections of the building are freshly painted and look brand-new under the glimmering sun. They basically are brand-new.

"You made it," Jules says through a smile. "Come on." She pulls my arm and leads me to the door. "Let me show you around."

I have never been inside the Sands on a point of principle. How could I set foot in a place so ostentatious in its differences from the town it was built in? But maybe that's the point. The foyer is vast and airy, giving the sense that I could step right onto the beach out the back. But we all know people have to get on the trolley and pay the Inn for beach access. Regardless, it's impressive with its tall ceilings and crisp white paint, the building iteration of a clean linen shirt.

To the left is reception. A long silvery marble desk runs about fifteen feet down the white tiled floor. It almost glows, beckoning guests to check in. I walk over, drawn by it all. "Welcome to the Sands, where you can let it all go," a handsome young guy says.

"Hi. Thanks." I lean on the desk, then lean away, afraid to scuff it.

He smiles, and it's ridiculously perfect. White straight teeth under full lips. I briefly wonder if this is a robot instead of a human receptionist. "Are you checking in with us today?"

I hear steps behind me, and Jules gently grips my elbow. "She's with me, Brent. Thanks."

He straightens, not that he was slouching before. "Ms. Peralta. Of course. Let me know if you need anything at all, Ms.…." He looks at me, but I apparently cannot speak.

"Brees," Jules supplies. "It's Ms. Brees."

He smiles that smile and nods. "Can I offer you a

complimentary mai tai, Ms. Brees? We whip up a fresh batch every morning, and they are to die for."

"Yes. Please," I manage.

"My pleasure." He turns away from us and scoops ice into a clear plastic cup, then fills it from the dispenser full of the greenish brown cocktail, somehow made beautiful with the fresh lime wheels floating in it. "Ms. Peralta, may I interest you?"

She smiles politely and tugs on the hem of her suit jacket as if I've put her in an impossible position of choosing professionalism or politeness. "I can't very well let my associate drink alone. Yes please, Brent."

He pours another and hands us each a drink. "Enjoy, and please don't hesitate to ask if you need anything. Again, my name is Brent, and it was lovely to meet you, Ms. Brees."

"Thank you, Brent." I lift my drink in gratitude and take a sip. "Holy shit, that's delicious," I whisper so only Jules can hear.

She laughs as we walk away from the reception desk. "It's the hook, you know?"

"The hook?" I take another sip. It's sweet and sour and perfect. I follow her down a hall with room doors on either side.

"Yeah. The first experience of a guest's stay is monumentally important. It sets the tone." She taps a card to the reader, and the door unlocks. "Walking into a place you probably spent too much money on puts you on your toes, looking for things to complain about. But if you're handed a delicious tropical drink as you're checking in to your room, you automatically think it's worth it." She shrugs and sips her cocktail. "It really is a low-cost way to make every guest feel like the VIP they dream of being. Puts everyone in a good mood." She sips again and groans. "The secret is fresh-squeezed limes. You can get away with cheap booze, but you can't get away with store-bought lime juice."

"Wow." I walk slowly around the guest room. It's not a standard boring hotel room. Every detail has clearly been chosen with care. It surprises me that the Sands feels so personal.

"What?" Jules follows my steps, and I can feel her eyes on me. "Good wow? Bad wow? The room or the cocktail?"

I turn on her, and she freezes, clearly eager for my opinion on everything. On the job she's done. "If you tell anyone what I'm about to say, no one will believe you, and I'll deny it until my dying breath." She places her drink on the nightstand, eyes wide. "Jules, please use a coaster." I slip the ceramic coaster under her drink.

"Okay. Lay it on me," she says, almost wincing.

"This is a standard guest room?"

She nods. "This is the show room. The sample room, if you will. We use it for promotional material, photo shoots, an example for our builders of what everything should look like." She spins in a slow circle, nodding. "This is the only complete wing so far. But it's still nice. Guests have access to the bar, the restaurant, the pool, the spa. And the construction is mostly out of the way, though we are running discounted pricing right now."

"It's beautiful, Jules." I drop my gaze to my drink, stuck in thought. Maybe I was entirely wrong about not only Jules but the Sands. What if there's some beauty to expansion?

"It's no Coral Bay Inn." She touches my hand. "And I'm not necessarily saying it belongs here." She sighs and rubs my wrist with her thumb. "I don't know what I'm saying, really."

"It's okay. I'm over it." I cover her hand with mine. "Things change. Places grow. And Oscar is right, Coral Bay needs more industry. There's plenty of space and tourists for the Sands and the Inn."

"Hey," she says as she takes the drink from my hand and places it on a coaster next to hers. She pulls me into her, kissing my neck.

I melt into her, tilting my head so she has access to more skin. "Hmm?"

"Given how the Meadows was set up and the layout of the Sands, I think we're pretty close to where the library would have been," she whispers.

I pull away enough to orient myself. She's not wrong. "So we could be standing where we had our first kiss?"

She nods, trapping a grin between her teeth.

"Come here," I say.

She looks too good in her black business suit and black heels and almost black hair. Gorgeous as ever. She grins, and her lips are on mine in an instant. It almost feels as if we're in that reading nook on the beanbag, her weight on me and her tongue warm in my mouth.

She pushes me against the small writing desk and groans, her hands moving up my thighs. "The one day you aren't in a dress," she says between kisses.

I chuckle and nip her ear. "You really give up easy, Ms. Peralta."

In an instant, she has me on top of the desk and is working on my jeans. "I'm no quitter, Breezy." She unbuckles them and bites my neck until I cry out.

"Fuck, Jules."

"I know, babe. We're gonna—"

The electronic lock on the door clicks, and Jules flies to it, latching the swing lock before the person can open it. I hop off the desk, fasten my jeans, and grab my cocktail, trying to act normal. I walk around the room as if I'm taking in every detail, but I know my face is on fire.

The door clunks against the swing lock. "Hello?" a woman calls through the small space.

Jules looks back at me to make sure I'm decent, then unlatches it. "Sorry about that." She laughs, and I notice her face is red, too. "I keep accidentally latching it out of habit. Come on in. I'm just giving a colleague a tour of our facilities."

The woman looks past her to me, and I wave. "Hey, there," I say.

"Oh, I'm sorry," she says. "I didn't mean to disturb you, Ms. Peralta. I was just making sure everything was in place for that commercial we're shooting in the morning."

She waves and grabs her mai tai. "Of course, yes. We're just finishing up here anyway." She turns to me. "Shall we go over what we discussed in my office?"

I nod a little too vigorously. "Yeah. Yes. Sounds good."

She winks and visibly holds back a laugh. We excuse ourselves and call for an elevator, which stops at the top floor—the seventh floor—and she leads me to her office. Of course, the office is beautiful with expansive views. The ocean glimmers out of west-facing windows.

"Ah, so there is an ocean view," I say.

She locks the door behind us and meets me by the window, her arms lacing around me. "Mm-hmm. I think it's the only building in town over two stories, so...yeah. Ocean view from up here."

The repairs on the Sands are ahead of schedule thanks to Oscar, and Jules doesn't live here. The headquarters for Peralta Inc. will always be in Atlanta. When she finishes overseeing this project, she'll be expected to leave. Again. And she hasn't hinted at wanting to stay at all.

But some things you can't hide. When she gets home to her kitschy beach house and parks the Range Rover, she sheds all of this and turns into the Jules I grew up with. The Jules whom I adore. She wears cozy sweaters and tees and wants to be a teacher. And she may even love me. She seems to love Coral Bay.

And I have always loved her. I wrap my arms over hers and hold her tight.

"Sorry for the interruption down there. I forgot that a lot of people have a key to that room."

I lean into her. "Do a lot of people have a key to your office?"

"Not a single person," she mutters against my skin. Her hot breath turns me on. Again.

"Mmm. That's good to know." I plant a hand on the window. It's reinforced by steel crossbeams and is no doubt rated for class five hurricanes; it can hold my body weight. "And can anyone see in these windows?"

"Not a single person," she repeats. "They're mirrored from the outside."

I drop my hands to the button on my jeans and undo it. "Interesting."

She pushes them over my hips and groans. "So interesting."

Giving myself to Jules is as natural as swimming in the ocean. Thrilling, but at the same time, it feels like home. Like Jules was always Coral Bay, and she was always mine. No matter who her boyfriend of the month was and no matter what guy she married. She made the wrong decision when she was seventeen, and that's okay. I only wonder—as she makes love to me against her office window—what decision she'll make this time.

I bite my forearm to keep from crying out as Jules hits a particularly delicious rhythm.

I come hard. I always do with her. She holds me as I catch my breath, my legs feeling like they may fail me at any moment. Once I've gathered myself, I turn and walk her back to her big, gorgeous desk. The idea of making a mess of her all over her fancy desk with her fancy papers and her fancy pens drives me wild. She lets out an *oof* as I back her into it, and she lifts herself onto the edge, trying to scoot things out of the way before they get trampled. A long, thick roll of paper falls off the edge of the desk and captures my attention.

"What's that?"

She waves it off and pulls my mouth to hers. "It's nothing," she mumbles between kisses, and I'm drawn back into her. Always.

CHAPTER SIXTEEN

Hanging with the boys never gets old. We were born in the same year, in the same town, and have known each other our entire lives. Sometimes it feels as if they're truly my own flesh and blood, and we are just different iterations of one being. Sure, I may be getting a bit carried away, but as I look at all of them smiling over their various drinks as Benny lines up his putt in minigolf, I'm overwhelmed with gratitude.

There's no amount of good I could have accomplished in a past life to earn this kind of family.

"Here you go," Jules says as she hands me a fresh beer.

I peck her cheek, careful to be discreet. "Thanks."

I know everyone knows. Benny and Austin helped me get ready for our "date," but something is keeping me from being open about Jules and me *reconnecting*. Especially when it comes to Oscar. It was a shock that he wanted me and Jules to hash it out so badly when she arrived because he was madder at her for hurting me than anyone. The guy was livid. I can't help but think he'll judge me for letting her back in. I don't think he meant for us to fall into bed together when he said he wanted us to be friends and work well.

Alas, here we are, trying not to kiss or hold hands during this super intense game of minigolf. Given we're all so close, competitions can be a bit...ruthless. Except for Austin. He truly could not care less about winning. That boy just wants a tasty drink and good company.

"Don't choke," Oscar shouts just as Benny takes his shot.

The purple ball ricochets off two bumpers before being violently rejected by the long alligator tongue that swings in front of the tunnel leading to the hole.

He turns on Oscar, face reddening. "Are you serious right now?"

"What?" Oscar holds up his hands. "Looks like you took a bad shot, brother. No one to blame but yourself."

Benny struts to me and Jules. "Breezy. We clearly outlawed any distractions as we take our shots in the summer of 2007. Back me up here." His seriousness makes me chuckle. I can't help it. "Breezy," he scolds. He drops his club in exasperation. "This is pure anarchy, and I will not tolerate it."

"Okay, okay," I announce. "Benny is correct. We outlawed distractions at the time of the shot. Therefore, it's a mulligan, and Benny gets to reshoot without an extra stroke being added to his score."

"Agreed," Austin says.

Oscar sips his beer and nods. "Agreed. But you're still being a baby. And you're still going to miss the shot."

Benny grabs his ball and places it on the rubber mat, lining up again. Everyone is quiet, and I half expect Oscar to shout again just to wind Benny up, but he stays silent. The ball traces its last path almost perfectly, ricocheting twice and getting rejected by the alligator tongue.

I don't dare laugh. I can feel Jules holding hers in next to me until just a little chortle slips out, and it's as if it sets fire to everyone else's laughter. Everyone except for Benny is hands-on-knees dying of gut-splitting laughter. Benny nods along, completely unentertained. "Okay, okay," he says. "It's all extremely hilarious, isn't it?" He rolls his eyes and plops on the bench next to the hole. "I'd like to see one of you jerks hit that shot."

"Okay," I say and hand Jules my beer. I pluck my pink ball from my pocket and set it on the rubber. The thing about minigolf and holes with alligator tongues is that you can't take it seriously.

I hit the ball without trying to time. It ricochets once, twice, then flies by the alligator's tongue and rockets down the tunnel, which spits it out perfectly in line for a—

"Hole in one," I say as the ball clunks into the plastic hole.

Benny's jaw drops, and Austin completely loses it, clapping and shouting and rubbing it in for his husband any way he can. Jules kisses me out of nowhere, her lips on mine quick and warm and tasting faintly of beer. It's a chaste peck, but it shocks me.

"Oh, come on," Oscar says. But he doesn't say it jokingly; there's a darkness, a disgust to his tone. "Are you fucking kidding me?" He throws his beer in the garbage and takes an aggressive step toward Jules.

I press a hand to his chest. "Oscar. Calm down. What's going on?"

His eyes narrow at her, and he grits his teeth. I'm not sure I have ever seen him this way. Sure, he carries an intensity that Benny and Austin don't, but this ire is new. He ignores me. "I wanted you to come here and repair the Sands. I wanted you to break ground on the Waters. I wanted you to be friendly with her and break the news gently. But you're fucking her, aren't you?"

"Oscar," Jules pleads. She clutches her chest. "I haven't told her because—"

"Because you wanted to sleep with her and run away again to make your parents money? Make Mommy and Daddy proud? Run home to your trophy husband, Jules. You don't belong here."

"Excuse me," I cut in. "What the hell is going on? And what is the Waters?" As I say it out loud, it hits me like a ten-foot wave. The beach trolley, the boardwalk, the *Waters*. It was never about sharing beach access with the Sands. It was about connecting the Sands with its future sister resort…the Waters. I step back, feeling like I may vomit. "Where is it being built?" I ask, but I already know.

Jules looks at me, desperation in her eyes. "Breezy, listen—"

I shake my head and close my eyes, not wanting to see her face when she says it. "Where?"

"On the east side of the Inn," she whispers.

I nod, swallowing down bile. Everything I feared would happen to Coral Bay is happening. And Jules, the woman whom I love—*loved*—is the one to destroy it. "Why do you need the boardwalk now?"

She grimaces. "Can we go somewhere and—"

"Tell me."

She nods. "The Waters will be like the Sands. Except the shops and restaurants will be separate from the rental units. We're building the shopping portion first and want the guests of the Sands to have access to it. We needed you to sign the contract before you knew about it because we knew you'd say no otherwise."

The bile creeps slowly up my throat. "Why right next to the Inn? There is plenty of beachfront property in this town. Why destroy our privacy and our view and turn my resort into an unrentable construction zone for years?" I bite my lip to keep my tears of frustration at bay. "How? How could you do this to me? Use me like this?"

She swallows hard. "We chose to build next to the Inn because we want to create a hub of entertainment for visitors, not just standalone attractions that they have to drive to and from. If the Sands and the Waters and the Inn and Crabby's are all connected, now we have a destination. A place to keep tourists spending their money with us longer. The Coral Bay Inn and Crabby's are beloved establishments. We wanted to capitalize on that."

Her gaze falls to her sandals before she looks at me again. "This was going to happen, Breezy, no matter what. It wasn't my idea. It wasn't my decision, and it was going to happen with or without me. This is what I came here to do. But how I feel about you...*this*"—she points between us—"this was not part of the plan. You and me—"

"Are over," I supply. "We're over, Juliette." I turn on Oscar. "I expected this from her. To be lied to and used and hurt. But I never expected you to betray me, to hurt me this way. To betray the Inn and Marge and this town." I shake my head, incredulous. "I can't even look at you."

His jaw is so tight, I expect him to shatter teeth, but I don't care. I am so done with him and Juliette. I turn to leave, but something nags me. I turn back. Jules looks up, hopeful. "Are you and Oscar seeing each other?"

Her eyes widen as if she's taken off guard. "No." She takes a step toward me. "Tanya, no. Oscar and I have never done anything except that night at the Palmetto Hill pool. And that was the worst decision. I only want you."

"Jesus," Oscar mutters. "And I thought this would be professional."

"The worst decision you've made? Really?" I scoff. "And fuck all the way off, Oscar. I'm sorry no one is ever professional enough or serious enough for you. Well, at least we're not as much of a lying prick as you, either." I shake my head, appalled by both of them. "I'm leaving, and I'm hiring a fancy-ass lawyer. There's no way that contract I signed has legal standing now."

I walk away, hearing Benny and Austin scramble after me. "Breezy," Benny calls.

I make it to my truck and turn. "Did you know?" I ask.

"No," Benny says.

Austin wraps his big arms around me and pulls me tight. "Of course we didn't know."

I collapse into him, tears welling, but I can't cry. Not here. I pull away and sniffle, wiping under my eyes just in case. "Can we go, please? I have to get out of here."

CHAPTER SEVENTEEN

I can't believe it," Aunt Pat says.

Benny, Austin, Aunt Pat, Uncle Trevor, and I gather around Aunt Pat's kitchen table, heads bowed and fingers twiddling. There's an anxiety brewing between us. It feels as if we just got news of a class five hurricane headed straight for us. Honestly, at this point, wipe it all out. The darker side of me would rather see Coral Bay destroyed than turned into the next Panama City Beach. An exaggeration, sure. But this just feels too big, too overwhelming.

"Really?" I ask. "You can't believe a Peralta is driven by money and greed?"

"No, smartass. That part I can wrap my head around just fine," Aunt Pat says. "The thing I just don't understand is Oscar. What is that boy up to?" She shakes her head, her lip trapped between her teeth as if she's working on a tricky puzzle. "What is in it for him? He loves this town as much as anyone."

"If not more," Benny says.

"Maybe he's getting a cut," Uncle Trevor suggests. He raises a hand before Austin can jump in and disagree. "I know, I know, it doesn't sound like Oscar. But in my seventy years of living, I've seen many a man and woman bend a knee to money and power. A lot of those people were just as shocking as it would be for Oscar to accept a bribe or a payout."

Austin shakes his head. "No, it just doesn't add up. Even when we were kids, he was the fiercest defender of Coral Bay, right alongside Breezy. There was nothing he wouldn't do for this town."

"And he hated Jules for being a tourist," Benny adds. "He could never truly get past that with her. He hated her parents and never trusted her."

"I should have never trusted her." I groan. "I thought I knew her better than everyone else. I thought I knew her on this deeper level. This inner version of herself that just wanted to settle down and be a teacher and live a simple life." I shake my head, willing away the tears again. "For a minute there, I really thought she loved me." A tear escapes, and I wipe it with the back of my hand. "Foolish. All she will ever do is take what she wants and leave."

Austin wraps an arm over my shoulders and gives me a quick squeeze. "So what's the plan?" he asks. "It doesn't matter why Oscar is working with Juliette. We need to do something."

"I think we hire a lawyer to look at the contract Breezy signed," Benny says.

There's a knock at the front door, and Aunt Pat stands to answer it. Everyone waits in silence. The door opens, and Aunt Pat says, "Nuh-uh, nope. Boy, you'd better turn right back around and get off my property." There's a muffled response that I can't hear as well as Aunt Pat's raised voice. "I don't care that I've changed your diapers. I don't care how many meals you've had at my table. I do not know you, Oscar Westinghouse. And now, you gotta leave before I call the cops."

We all know the cops wouldn't do anything to Oscar, but hearing Aunt Pat's anger…it's enough to make someone run.

The door slams, and she rounds the corner, her cheeks red from the altercation. She plops back in her chair and crosses her arms. I don't think I've ever seen her this mad. Not even when my mom showed up in the middle of the night banging on the windows and looking for money.

"Well," she says. "That was Oscar."

I can't help but laugh. "No. Really? We couldn't tell."

Benny and Austin try to smother their own laughter as Uncle Trevor's lips curl into a grin.

"You're all just a lot of smartasses, ain't ya?"

"Yes, ma'am," Austin says through his laughter, his words hiccupping on each chuckle.

"Oh, it feels good to laugh." I wipe my eyes and sigh. "Okay, I'm getting myself together. I promise." We all take a moment to regain our composure, but I notice Aunt Pat's features softening, her shoulders relaxing. "Right. I am going to contact a lawyer in the morning and start from there."

"We can all chip in. I know lawyers are pricey," Benny says.

"Thank you. That means so much to me, but the Inn has some cash saved up right now, and I'd like to keep this professional. Strictly involving the Coral Bay Inn and Peralta Inc."

He nods. "I get it. But the offer stands."

"I love you guys," I say as I excuse myself from the table. "I'm going to go home and start researching lawyers. Try to get the ball moving on this." I bow and kiss Aunt Pat and Uncle Trevor on the cheek.

"Tanya." Uncle Trevor grabs my wrist and tugs me back. "I'm proud of you. Patty is proud of you. And I know Marge is proud of you. We love you."

I can't find words. My heart is too heavy with pain and love. I kiss him again and leave. The night is crisp, or as crisp as a night can be in the panhandle of Florida in December. I tug my sweater tighter around myself as I walk home. My phone pings in my purse, and I know it's Juliette. She's texted me a few times already today, begging to talk to me. As if she could say anything to remedy this mess. It is what it is, and she is who she is. That's that. And I don't owe it to her or to anyone else to forgive her.

I've done that once already, and it didn't work out well for me.

I pull out my phone regardless. It's not Jules. It's Oscar.

Meet me at my office. Please, Tanya. Whether you like me right now or not, we're family. At least hear me out. Please.

"Fucking hell," I mutter into the night. Then type, *Fine. I'll be there in ten.*

❖

Oscar's office is neat and orderly, exactly what one would expect a mayor's office to look like. An American flag hangs in the dark corner where the wall meets a bookshelf. It feels as if it's guarding something. Maybe the big mahogany desk with documents and manilla folders stacked like pillars, Coral Bay in paper form. A photo of us as kids sits in the middle of the bookshelf. We're about ten, wet-haired and sunburnt from another beach day. The four of us are pulling each other close, arms linked over shoulders and smiles bright. I love that photo.

It was before Juliette arrived in town three years later.

Looking at the photo, it feels like something's missing. Feels like she's missing. But that would mean that she belonged at some point. I don't know, maybe she did. I've been in Oscar's office countless times, but it feels different tonight. The building is quiet, and most of the lights are already out. It feels heavy here. Oscar walks behind his desk and pulls a folder from the filing cabinet beneath. He nods for me to sit.

"I don't want to sit," I say, unwilling to assume even the most insignificantly submissive position. I'm angry. And I'd like to stand in my anger.

"Okay." He walks to my side of the desk and drops the folder in front of me. His shoulder is warm against mine, and I lean away. "Take a look." He flips the envelope open and steps away.

It takes me a minute to figure out what I'm looking at. Numbers swirl together in a black vortex. "What is this?" I ask, too frazzled to focus on what I'm looking at.

He grimaces, the shadows pooling under his features,

bringing to light how tired he is. All I see is pure exhaustion. "It's the city budget."

Now the numbers begin to make sense. The categories. The bottom line. While I've had to learn a lot about finance, running the Inn and Crabby's, I wouldn't consider myself an expert. But it's not hard to see what's going on here or how bleak a situation Coral Bay is in. We're almost completely bankrupt. I'm quiet as I absorb this information.

"The city's revenue has been trending down for decades, and we're just about flat broke, Breezy." He takes the stack of paper from my hands and flips to another page and hands it back. This page breaks down industry and growth or lack thereof. Fishing has remained steady, with just a minor decline in revenue. Tourism has also remained steady but steadily low. "As the cost of running a town increases dramatically and hurricane after hurricane hits, pandemics happen, life happens...our revenue hasn't increased in years. We're not even keeping up with inflation at this rate." He shakes his head. "Coral Bay is just a dying town with no life force. Nothing."

I stay silent. I don't know what he expects from me, so I close the envelope and hand it back to him. "I don't see how this is relevant to me."

He laughs and shakes his head. It's a dark laugh. "If you can't see how this is relevant to you as the owner and operator of the Coral Bay Inn, then I don't know how to break it to you, Tanya." He sighs. "We're fucked. If no changes are made, this town will slowly fade away. Who would want to come here for vacation when there are literally two restaurants, and one is attached to a damn gas station."

"So you just throw us to the wolves? Let the Peraltas do whatever they want? Let them ruin my resort for however many years construction lasts? Doesn't sound like this benefits Coral Bay Inn at all."

He groans and runs a hand through his hair, leaving him

looking a bit frazzled. "Before Sasha made landfall, we could already see a massive bump in revenue from tourism with the Sands. And sure, we facilitated securing contractors for Peralta Inc., but Breezy, you have no idea how much tax we make from their business. It's the jolt we need to sustain. To grow, even. And when the Sands is up and running, and one day the Waters, that only helps your business, too. It's beneficial to everyone involved. You just have to think of it as an investment that will pay off in the future. The Inn will always be booked out."

I chew my lip, hating every word. Hating that I know he's right. Deep down, I know. "Oscar..."

"What?"

"I don't want to lose this place," I say. I feel a rumble in my chest, and tears gather in my eyes. It feels like a battle I just can't win, and for the first time, I'm not even sure I'm on the right side anymore.

He rubs my back gently, and I let him. "You know I love this town just as much as you do. I'm trying to make the best decisions possible for it. Someone needs to step up and make this call." He takes a deep breath and squeezes my shoulder. "I refuse to let Coral Bay fade away. It's my heart."

"Don't build a wall of high-rises between the town and the ocean. Please. The ocean is the beating heart of Coral Bay. It'd be so wrong, Oscar."

"I won't let that happen," he whispers.

I turn on him. "You say that now, but it's a slippery slope. The money starts coming in, and why would you stop it? So we keep giving building permit after building permit, and boom"—I smack my hands together obnoxiously close to his face—"wall between us and the ocean."

He groans, clearly losing his patience. "Tanya..."

"You know that contract you had me sign is bullshit. I could fight it. In fact, I'm calling a lawyer tonight about it." I plant my hands on my hips for emphasis. *I am not messing around, sir.*

"I know," he says softly, clearly feeling some kind of shame.

He considers his shoes for a moment, then pops his gaze back to me. "What if I could guarantee you that things won't get out of hand? That building permits will be given out sparingly." He taps his chin as he thinks. "Like, maybe we have three permits available every year. Would you sign the contract then?"

I grab the photo of us. We were so young. Things were so clear and easy. High-rises were evil, and tourists were evil, too, but they're the kind of evil that gives us money. It hurts to think of this town commercializing beyond recognition. I can't imagine driving down Ocean Avenue and not being able to see the ocean. It'd be claustrophobic and just so wrong.

"I like that idea," I say and set the photo down. "But it's not good enough."

His brows rise, and he stretches across me to fix the angle of the frame. His cologne is spicy and subtle. "It's not enough?"

"No. I want you to enforce strict building height limits, and I also want you to enforce some kind of maximum building density. Like…" I struggle to find words to explain what I mean. "Like, there can only be one building per half mile of beachfront. Or something like that."

He rolls his eyes. "Breezy. That's ridiculous, given the plan is to build a little downtown area around the Waters and the Inn."

"Fine," I shrug. "Then, there can only be one building per half mile of beachfront *on average*."

"Drafting these bills and signing them will take time," he warns.

I brush him off. "They'll be passed unanimously, and you know it. I don't know if I can give you more than this."

He nods slowly. "A density maximum and a building height limit?"

"That's right."

He extends his hand and grins. "It was a pleasure doing business with you."

I shake his hand and grimace. "Dick," I mutter.

He just laughs, and a thick quiet falls over us. I don't know what to say as he leans on the table and stares at me. His eyes are sincere, if not a little sad. "This was all my idea," he admits.

"Okay…"

"She had nothing to do with it." He pushes off the table and shakes his head. "I mean, of course it was her job to come down here and build the Waters, but the contract and the boardwalk is on me."

I digest his words slowly. They're often hard to swallow these days. "Why did you completely lose it on her at minigolf? You were deceiving me just as much."

"Because she hurt you, Breezy. She hurt you, and she's just going to take what she wants and disappear on you again for another sixteen years." His eyes narrow in anger. "I understand this is business, and this is a decision I've made for the sake of the town, but to sleep with you while she's planning to build next to your property? I just couldn't stomach it." He rubs a spot on his desk that looks completely clean.

"If you don't trust her, why are you doing business with her?" I ask.

He looks at me. "I didn't say I don't trust her."

"Look, I have to sort my feelings about Jules on my own and at another time." I wave him off, confused and annoyed. "Do you have the building plans?"

"Yes." He ticks a finger and walks behind his desk, pulling open a drawer and taking a long cardboard tube from within. He pops open the cap and carefully pulls the plan for the Waters. "Here," he says as he spreads the document before us.

I don't understand every single detail, but again, I grasp the general direction of what is being built where. The "what" being the Waters, and the "where" being *partially on my property*. I know the Inn's property line by heart, and I bet Osar and Jules have no idea that I know it so well. When I look at the blueprint, I see a clear edge of one of the Water's building on our land.

"Interesting proximity to Crabby's, huh?"

He looks over my shoulder. "What do you mean?"

Maybe Oscar doesn't know these plans encroach on my property. Suddenly, this feels like information I should keep close to my chest. "Nothing," I say. "Hey, do you mind if I take a picture of these? I'm meeting up with Justin soon and want to make sure we have a plan for exactly where construction will be affecting us."

He nods. "Of course."

"I still love you," I say and pat his arm. "I hate all of this, but I still love you, Oscar. And I forgive you for lying to me."

"It was hardly a lie. More like a 'left out key information' kind of moment."

I loop my purse over my shoulder and shrug. "Whatever helps you sleep at night, brother."

"I love you, too, Breezy," he calls after me.

CHAPTER EIGHTEEN

I drive to the Inn straight from Oscar's office with the building plans in my front seat. I know for a fact that they'll be encroaching on my land, but I need to find our property map in my office before I can make a plan. I turn into the bustling parking lot, pleased to see business is popping for this Wednesday evening.

A few of my staff greet me as I speed-walk through the hallway to the offices, then shut myself in mine. I find the little file cabinet key in the small lockbox under my desk and pop it open. The map isn't hard to find, and I lay it out on the table, then lay the Waters's plan right next to it. I trace along the lines and nod. *Yep.* I just found myself a huge bargaining chip. There's no way they would risk building on someone else's property. There must have been a mistake when they purchased the land. Or someone must have seriously overlooked something when they were making these plans.

I teeter on my back chair legs and think. It's not a part of our property that we need, necessarily. And if I let them break ground and invest into this set plan they have, then tell them they are on my property, it puts them in a greater position of stress and will make them more willing to negotiate with me. Or they can waste the obscene amount of money they've already sunk into the project and move it down the beach by a hundred feet. Up to them.

I take a deep breath and exhale slowly. At least now I have a modicum of control in this situation.

"Hey."

I look up to find Juliette letting herself into my office. "Don't even feel like you need to knock, do you?"

"I knocked," she says defensively. "You just didn't hear it."

"And how did you find my office?" I ask, increasingly annoyed.

She rubs the back of her neck, looking tired and worn down in her all-black attire. "Wren helped me out."

I roll my eyes. "Of course she did. I wouldn't put it past you to actually steal her from me."

She walks in front of my desk and lingers. "And I wouldn't put it past you to blame me for 'stealing her' instead of realizing your employee left on her own free will for an opportunity that she decided suited her better."

I lean back in my chair and give an exaggerated shake of my head. "Oh, well, excuse me."

"Come on," she says. "Don't take it like that."

"Don't take it like that?" I stand and smooth my hair, feeling a little out of control. "Why don't you try telling me exactly how you meant for me to take that?"

She crosses her arms and takes a step forward. "You know what, Tanya?"

"What, Juliette? Tell me."

"I've apologized so many times to you that I'm pretty sure it makes up at least ninety percent of our conversations, but maybe you want to hear just one more time." She holds up a finger, her tone angry. Eyes so dark. "I'm sorry I wasn't born in Coral Bay. I'm sorry I had to leave you when my family went home for the summer. I'm sorry my parents had a plan for me, and I felt I had to follow it. I'm sorry I was a child and didn't know what to do. I built a life, and I lived it the best way I could."

She stares, her chest rising and falling. The quiet in my office is stifling as I walk around my desk to face her. "What an apology. Yep. That's all I needed to hear right there. Why don't we just kiss and make up, and I'll give your greedy family every little thing they want? Can't keep their grubby little paws off it anyways," I spit. It's venom. And she absolutely deserves it.

She gives a breathy little chuckle and shakes her head. "It must be so hard being that sanctimonious." She takes the few steps to land right in front of me. "I know you think you're entitled to this town. You think you know what's best for it. You're like a sick mother, keeping her child from growing up, going out, and becoming their own person. You'd rather watch Coral Bay die a slow and painful death than watch it grow and evolve into something beautiful. Into something that can survive and last forever."

I press a finger into her shoulder and say, "You're feeding your parents' company by sucking the tax dollars—"

"My God." She flails her arms and frees herself from my accusing finger. "What do you think taxes are for, Tanya?" She stares, her brow arched in a menacing glare. I stay silent. "Yes. We were given a government grant. Weren't you?" She points at me.

"Yes, but we are a local—"

"Guess who else is local?" Her eyes widen. She's completely lost all decorum, and it makes me nervous. For the second time, I wonder if I'm on the wrong side of everything. "Every living soul who works in the Sands and who will work in the Waters. The town needs more money. The town needs more resources. The town needs more industry and revenue so it can finish rebuilding and begin to reinvest in itself." She sighs, long and loud. "I'm sorry for lying. I'm sorry for leaving and never reaching out. But Tanya, Coral Bay can be so much more than this. We could rebuild schools, repair the terrible roads, invest in a community center. I know Oscar agreed to building density and height limitations. The Waters is within all those specifications. I wish you could see this is a good thing."

We're quiet for a beat as I digest everything she just threw at me. I didn't know she felt this way. Didn't know she felt so passionately. Her palms face upward, and her mouth is slightly open. She looks exasperated.

"You always said I was just a tourist," she whispers.

I exhale a small chuckle through my nose. "You are. A very angry one."

Her lips twitch upward, and she shakes her head. "Well, you've been a very angry townie."

"Yeah, I guess I have." I sigh and lean against the edge of my desk. "I hate when things change."

"Welcome to being human," she says with a laugh. "No one likes change. It's hard and painful, but it's the only way to grow."

"I know." I stare at my shoes and wonder if I'm just…weak. Is that the problem? "I hated you for always leaving. Coming, going, never being mine. I hated my mom for coming, going, never being mine. Hate the hurricanes and the Sands. But damn, I love Coral Bay and my family."

"How is your mom?" she asks gently.

I shrug. "No idea. Haven't heard from her in years. And I think I'm at peace with it. Not everything has to be tied with a bow."

"Yeah. I get it. Relationships are complicated." She walks next to me and leans against my desk, too. "If it matters, I dreaded every time we had to go back to Atlanta. I didn't like my friends, and nothing felt right when I wasn't here. Ever. Nothing felt right when I wasn't with you."

"Jules, don't say it if you don't mean it. I loved you, and you just—"

"I loved you, too." She turns to me and grabs my hand. "Since the day we met, and I've never stopped."

I shake my head, completely taken aback by her admission. "That can't be true."

"It is. And it's not the first time I've told you." She rubs my hand with her thumb and drops her gaze, seeming to gather confidence or strength or both. "There was never any pen pal assignment."

I feel my eyes go wide. "What? What do you mean?"

"I lied that day on the beach. The day we met. There was no assignment. I just knew that I wanted—needed—to be a part of your life somehow." She bites her lip and shakes her head. "It's the wildest thing, babe. I just knew we were connected. Like, I don't think I believe in past lives or soulmates, but I can't describe it any other way. It just felt like I had known you before, and you were supposed to be someone very important to me." She looks at me, her gaze deep. "And I'm pretty sure you felt it, too."

I take a moment before I respond. This is all so...*much.* Everything she's said about my refusing to let Coral Bay grow into itself. About how she's felt about me all these years. It's a lot to take in. "But you...you got married to someone else."

"I also cried for months after I left Coral Bay the last time. I cried so hard and so often that my parents made me go to therapy before they let me go to college. I could barely eat."

Her words hit me right in the heart. It tears me apart to think of her struggling that way, the same way I was. And I thought I was the only one not eating and drowning in tears. But we were together even in that. "I hate that, Jules. I hate knowing you were in pain."

"I know you were, too."

I pull her into me, and she rests her head on my breasts. We sit that way for a while, me holding her in silence, rocking softly. It almost feels like coming home.

"You know Jim never had my heart. Oscar never had my heart. No one else has ever had my heart," she whispers against my chest. "Only you."

I drop my arms, and she pulls up. My breathing is rapid and uneven. It's overwhelming, feeling like I'm about to give in to her again. It makes me feel out of control, foolish, and like I'm reliving the same mistake over and over. "Jules. This scares me."

Tears well, and I shake my head. "I don't know if I can do this again with you. You left. You lied to me. You broke my heart, and I don't want to go through it a third time." I let a tear fall, and she brushes it away softly. "It hurts too much."

She nods slowly, her eyes soft and sincere. "I know. I know, love. I wish I could change my decisions. I know I could have done so much better by you. But I can't go back. All I can do is take today and start living the life I want. The one I was meant to have."

"I don't understand," I say. "What does that mean?"

"It means I need a little time to sort through some things. I know, given today and everything I've put you through in general, you don't trust me. As things stand, you can't do this with me." She points to both of us. "I understand."

"I want to, I just…" I wince.

"I know, my love. I know." She leans in and kisses me softly on the cheek, not taking too much but giving me calm. "That festival is next week, huh?"

I nod, unable to speak with her kiss sinking through me. Damn her and her sinking kisses.

She stands and tucks her hands in her pockets. The gesture makes her look young, almost innocent. "I'll see you there?"

"Of course." I chuckle. "We're only contractually obligated to hang out and get dunked by travel reviewers together."

She rolls her eyes and walks backward toward my door. "You know, I think Oscar just wanted to bring us down a peg, that scoundrel." She winks, and it sends me.

I grin and roll my eyes, too. "Complete scoundrel, that mayor of ours."

"Thank you for talking to me, Tanya. I'll see you next week, okay?"

I nod. "Yeah. Okay. Get home safe."

"Night." She walks out of my office and closes the door behind her.

I walk behind my desk and collapse in my chair. "What in

the world just happened?" I whisper to myself, clutching my heart.

I swivel in my chair to look out my office window. It has a perfect view of Crabby's below. People are laughing, eating, drinking. It's almost like a silent movie, watching them from above. Juliette wasn't wrong. Oscar isn't wrong. Sure, they were complete assholes in how they went about doing what they thought was best for Coral Bay. Well, Oscar did what he thought was best for Coral Bay, and Jules did what was best for herself and her family's company. But maybe I was wrong. Maybe things aren't so black and white. Maybe the Sands and the Waters will have a symbiotic relationship with our town, and I need to grow up and stop standing in the way of it.

Then, there is me and Jules. And Jules confessing her love for me for the second time. I let my head fall softly against the cool window. There was never any pen pal assignment...she made it up to keep me close, as if I wouldn't have written all those letters anyway. I would have. Leaving me tore her apart, too.

I grab my purse and walk down to Crabby's in a hurry. Wren is slinging drinks behind the bar, tickets printing almost nonstop behind her. Her support bartenders tonight are skilled and fast. Even though it looks like they're behind, they have it under control.

"Hey, Breezy. All good?" she asks as she rinses out a shaker and free pours a perfect two ounces of tequila.

"All good, yeah." It's busy and loud, and I'm shoulder to shoulder with the rest of the bar patrons. She shakes the margarita, and I wait for the loud *thunking* of ice to stop. "Hey. Do you think Coral Bay needs to grow?" I ask. It's such a vague question. Such a broad thing to ask someone in the middle of the dinner rush as they're knocking out drink orders and trying to get out of the weeds.

"For sure," she calls over her shoulder. "Definitely needs some revitalization. Would hate to see another school shut down." She serves the drink.

"So, like, more businesses?" I shout. I'm ridiculous.

"Yeah," she shouts back, then takes another order from a woman at the other end of the bar. She walks to my end and sends the order through the POS. "More businesses, more growth, more resources. Simple."

"Simple." I nod. "And you don't think Coral Bay would change too much?" I ask in a raised voice, trying to be heard over all the clanking glasses and chatter.

She shrugs. "If we don't change at all, it's kinda a moot point. Right?"

"Right," I say, probably not loud enough for anyone to hear. Bar guests are beginning to take an interest in me and my weird questions. "Okay. Thanks, Wren. Sorry for the interruption. Y'all are crushing it tonight."

"No worries. See ya tomorrow, boss."

"Don't call me that," I yell.

I drive home with the windows down like always, listening to the whooshing heartbeat of the ocean. The moon is bright, and everything is peaceful. Except my heart. Resisting all this change, all this construction, all this growth feels wrong. But I'm so scared to give in. Not only will I leave myself vulnerable again, but Coral Bay will be vulnerable. I swerve to avoid one of the bigger potholes but catch the corner of it. The force of it makes me jump in my seat. Maybe Coral Bay already is vulnerable.

CHAPTER NINETEEN

Oscar's festival turns out to be pretty amazing. I walk up Ocean Avenue, which has been completely blocked off for five blocks. Tents, carnival games, and food stands line the streets. People carry to-go drinks from Crabby's as they walk from booth to booth. It's pure joy, really. Children run by, laughing and playing, snow cones dripping bright blue and red down their wrists. It's Coral Bay, but it's…livelier. Happier. Brighter somehow.

"Breezy," Austin and Benny call from the booth to my right. Their two kids are focused on trying to toss rings on old-school glass bottles. I'd bet they have their heart set on the giant alligator stuffed animal hanging on the prize display.

"Hey, guys." I give them both a giant hug and let their calming energy settle me. I release them and say hi to the little ones. They're too in the zone to do more than greet me causally over their shoulders.

"Kids," Austin says and rolls his eyes.

"They really want to win that gator and have almost blown all their allowance on trying," Benny explains.

I laugh. "I had a suspicion that's the one they were after." I rummage through my purse, looking for the loose dollar bills I thought I had. "I think I may have some spare ones in here somewhere."

"Nope." Benny pulls my hand out of my purse. "No, no, no. These little gremlins have been warned over and over not to blow all their money in one go. They're going to have to learn their lesson."

"Ah." I close my purse. "I see."

"Plus, they're kids. They don't need money to have fun. We never did," Austin says.

Benny scoffs. "Except for the booze and the wee—"

"Can we not say that in front of the children?" Austin interjects.

"Oh please, they wouldn't notice if the next hurricane hit right now," Benny says.

Austin shrugs. "Touché."

"You need a drink, Brees." Benny sips his margarita and grins. Everyone here seems so happy. It could be the drinks and the sunshine, sure. But I think it's more than that. There's an energy about this festival. Maybe this is a hint of what Coral Bay could grow into one day.

"You're absolutely right. Have you seen Oscar?" I hadn't seen him or Juliette since last week, when I had a blowout fight with both and a very confusing resolution with both. But I have done a lot of reflecting since then, and I am eager to see them. Well, I am eager to see Oscar and anxious to see Jules.

Benny wipes his mouth with the back of his hand. "Yeah. He's up by Crabby's with Jules and some local news folks."

"Okay. Great. I'll catch up with you guys later. I'm going to go check in with them."

I begin to walk by, but Benny catches my arm. "Brees, listen. Maybe all this"—he lifts his drink to encompass the festival—"isn't so bad."

Austin wraps an arm around my shoulders and squeezes. "We've done a lot of thinking, and maybe with a few more businesses and a little more revenue, these guys can have a more secure future." He nods to Joey and Layla. "The school district's budget is just sad at this point. Everything is getting cut that isn't the basic core curriculum 'cause they can't afford to pay the teachers."

"Okay," I say and slink out of his arm. "I know. I kind of came to that realization, too."

"Have you talked to Aunt Pat?" Benny asked.

I nod. "All week. She was still pissed about Oscar and Jules lying to me and messing around with my property lines, but I don't even think they realize."

"Gonna tell them?" Austin asks.

"I have a plan for that." I grin, thinking about the scheme I've cooked up. "Okay, I'm going. Love you, guys."

"Love you, Breezy," they call after me.

I weave through the festivities, saying hi and chatting to all the folks I know and love along the way. For all the commotion and energy, it still feels like home. I spot Oscar and Jules chatting to a couple of strangers, one wearing a jacket with *Coral Bay Today* written on the back.

"Hey, there," I say, and they all turn to greet me.

"Breezy," Oscar says and tugs me into their circle. Jules catches my eye and smiles at me as Oscar introduces me to the news representative and reviewers.

Oscar is wearing his standard starched white guayabera and pressed slacks. His sunglasses are tucked in his breast pocket, and his hair is perfectly smoothed back. He must be the most handsome mayor in America. Jules does not look like she's representing Peralta Inc. She wears light jeans with the cuffs rolled a few times, turning them into capris, a black belt, and a nice light green T-shirt. Her jeans will be quite soggy if we get dunked.

"Oh shit," I mutter to myself.

Oscar is lost in conversation, too far gone into business mode to hear me, but Jules lifts a brow and mouths, "You okay?"

I nod and wave her over. She politely excuses herself from the person on her right and walks to the other side of the small circle to me. My stomach sinks with the weight of all the butterflies.

She looks so effortlessly beautiful, casual, and at home. "Hi," she says so only I can hear her.

"Hey. Missed you," I admit.

"You have no idea." She brushes her fingers down my forearm. "So what are we saying 'oh shit' about?"

I look at myself and hold out the hem of my dress. "Oh shit…I'm wearing a dress for the dunk tank." I laugh, shaking my head. "I clearly did not think this through. I'm going to end up flashing the entire festival."

"Would it be so bad?" She winks, and I smack her arm.

"Jules," I scold. Oscar flashes us a look as if we're his kids, and we're misbehaving in front of company. "Sorry," I mouth.

"There's plenty of time to run home and change. The dunk tank isn't until the end of the night. We've got another"—Jules checks her watch—"five whole hours."

"Okay. Yeah. I'd better go put on some pants." I wave at Oscar. "Hey, I'll be back soon. I forgot to wear something dunk tank appropriate."

He chuckles. "Okay. Don't be too long."

I start walking away and realize Jules isn't following. "You coming?" I ask.

Her eyes brighten, a smile breaking over her lips. "You want me to?"

"Yes."

She says good-bye to the small group and walks with me back to my car. It's strange, the intimacy of being in a large group. In a loud place. It feels as if it's just me and Jules under this blanket of the festival. "It's wild, huh? Seeing Coral Bay this way," she says.

I nod. "It's beautiful, actually. I'm beginning to think that maybe you and Oscar are on to something."

She shrugs. "Yeah, I think we are. You know Oscar wouldn't do anything that wasn't in the best interest of this place, even if, to the outsider, it seems against everything Coral Bay is."

"I know. Looking at it now, with all this energy and vibrancy, somehow, it's more Coral Bay, not less."

She grins, her dimples deepening and soft crow's feet forming. "I'm glad you feel that way."

The sounds start to fade as we reach my truck and get in. We close the doors, and everything melts away. I can hear her breathe. My hand lies on the bench seat between us for all of five seconds before her hand is holding mine. We sit in the quiet for a moment longer, just absorbing each other's company before I speak again.

"I think—"

"I quit my job," she interjects.

"What?" I lean away so I can see her in her entirety. I am in complete shock. "You mean, you quit Peralta Inc.?"

She nods. "Last week after we spoke. I agreed to get my replacement up to speed on the development in Coral Bay, then I'm done."

I'm momentarily speechless. I don't notice I'm death gripping her wrist until she smiles and wiggles to loosen it. "Are you okay?" I ask. It's the only thing that floats to the top of all the questions I have and emotions I'm feeling.

"Best I've ever been." I believe her. She looks…at ease.

"And your parents? Are they okay with it?"

She chuckles. "See, the thing is, I am a grown-ass woman. And I have been sad my entire life trying to make sure my parents were 'okay with it.' But I'm tired of being sad. I never wanted to work in real estate. I never wanted to marry Jim. It's time I start living before life passes me by."

"So they're pissed?" I ask through a laugh.

"Oh yeah." She chuckles. "They haven't really spoken to me, but they'll have to figure it out sooner or later."

"Wow. I can't believe it." I squeeze her wrist more gently this time. "I'm so proud of you, Jules."

She smiles, a sheen of wetness in her eyes. "Yeah?"

"Of course. I can't imagine what it took to make that decision and choose to be true to yourself after all these years."

She nods. "I'm glad someone is proud of me."

I let this news sink in for a moment. Juliette Peralta is single. Juliette Peralta quit her job. "What does a Peralta do if they're not working for Peralta Inc.?"

"I have no fucking clue." She shrugs. "I think I'll take this year to finalize the divorce, get my life sorted, move, and relax. Then, maybe go back to school."

I smile. "That sounds perfect." We sit, holding each other's hands. Something keeps me from turning on my engine and driving. This moment...I'm not ready for it to end. "I got the building plan for the Waters from Oscar's office," I say.

She rubs the backside of my hand. "Oh yeah? You approve??

"Yeah, except for one pretty major thing."

"What's that?" she asks, sounding more than a little concerned.

"Seems that Peralta Inc. didn't have my property map of the Inn when they designed it. As it is, the Waters will be built one hundred feet onto my property."

"What?" She gasps, completely horrified. "Oh my God, that is a *huge* fuckup. Someone is definitely getting fired over this." She drops my hand and fishes her phone from her back pocket. "I'll call my father right now and have them stop everything."

"Wait," I say, reaching for her wrist. "What if we didn't?"

She quirks a brow and lowers her phone. "What do you mean, what if we didn't? It's your property, Tanya. This is completely unacceptable."

"I know. But if they get into construction first, then they have already sunk millions into the plan and will do anything to keep it as is."

She tilts her head. "You want to force them into a payout?"

"I mean, yes...but think of it as more of a forced donation to the school district. We both know Peralta Inc. has the money, and they would have to spend it scrapping their project and moving it off my land anyway. Why not save them the time and just settle it with a simple reallocation of funds?"

"Damn, Breezy." She smacks her thigh and laughs. "I'm so lucky I won't be the one having to go toe-to-toe in negotiations with you."

"You're not mad?"

"Mad?" She points to herself. "Me? I think it's brilliant. I don't give a shit what happens to Peralta Inc., and quite frankly, this won't affect them at all. I say go for it. I'll help."

"Really?"

"Yes. Really." She checks her watch again. "We should probably head to yours before we get in trouble with Dad."

I chuckle and start the truck. "Oh gosh. Oscar is such a dad."

❖

We pull into my driveway and park, the quiet of my truck falling heavy on us. With all this new information, the space between me and Juliette feels saturated. She stares, holding my gaze as if she's about to lean in and make it rain on us. It's an overwhelming feeling, being on the precipice of so much.

I open my door. "We should…"

"Yeah," she says and opens hers.

We walk quietly to my front door. She stops behind me as I search through my purse for my keys. I feel her breath in my hair as her hands find my hips. "Jules." I groan and lean into her, forgetting about my keys entirely.

"Breezy," she whispers into my hair. "Let us in, baby."

I nod against her chest, and her grip tightens on me. I'm already soaked for her, a sweet buzz humming through my entire being. I push back harder into her, and she brushes my hair away from my neck. She plants a hand on the door in front of me and sighs in my ear.

"I need you," I whisper.

She kisses my neck and scrapes her teeth along my jaw. It makes my legs shake. "Then open the door."

I take a deep breath and find my keys. It takes a few attempts to get it in the lock. We walk into the privacy of my living room, and I drop my purse in the corner. "Can I get you anything?" I ask, my voice as shaky as my legs.

"No, thank you. You should go change, right?"

My sundress has wooden buttons all down the front, and I unbutton the first one, walking backward toward my room. "Do you want to come help me? These buttons always give me a hard time."

She nods, following me down the hallway. I open my door and let her in, closing it behind us. My room is dark, except for the sunlight peeking through the edges of the curtains. It's the perfect amount of light to see everything but to feel held in darkness. She turns and pushes me gently against my door by the hips. She nips my collarbone as she works on my buttons, one by one, freeing me from this cotton.

She kisses down my chest, claiming the skin she exposes as hers. Always hers. Until she unclasps the last button and pushes the dress off my shoulders. She sinks to her knees, dragging her mouth to the waistband of my panties.

"Fuck." I groan and try to push against her mouth, but she won't let me.

Instead, she anchors me against the door by my hips and mutters, "Be a good girl."

"Oh my God, Jules. Fuck, baby." My nipples strain against the fabric of my bra, my pussy aches, hot and needy for her. The image of her on her knees in front of me makes me pant.

She slips a finger inside my wet panties and runs her knuckle over the length of me. My entire body shudders. Then she pulls them entirely to one side and presses her mouth to me, kissing me softly.

I can't bear another second of this teasing. I'm hers. "Please. I need you inside me. I need you to fuck me, Jules. Please," I beg.

She stands and tucks her thumbs in my waistband, pushing down my underwear as I unclasp my bra. I am completely naked against my door as she kisses me hard, the taste of me on her tongue.

"It's not fair," I say between kisses.

"Hmm?"

"Take off your clothes," I command.

She pulls away in a hurry and tears off her shirt and pants. She drops her bra by her feet and kicks off her panties to join her shirt. Jules is the most beautiful woman I've ever seen, her curves illuminated by the soft sunlight.

"Now come back," I say.

She's everywhere. Her mouth closes over my nipple as she massages the other between her fingers until I wonder if I could come just from how she sucks my tits. She drops her hand down my stomach, letting her fingers trail lightly down my skin until she hits all my hot wetness. I spread my legs for her, and she pushes two fingers into me as she sucks my neck now.

I moan as she fucks me against my door. The hinges creak with each of her thrusts, and I grab fistfuls of her hair, pulling her harder into me. I want her to leave a mark. Need her deeper. I lift a leg and curl it over her hip, giving her more access, and she uses it. I feel myself tighten around her fingers. I know I'm going to come fast and hard with the way she's fucking me, her thumb rubbing over my clit as she strokes me.

But I don't want to come. Not yet. I drop my leg and give her a little shove backward.

"You okay?" she asks, all breathy and hot.

"I just don't want to come first this time," I say as I walk her back to my bed. She lets me push her onto it and cover her with my body.

She laughs and pulls me into her. Her naked body feels like

home under mine. "I love you, Tanya Brees," she whispers into my ear.

"I love you, Jules."

I kiss my way slowly down her perfect body, her skin so soft and warm against my lips. She shudders when I nip at her hip bone and cover her breast with my hand. My lips meet hers, and she's as hot and soaked as I imagined. I breathe her in as she pushes her hips up to press herself harder against my mouth, and we moan together.

I fill her with my fingers and make love to her until her thighs begin to shake, and she tightens around me. Her breathing is ragged as she comes hard. I slow my movements. Gentle. Long. She shudders through the waves of her orgasms. One after another. Smaller and smaller, until she's spent. I crawl up her body, and she gathers me in her arms.

I nibble her ear, completely content. "You always did come in waves," I whisper.

CHAPTER TWENTY

"Where have you been?" Oscar scolds as Jules and I walk down the steps of the boardwalk to the beach in front of Crabby's. "It took forever."

Jules bites down a grin as I weave some tale about having to pick up Aunt Pat, who was running late, and give her a ride. I specifically leave out the part about me and Juliette taking a detour to my bed for a solid two hours.

"Okay, whatever," he says in exasperation. "The two travel bloggers are at the bar going over their notes on the festival. Let's go inside and chat while they finish setting up the dunk tanks on the beach."

"I still don't understand why we have to get dunked," Jules complains as we follow him inside.

I don't see the bloggers from before, but I do see Benny, Austin, Uncle Trevor, and Aunt Pat chatting with Wren and enjoying a drink at the bar. My heart leaps at the sight of them. Together in my restaurant. Juliette by my side and a world of possibility ahead. For the first time, everything feels right. I am not scared of losing. Not scared of change. I'm excited for the future, whatever it may hold.

"They must have disappeared somewhere," Oscar says.

I squeeze his shoulder. "Oscar, this whole festival is amazing. I am so wildly proud of you. You did it. Now can you relax for just a moment and come have a drink with our family." I nod to the bar where Jules has joined them. She chats with Aunt Pat, and I know they will be okay. Aunt Pat will forgive her as easily as I did. "Look at all of them," I say.

His brow softens, and he smiles. "Yeah. Look at them." He sighs and shakes his shoulders. "I guess a Cuba libre couldn't hurt."

I smile and turn to the bar. "Wren, can we get a Cuba libre and two guava sours? Thanks."

❖

The sun begins to set down the beach as most of the town gathers in front of Crabby's to listen to Oscar's speech and to watch me and Jules potentially get dunked. I reckon it's possible for us to escape dry if the bloggers have bad aim. But I'm keeping my hopes low.

Oscar talks about his love for Coral Bay and his hopes for its future. He details his plans to build more revenue streams and how that money will work to make Coral Bay a better, stronger, and safer version of itself. How there will be more resources flowing into our school system, our hospital, and our infrastructure. He even announces that "Peralta Inc. will be breaking ground on a new property that will be located right here next to Crabby's. It will be called the Waters and have multiple restaurants and shops, including a hotel for visitors."

The crowd is quiet as they digest the news. They probably don't know how to feel about it. Oscar announced it in such a way that it's clear this is where all the revenue he was speaking about will come from. But it's scary. A low murmur rumbles through them until Aunt Pat walks to the front next to Oscar and takes his mic.

"Excuse me," she says, and everyone turns their attention to her. There are a few cheers and hollers for her.

A random person yells, "We love you, Pat!"

She grins and shields her eyes, trying to make out the faces of all the people in the crowd. "I love you all, too," she says. More cheers. "Now, listen. I know the sounds of this new construction is scary. Hell, I was scared when I first heard about it, too. But let me tell you something. I've lived in Coral Bay my whole life, and I love this town with my whole heart. That's why it's so sad to watch it die over the years. How many family-owned shops have we witnessed shut down? We lost entire schools. Our population is declining. Rapidly."

She scans the crowd, letting everyone see her face. This is *Aunt Pat*. The most beloved figure in our community. "Mayor Westinghouse is taking action for us. *Finally.* Now, I've known Oscar since he was born." She turns to him and smiles. "Boy, how many meals have you had at my table?" He chuckles and shakes his head, his eyes misty. He's speechless. "Let's just say, I know this man through and through, and I trust him to do what is best for Coral Bay." She winks at him then turns back to the crowd. "Now, where's my drink?"

Uncle Trevor walks up and hands her a plastic cup of white wine and kisses her on the cheek. The crowd erupts into cheers. "Yep. I recommend you get you one like my baby, here. Thank you, honey." She lifts her cup. "Here's to Mayor Westinghouse, Peralta Inc., and Coral Bay."

The crowd claps and hollers, and Oscar thanks Aunt Pat for vouching for him. "Never thought I'd see that happen," I say as she walks past. She winks and finds Uncle Trevor again.

"Thank you, Pat. Now, how about we give our guests of honor the chance to dunk the GMs of Coral Bay Inn and the Sands?"

I squeeze Jules's hand as everyone cheers, and she looks at me. "Are you going to leave?" I ask because I need to know what this is. I need to know what I have in her.

She holds up a pinkie. "Never again. Not without you."

Juliette Peralta broke a pinkie promise to me a long time ago, but I forgave her for that. We moved on from that. I wrap my pinkie around hers and smile. "The tourist and the townie."

She laughs. "Two townies. I'm not a tourist anymore."
"Deal," I say.
"Deal."

❖

It feels so ominous, sitting in the dunk tank, awaiting my fate. The two bloggers really do suck at this. I know Oscar is itching to dunk one of us. I look over at Jules in her own tank, white-knuckling the plastic seat.

"Mind if I take a turn?" Oscar asks.

"Oh, I'd love a turn, too," Benny says.

Jules looks straight at me. Her midnight hair blowing in the evening breeze, the orange glow of dusk highlighting all her—

She plunges straight into the water with a splash, and I laugh hysterically at her as she surfaces. I knew Oscar was going to—

My seat disappears from beneath me, and I plunge into the shallow water. Serves me right. I take an extra second to enjoy what I've always loved about being underwater. The weight of it on my skin. How all the noises quiet. The pressure in my ears...

I break the surface and wipe the water out of my eyes. I look over at her as she stares at me, and I know in that moment that Juliette Peralta will always be my deep end.

EPILOGUE

Jules groans and rolls her eyes. "I still cannot believe you're letting him cut the ribbon," she says.

Mr. Peralta stands in front of the crowd with a giant pair of scissors that he insisted on using to cut the ribbon during the grand opening ceremony for the new middle school in Coral Bay, fittingly called Meadow Breeze Middle. *Go Pirates!* A big plaque with the Peraltas' name thanking the family for its generous donation sits right underneath the school's main sign.

I squeeze Juliette's hand. "Babe, it benefits everyone to let the town think this money was donated from the goodness of your father's heart."

"You're like the Batman of Coral Bay, saving the day behind the scenes and everything." She bites her lip and quirks a brow. "It's pretty sexy, I have to say."

"I'm very glad you think so." I kiss her dimple, then watch her father cut the ribbon to the school he once demolished. Everyone cheers, and I just smile, thinking how five years ago, Jules showed back up in Coral Bay and changed my life. How twenty years ago, I could have never imagined Coral Bay getting a beautiful new school, our roads being mended, and our workforce strengthened. And Juliette holding my hand, a ring on each of our left ring fingers.

We let go to clap for her father, then find each other again.

"You think he'll ever forgive me?" I ask.

"For forcing him into giving away millions of dollars and corrupting his daughter?"

I grin. It never gets old. "Yeah. For that."

She laughs and shakes her head. "No, babe. Not a chance."

I pull her in for a hug, marveling at how the way she feels and the way she smells still gives me butterflies. She kisses me softly. And how her kisses still sink. I press my lips to hers one more time, then pull away. I nod to the school. "Can you believe your first day is on Monday?"

"Holy shit." Her eyes widen, and she shakes her head. "Am I ready for this?"

"You've always wanted to be a teacher, Jules. You're so ready for this. And the fact that they have an Introduction to Finance course in middle school is amazing. Kids need to learn how to handle their money and invest for the future. And you, Mrs. Brees, have all the experience in the world to help them learn. Okay?"

She bites her lip and nods. "Okay."

"You want to bust out of here and head to Aunt Pat's early?"

Her father takes the mic and begins to explain how he felt it in his heart that he needed to make this generous donation.

"Or do you want to stay and listen to this shit?"

She rolls her eyes. "No, thank you. I think I'm ready for a cocktail."

❖

Aunt Pat and Uncle Trevor have cooked a feast for this celebration. Three types of shrimp, mashed potatoes, and more bottles of wine than we could possibly drink. Austin shakes up some of his famous spicy margaritas for the first round and pours everyone a drink. It sets my heart on fire to see us around Aunt Pat's table. We're almost forty now, and so much has changed.

But at the same time, nothing has changed. We're still all here. Together.

The table has a small pile of gifts for Juliette's first day of teaching on Monday, and they may or may not be coordinated. I lift my glass and stand.

"Jules, I think I speak for everyone when I say that our lives and this town changed for the better the day you arrived nearly twenty-five years ago. It's been a wild ride, but you've touched all our hearts and made Coral Bay a better place. And now, you're starting a new adventure on Monday, and we couldn't be prouder of you. Cheers, my love."

We toast to Jules and sip our drinks as Benny hands her a gift. "Okay, time for presents."

"Okay," Jules says, and I can tell she's a little nervous. She takes the rectangular box from Benny and unwraps it. "Oh my gosh, this is perfect." It's a lava lamp just like the one that was in our favorite classroom in the old Meadows.

"It's the same," Benny says, clearly excited.

She clutches it to her chest. "It's perfect. Thank you."

Austin hands her a gift next. It's a small one, and I know exactly what it is. "This was strangely hard to find," he says. "We're getting old, guys."

"Oh, I know what this is. Nothing else is the shape of a CD," Jules says. She unwraps it and claps. "Yes. The Blink-182 album from that night. I love it so much."

Austin grins. "It's probably not appropriate for your students, so only listen to it after school."

"Noted."

Oscar pats his larger gift and nods for her to come open it. "They don't really make these like they used to. Austin is right. We're getting old."

Jules unwraps the boombox and squeals in delight. "I can't believe you guys. This is incredible."

"Just one thing missing," I say.

She raises a brow. "No, you didn't…"

"Oh, I did." I hand her a box, and she unwraps it. "The first man I was ever truly jealous of."

She gasps. "Skeeter the skeleton, oh my God, babe. We have to put him together tonight."

"We will. I know it's random to have in a finance class, but that's what makes it fun. Your classroom will be the kids' favorite by far." I wink. "You'll be their favorite teacher by far."

"I love you." She plants a kiss on me. "Thank you all so much. I'm…I'm overwhelmed."

"We love you, Jules," Oscar says and lifts his drink.

We toast to her again as she wipes a tear from her eyes. Then everyone digs into the food and the drink and the company. It's almost like Thanksgiving. Jules squeezes my thigh under the table and leans into my ear.

"Want to go on a little stroll after dinner?"

I pull her hand into my lap. "I'd love that, we can all walk to—"

"No, no. I meant just you and me. Maybe we can walk to the playground and…swing."

I scoff. "You're terrible."

"You love it."

"Hey," Benny shouts, and we both startle away from each other. "Stop your canoodling and listen up. We're going for a night swim after dinner. So get yourself a to-go drink and emotionally prepare yourself to be pushed in a pool."

"Whose pool?" I ask.

He shrugs. "Does it matter? The first pool we see. It's Coral Bay, everyone is family." He points at Oscar. "And we're rolling with 'beloved Mayor Westinghouse.'"

Oscar socks him in the shoulder. "You're always such a prick."

"That actually sounds perfect," I say. Then I turn to Jules. "Rain check on the, you know…"

"Yes. Rain check on the booty call." She laughs. "I know how you like to plunge into a deep end."

I kiss her knuckles and stare into those eyes I adore. Everyone fades. The laughter drowns. I can feel the pressure in my ears. "My love, you are my deep end."

About the Author

Ana is an award-winning author of Sapphic romance. She worked in the Pacific Northwest wine industry for eight years and now lives in her hometown of Atlanta. She loves all things fermented or distilled, walking the local trails, and eating pastries. So many pastries. She is currently working on her next book and dreaming of a beach trip.

Books Available From Bold Strokes Books

Can't Buy Me Love by Georgia Beers. London and Kayla are perfect for one another, but if London reveals she's in a fake relationship with Kayla's ex, she risks not only the opportunity of her career, but Kayla's trust as well. (978-1-63679-665-9)

Chance Encounter by Renee Roman. Little did Sky Roberts know when she bought the raffle ticket for charity that she would also be taking a chance on love with the egotistical Drew Mitchell. (978-1-63679-619-2)

Comes in Waves by Ana Hartnett. For Tanya Brees, love in small-town Coral Bay comes in waves, but can she make it stay for good this time? (978-1-63679-597-3)

The Curse by Alexandra Riley. Can Diana Dillon and her daughter, Ryder, survive the cursed farm with the help of Deputy Mel Defoe? Or will the land choose them to be to the next victims? (978-1-63679-611-6)

Dancing With Dahlia by Julia Underwood. How is Piper Fernley supposed to survive six weeks with the most controlling, uptight boss on earth? Because sometimes when you stop looking, your heart finds exactly what it needs. (978-1-63679-663-5)

The Heart Wants by Krystina Rivers. Fifteen years after they first meet, Army Major Reagan Jennings realizes she has one last chance to win the heart of the woman she's always loved. If only she can make Sydney see she's worth risking everything for. (978-1-63679-595-9)

Skyscraper by Gun Brooke. Attempting to save the life of an injured boy brings Rayne and Kaelyn together. As they strive for justice against corrupt Celestial authorities, they're unable to foresee how intertwined their fates will become. (978-1-63679-657-4)

Untethered by Shelley Thrasher. Helen Rogers, in her eighties, meets much younger Grace on a lengthy cruise to Bali, and their intense relationship yields surprising insights and unexpected growth. (978-1-63679-636-9)

You Can't Go Home Again by Jeanette Bears. After their military career ends abruptly, Raegan Holcolm is forced back to their hometown to confront their past and discover where the road to recovery will lead them, or if it already led them home. (978-1-636790644-4)

A Wolf in Stone by Jane Fletcher. Though Cassilania is an experienced player in the dirty, dangerous game of imperial Kavillian politics, even she is caught out when a murderer raises the stakes. (978-1-63679-640-6)

The Devil You Know by Ali Vali. As threats come at the Casey family from both the feds and enemies set to destroy them, Cain Casey does whatever is necessary with Emma at her side to bury every single one. (978-1-63679-471-6)

The Meaning of Liberty by Sage Donnell. When TJ and Bailey get caught in the political crossfire of the ultraconservative Crusade of the Redeemer Church, escape is the only plan. On the run and fighting for their lives is not the time to be falling for each other. (978-1-63679-624-6)

One Last Summer by Kristin Keppler. Emerson Fields didn't think anything could keep her from her dream of interning at Bardot Design Studio in Paris, until an unexpected choice at a North Carolina beach has her questioning what it is she really wants. (978-1-63679-638-3)

StreamLine by Lauren Melissa Ellzey. When Lune crosses paths with the legendary girl gamer Nocht, she may have found the key that will boost her to the upper echelon of streamers and unravel all Lune thought she knew about gaming, friendship, and love. (978-1-63679-655-0)

Undercurrent by Patricia Evans. Can Tala and Wilder catch a serial killer in Salem before another body washes up on the shore? (978-1-636790669-7)

And Then There Was One by Michele Castleman. Plagued by strange memories and drowning in the guilt she tried to leave behind, Lyla Smith escapes her small Ohio town to work as a nanny and becomes trapped with an unknown killer. (978-1-63679-688-8)

Digging for Destiny by Jenna Jarvis. The war between nations forces Litz to make a choice. Her country, career, and family, or the chance of making a better world with the woman she can't forget. (978-1-63679-575-1)

Hot Hires by Nan Campbell, Alaina Erdell, and Jesse J. Thoma. In these three romance novellas, when business turns to pleasure, romance ignites. (978-1-63679-651-2)

The Land of Death and Devil's Club by Bailey Bridgewater. Special Liaison to the FBI Louisa Linebach may have defied all odds by identifying the bodies of three missing men in the Kenai Peninsula, but she won't be satisfied until the man she's sure is responsible for their murders is behind bars. (978-1-63679-659-8)

McCall by Patricia Evans. Sam and Sara found love on the water, but can they build a future amid the ghosts of the past that surround them on dry land? (978-1-63679-769-4)

Promises to Protect by Jo Hemmingwood. Park ranger Maxine Ward's commitment to protect Tree City is put to the test when social worker Skylar Austen takes a special interest in the commune and in Max. (978-1-63679-626-0)

Sacred Ground by Missouri Vaun. Jordan Price, a conflicted demon hunter, falls for Grace Jameson, who has no idea she's been bitten by a vampire. (978-1-63679-485-3)

When You Smile by Melissa Brayden. Taryn Ross never thought the babysitter she once crushed on would show up as a grad student at the same university she attends. (978-1-63679-671-0)

A Heart Divided by Angie Williams. Emmaline is the most beautiful woman Jack has ever seen, but being a veteran of the Confederate army that killed her husband isn't the only thing keeping them apart. (978-1-63679-537-9)

Adrift by Sam Ledel. Two women whose lives are anchored by guilt and obligation find romance amidst the tumultuous Prohibition movement in 1920s California. (978-1-63679-577-5)

Cabin Fever by Tagan Shepard. The longer Morgan and Shelby are stranded together, the more their feelings grow, but is it real, or just cabin fever? (978-1-63679-632-1)

Clean Kill by Anne Laughlin. When someone starts killing people she knows in the recovery world, former detective Nicky Sullivan must race to stop the killer and keep herself from being arrested for the crimes. (978-1-63679-634-5)

Only a Bridesmaid by Haley Donnell. A fake bridesmaid, a socially anxious bride, and an unexpected love—what could go wrong? (978-1-63679-642-0)

Primal Hunt by L.L. Raand. Anya, a young wolf warrior, finds herself paired with Rafe, one of the most powerful Vampires in the Americas, in an erotic union of blood and sex.(978-1-63679-561-4)

Snake Charming by Genevieve McCluer. Playgirl vampire Freddie is on the run and a chance encounter with lamia Phoebe makes them both realize that they may have found the love they'd given up on. (978-1-63679-628-4)

Spirits and Sirens by Kelly and Tana Fireside. When rumored ghost whisperer Elena Murphy and very skeptical assistant fire chief Allison Jones have to work together to solve a 70-year old mystery, sparks fly—will it be enough to melt the ice between them and let love ignite? (978-1-63679-607-9)

Aubrey McFadden Is Never Getting Married by Georgia Beers. Aubrey McFadden is never getting married, but she does have five weddings to attend, and she'll be avoiding Monica Wallace, the woman who ruined her happily ever after, at every single one. (978-1-63679-613-0)

Flowers for Dead Girls by Abigail Collins. Isla might be just the right kind of girl to bring Astra out of her shell—and maybe more. The only problem? She's dead. (978-1-63679-584-3)

Rainbow Overalls by Maggie Fortuna. Arriving in Vermont for her first year of college, an introverted bookworm forms a friendship with an outgoing artist and finds what comes after the classic coming out story: a being out story. (978-1-63679-606-2)